RAE WILLIE CHAPPELL WAS DEAD, OR WAS SHE?

Certainly the famed country singer wasn't dead to her fans, who bought her records in the millions decades after headlines screamed she had burned to death in her trailer.

Certainly she wasn't dead on the bestseller lists, in a book that revealed the steamy sex going on in the trailer.

Certainly she wasn't dead in the mind of a killer who kept her memory alive by ritual murders to mark the date in blood of that fatal fire.

Certainly she wasn't dead on a phone line as her son heard a voice that pushed him to the brink of madness.

Was Rae Willie Chappell dead? Nashville cop Rider Chappell only knew one thing for sure. Whether his mother was dead or not, the victims he kept finding one after another certainly were. . . .

MIND GAMES

by
Seth Kindler

AN ONYX BOOK

ONYX
Published by the Penguin Group
Penguin Books USA Inc., 375 Hudson Street,
New York, New York 10014, U.S.A.
Penguin Books Ltd, 27 Wrights Lane, London W8 5TZ, England
Penguin Books Australia Ltd, Ringwood, Victoria, Australia
Penguin Books Canada Ltd, 10 Alcorn Avenue,
Toronto, Ontario, Canada M4V 3B2
Penguin Books (N.Z.) Ltd, 182–190 Wairau Road,
Auckland 10, New Zealand

Penguin Books Ltd, Registered Offices:
Harmondsworth, Middlesex, England

First published by Onyx, an imprint of Dutton Signet,
a division of Penguin Books USA Inc.

First Printing, February, 1996
10 9 8 7 6 5 4 3 2 1

 REGISTERED TRADEMARK—MARCA REGISTRADA

Printed in the United States of America

PUBLISHER'S NOTE
This is a work of fiction. Names, characters, places, and incidents
either are the product of the author's imagination or are used ficti-
tiously, and any resemblance to actual persons, living or dead,
events, or locales is entirely coincidental.

BOOKS ARE AVAILABLE AT QUANTITY DISCOUNTS WHEN USED TO PRO-
MOTE PRODUCTS OR SERVICES. FOR INFORMATION PLEASE WRITE TO
PREMIUM MARKETING DIVISION, PENGUIN BOOKS USA INC., 375 HUDSON
STREET, NEW YORK, NEW YORK 10014.

ACKNOWLEDGMENTS

The germ of this plot was suggested by my agent, Clyde Taylor, a former editor and major publisher. When I asked him why he didn't write his own novels based on some of the great ideas he has suggested to me in the past, he answered, "Writing's too much work."

I am extremely appreciative to husband and wife medical examiners Drs. Charles and Gretel Harlan, who not only returned my calls, but also spent precious time explaining forensic medicine to this former premedical student who knows just enough to be dangerous. The advice from friend (and longtime caregiver to my seven cats) Dr. Dave Elliston, DVM, was most invaluable.

I'd also like to thank Don Aaron and Lt. Tommy Jacobs of the Nashville Metro Police Department for the tour of the Homicide Division. The people who work there will notice that I again took a couple of liberties with the location of their offices.

Betcha can't say "toy duck" five times fast.

Chapter One

Fetid.

—the July heat,

—the putrefying horse,

—the collective conscience of the men who stood helplessly and watched.

Summer *heat* is spine-soaking and legendary for the Cumberland River Valley, once the river has left the spring-fed altitudes of "The Plateau" seventy-five miles to the east. Stewing heat demons jittered and danced above the road, the roofs of farm buildings, and the tops of the police vehicles that were strewn haphazardly around the barnyard. Two red-tailed hawks screeched in the distance, but neither seemed to posses the necessary enthusiasm for the hunt. They floated on great bubbles that rise from Sol's boiling pots—plowed earth, dark green leaves, gray rock outcroppings.

The dead *horse* lay on its side like an unconscious wino in one of Lower Broad's alleys. A swarm of angry bluebottle flies regrouped and reattacked when repelled by some of the hardier onlookers who had bent over to examine the animal more closely. Here was a prize worth fighting the humans for. A mare, she was solid brown, except for white fetlocks on stiff front legs that stretched toward a large citadel of weeds grown too hardy for the pasture animals to breech and trample. The ground was gouged in several places. Perhaps in her final spasms the animal had tried to pull herself from the jaws of death by crawling for the safety of the bush.

The *consciences* of the dozen men assembled weighed unbearably heavy with inherent shame. Subdued guilt bubbled and gurgled annoyingly as questions like, "Where were you when this happened? Why didn't you stop it?" were asked over and over.

"Go ahead, Doc. Let's get it over with."

The balding head of the medical examiner was pouring sweat as he knelt by the horse's belly. The man's stomach slopped over his belt in testimony of too many on-duty junk-food meals for too many years. A V-shaped blotch of wetness slowly crawled down the back of his white shirt as he began to cut the ornate sutures in the horse's belly.

The five-foot wound had been sewn closed with thick rawhide stitches that had then been meticulously decorated with silver studs and rhinestones. Intertwined with the lacing were a number of elaborate silver spangles and golden braids composed of exotic tapestry threads. The stunning decoration ran in a ruler-straight line down the *linea alba*—the two-and-a-half-inch-wide center line where the right and left abdomen muscles joined, and the stitching would immediately capture the interest and envy of any serious artisan.

Each one of the men watching was bracing hard mentally for what he knew was going to ooze from the horse's belly once the five-foot wound was reopened. It was because they were reasonably sure of what would be found that the medical examiner had been summoned.

Before the doctor had been allowed near the animal, the lab crew had vacuumed the immediate area around the horse for hair and fabric particles. Filters would allow the dirt and grass to be separated from any clues. A portable laser had hosed the animal's smooth surfaces—nostrils, lips, eyeballs, and hooves, in vain—searching for latent fingerprints. It had taken four men to flop the stiffened carcass over so that the ground beneath could be vacuumed and photographed. A large bloodstained swatch on the grass signified where the gut pile had lain. Animals—possums, foxes, coyotes, turkey vultures, and several other species of scavengers had undoubtedly feasted well. Not a scrap was left. They had also nibbled on the horse in several places.

The dry earth was too hard for footprints. Extensive pictures had already been taken of every square inch within a thirty-foot radius. A rough map with dimensions had been scratched on a pad showing the dead horse's relationship to clumps of bushes, fences, gates, the woods. The animal itself had been scrupulously photographed and videotaped from every conceivable angle, especially the decorated sutures. Detective Lieutenant Chapell knew these stitches would match the file pictures of the other four unsolved crimes that had been spread unevenly over a period of fifteen years. And now number five. There had been hope that the killer had given up ... or jumped off a cliff. The last travesty had been over five years ago. The murders were legends in police circles—nothing like them in the entire world before or since. Nor could the detective remember ever seeing anything resembling this kind of *artistry* before. Not on the gaudy performance suits, at six or seven thousand dollars a copy, that were worn on stage by the Porter Waggoners and Little Jimmy Dickenses at the Grand Ole Opry; not the decorations found on the most ornate tapestries and draperies in state museums and historical homes; not in the elaborate cornrowing of the Afro-American elite; not even the most expensive decorations found year round in the Yule Shoppe in the Green Hills Mall or Barbara Mandrell's Christmas shop on the triangular corner across the street from the Hall of Fame. The decorative sutures were one of a kind.

"Must have taken hours to do that."

Bob Trellis, the assistant D.A., seemed to be reading Chapell's mind.

"Yeah. What I'm wondering is if that poor woman regained consciousness while he was doing it. Did the bastard get his rocks off listening to her scream? Could he feel her kicking and clawing through the skin? God Almighty, that would be horrible—being trapped inside. The smell alone . . ."

The men turned together at the sound of the farmer and the official police photographer hurling their breakfasts onto the dew-covered early morning grass. The M.E., his breath clearly audible through the gas mask's filter, had removed about two feet of the stitches, and a bloodied bare foot and ankle had slipped through the gap into the morning air. With them came a smell worse than anything imaginable by the men watching. Chapell wondered, if the woman had been alive, would the air feel cool compared to the inside of the horse?

Two more uniformed officers turned away gagging. Chapell could see that most of the men were on the verge of losing their stomach contents, and these were tough men—men who had seen human brains splattered on walls, furniture, sidewalks, and car dashes for ten, twenty years.

Desperate for a distraction, the detective began to lecture softly to the D.A. "Plenty of room in there, you know."

"What?"

Trellis was a bit incredulous at the incongruity of Chapell's demeanor at a time like this; however, he quickly grasped that the cop was assembling a quick-form defense mechanism to keep from buckling.

"The inside of a horse."

"Oh?"

"The stomach of an average-sized horse will hold ten gallons, and there are sixty feet of small intestine. The large intestine alone will hold two hundred pounds of feed."

Realizing that here was an opportunity to fortify himself, Trellis allowed Chapell to draw him in, in spite of the repulsion of another one of Detective Lieutenant Rider Chapell's lectures. He said, "Go on."

"The diaphragm is bell-shaped. Big lungs. They fill in the spaces on top of the flange. Big heart. Actually, there would be plenty of room without ever involving anything above the diaphragm. Cleaning out the anterior viscera would probably get very messy unless you cracked the chest, and that would be serious work with a good six-pound ax."

"How does he kill the horses? I mean, you just don't walk up to the animal in the middle of the pasture and stick a needle in it. The vet said the horse hadn't been shot."

"He probably poisoned her—always a her, never a stallion or gelding. Could have used a pail of sweet feed—corn, oats, molasses. Lace it with something. Walk into a field where the horses can see you with a pail in your hand, and one or two will come to you—even in the dead of night. We'll know after the vet does a necropsy."

The D.A. turned and looked at the cop with dismay and said, "Rider, where in the hell do you learn all that stuff?"

"Well, I grew up with horses, but I read a lot. Everything I can get my hands on. Always have—since I was a kid."

"Well, the old man said the animal was a twenty-five-thousand-dollar Walker. I guess he'll be getting an insurance check."

The 911 call had come into the Nashville Metro Police department at 5:45 that morning. After the operator had calmed the nearly hysterical farmer down, the man had said he had a dead horse that probably had a dead woman inside. Chapell was rousted from bed, along with the assistant D.A., the medical exam-

iner, the police photographer, and a three-man lab
crew. By the time the detective lieutenant had arrived
at the farm on River Road, a veterinarian, four of
the seven men on his Murder Squad, three uniformed
officers and a state policeman were already on the
scene. The half-conscious thought went through Chapell's mind that there were too many people there. Evidence might have been destroyed with all those bodies
tramping around. However, if this murder was like the
others over the years, there'd be a chronic lack of
evidence. This killer didn't make mistakes.

Chapell had made the elderly farmer go over the
story again. The man had missed his prize Tennessee
Walker and he'd gone looking. It hadn't taken long.
She was less than a half mile from the barn, lying at
the back of the pasture not far from where the woods
began to climb the river valley's ridge. The farmer
knew what he'd find inside her when he saw the incredible stitches in the dead animal's belly. The same
thing had happened ten years before less than a mile
down the road. It wasn't the kind of event that escapes memory.

Within four minutes, the M.E. had removed three-
quarters of the incision's sutures. Before he could fin-
ish, and before the ambulance crew or the doctor
could reach and catch her, the nude woman tumbled
from the cavity onto the pasture's grass, where she
flopped unceremoniously onto her stomach. She was
covered in gore. The back of her head revealed several
bald patches where she must have torn her own hair
out in the midst of hysteria. There was a large clump
of it clutched in her left hand in a classic *cadaveric
spasm.*

"Anybody see the duck?"

Chapell had moved in closer, while several of the
men had turned away as the nausea worsened. He had
donned rubber gloves and a filter mask like the two
ambulance attendants were wearing. He kept a supply
of both in a plastic box in the trunk of his car. They

had come in handy more than once over the years when decomposing bodies had been discovered. Aware of what he was probably going to face, the M.E. had brought the gas mask he used when performing postmortems on decomposing bodies. More effective than the simple filter mask, it still wasn't a great deal of help. Most medical examiners would admit that the saving grace was the fact that after three or four minutes of constant exposure to stench, the nose desensitizes and the smell is almost bearable.

"Pictures. Tommy, can you do this?" He had turned to the photographer, his voice muffled by the rubber mask.

"Yeah, I'm okay." The photographer had been videotaping the doctor's work when the woman tumbled from the horse. He had a green tinge about his face, but he dutifully moved in and still-photographed the woman on her stomach. Even through the glaze of the horse's blood and gore, the purple marks of lividity, interrupted by a few faint white creases that were caused by the way her body had been cramped into the space, could be seen sketched across the parts of the woman's skin which had been closest to the ground. She had been lying on her side. Without the heart to provide pressure, gravity usually causes the blood to settle and pool.

The tiny film-advance motor in the camera ground and wheezed as the man moved from the head down the length of the woman, then back again, but at different focal lengths and angles.

"Okay. I've got enough. Turn her over."

"Boys, give me a hand. Let's put the bag down and turn her into it." The doctor had addressed the ambulance team. One of the men dropped the body bag he was holding, and both of them opened it and flattened it on the grass. Reluctantly, they kneeled and helped the doctor turn the woman over. The stench . . .

"There it is. Son of a bitch! How could a human being do this to another human being?"

The child's bath toy, a yellow toy duck, had been trapped beneath the dead woman on the grass.

Wild eyes, coated with blood and bits of gore, were open. She had, no doubt, been staring in horror at a final mind image projected on the pitch-black inside of the horse. Her face was relaxed. Contrary to many horror stories, death reposes the muscles. There was no frozen rictus, no painful grimace.

"Some noticeable rigor, bottom half of the body only."

The M.E.'s practiced eye had noted the body stiffness as she had rolled from the horse. The woman's knees were frozen, bent slightly into the air. Stiffness at the waist kept them from flopping to one side. Panic and terror would have generated an excess of lactic acid, and with the combined residual heat of the horse, along with the woman's small size, rigor mortis had probably been initiated early—perhaps in as little as a couple of hours. Rigor begins in all the muscles at the same time, but it is first noticeable in the smaller muscles of the face and neck as the protoplasm in the cells acidifies. The resulting gel causes the muscles to become rigid. It can take as much as twelve hours for rigidity to involve the entire body, depending on temperature and the onset of decomposition. It appears to move slowly down the torso until the large muscles in the legs stiffen. As decomposition sets in, the process slowly reverses itself, the face and jaws relaxing first.

"Taking her temperature would be a waste of time. The horse would have cooled significantly when he eviscerated it, so we wouldn't have a constant cooling gradient."

Had the doctor taken the temperature, he would have made a small incision in the lower-right chest over the liver, then carefully threaded an old-fashioned glass thermometer through the ribs into the body's core.

"I'm guessing she was killed night before last."

"In other circumstances, she would be a beautiful girl. How old, Doc, twenty?" Chapell was still squatting beside the doctor.

The muffled voice answered, "Yeah, nineteen, twenty. Five-two, a hundred ten pounds maybe. What an incredible sacrilege. See these spots of putrefaction?" He pointed at several dark spots on the right and left side of her abdomen that would have been a greenish shade had they not been covered by the coat of blood. "They wouldn't get that kind of start just since last night. Got to have been the night before last."

"Farmer said he saw the mare two afternoons ago but not yesterday—it's gotta be the night before last."

The doctor perfunctorily pressed the tip of a finger into one of the purple lines of lividity showing through the woman's left side. Had she died just a few hours before, lividity marks may have shown, but the blood might not have already clotted in the tiny vessels— the area would have blanched as the liquid was pushed aside. The M.E. came back to reality when he noticed something new on her arm.

"Oh, look here—we've got some petechiae, pupura."

"English . . ."

"Tardieu spots. The capillaries involved in *livor mortis* rupture from the accumulated pressure, and the blood shows up on the skin as spots. Usually takes eighteen to twenty-four hours. It's also a good sign of asphyxiation. If she's the same as the others, postmortem will show she was anesthetized before he put her in there to suffocate. I can't imagine what it would be like when she regained consciousness."

"Well, if past experience holds up, I don't think it's going to take us very long to find out who she is, Bob. We'll find there's an up-and-coming country singer missing." Chapell had turned to face the D.A. Trellis had found his second wind and joined the detective.

The other men kept their distance. Some of them had already left for their cars, retching uncontrollably.

"David, you got a tag?" Chapell had directed the questions to one of the lab crew who was standing a few feet away.

"Just a second." The officer had already consulted his case notebook to find the next sequential number that should be written on the evidence tag to identify the duck. He'd written the number in the notebook and was in the progress of writing it on the tag. He handed the tag to Chapell, who initialed it, then carefully attached it to the duck's neck by twisting its two wires together. He would have also initialed the duck directly with an indelible pen but the toy was wet with blood. the lab officer then made a brief description in his notebook of the duck after the number he'd assigned to it. More than one case had been lost in court because evidence as conspicuous as this famous little yellow duck had been mislabeled or misidentified.

"Bag?" The officer handed Chapell a paper bag. Paper, rather than plastic, would allow the blood to dry and not rot. Chapell carefully manipulated the toy into the bag without touching it, then handed the bag to the officer who would do the labeling.

"Well, it's in the hands of Forensics now. I don't think the fat lady's gonna sing even if I stay. Gene?"

"I want another minute or two. I'll see you back at the office."

The detective lieutenant turned from the scene and began the walk back to the car. The smell of death pervaded the pasture heavily, and in respect, the morning had begun a requiem. A despairing sun had quietly left the scene in order to allow caissons of gunmetal nimbus clouds their funeral-march entrance from the southwest. Even the hawks fell silent in deferential silence. Soon nature would attempt to cleanse the pasture with a summer morning rain.

*   *   *

The 1,368-foot WSMV television tower on Knobb Hill kept Chapell under surveillance for a full five minutes as he emerged from River Road, drove the half mile on Charlotte to the interstate entrance, then headed east toward downtown Nashville. The station had been the home of WSM radio studios before it was bought out. The new owners had added the V to sever all ties. The radio station had moved across town and had continued to broadcast the Grand Ole Opry, which it had been doing since the nineteen twenties. Until it was discontinued in the mid-eighties, the station's "Waking Crew" show had been the longest-running live radio program with a live band in the entire United States. The "Waking Crew" and its sister television show, the "Noon Show," which also used a live band, had served as showcases for countless hundreds of country stars and wannabes. For decades many of Nashville's musicians had augmented their livelihoods playing the two shows. There were "charts" to be arranged and copied for all the stars performing, while a constant flow of musicians and subs flowed through the station on a daily basis. TNN, the cable country music station, had taken up some of the slack for players who performed live on radio and TV. The first year "Music City Tonight" had been on the air, the show paid its band members and backup singers $80,000 a year—contractors made more. Live performances didn't leave much room for anything but the best players. You didn't have to screw up very many times not to be asked back.

Chapell recalled his sister, Gale, telling him about subbing one time for one of the backup singers on a "Nashville Now" show. The group's alto had blurted out her part in the wrong place—in a rest!—when absolutely nothing was happening in the band. The girl quickly grabbed the pencil that was lying on the music stand and wrote, "STEP-OUT—MORE $." A step-out solo in a recording session usually paid more than just singing back up. The television audience was never privy to the woman's sense of humor, but they probably heard the clam. "Live" was tough. Very tough.

The silver Cherokee slid into a parking place in the garage almost on its own. Chapell's mind was too hard at work to bother with driving a car. The Toy Duck cases were legendary not only in Nashville, but in police studies around the world. Like the majority of *mystery* homicides—murders in which the killer's identity wasn't readily known the way it was in family squabbles, drunken brawls, or friends shooting each other in a fit of passion—the killer had never been caught; the killer had never even come close to being caught. No clues.

"Toy Duck?"

The word had got around quickly. Chapell had made the short walk up the sidewalk to enter the building's side door. The sergeant on the desk had once served under him. The man had been shot seven times by a drug dealer in East Nashville. The cop had recovered, but not enough to go back on the street.

"Yeah, Sandy. Hey, keep the media out of it as long as you can, will you? Warn your guys not to leak this one. We need to run all the usual programs to find the woman's family before we turn to the unidentified-body routine in the media. Her folks don't need to hear about it on TNN unless we can't find who she is any other way."

"Sure, Rider. But you and I both know it won't keep for more than a few hours. That farmer's probably got a book deal and a TV movie in the works already."

"Not unless he's stopped puking."

Chapell ran the fire stairs to the first floor, then ran the next two floors on the half circle of inside stairs that filled much of the three-story, brown brick atrium anchoring the core of the building. Using the stairs rather than the elevator had to be good for at least five pounds a year.

He glanced upward at the decorative translucent-glass dome in the roof to see if there were any pigeons fighting for position at the top. The department ran an ongoing feud with the birds to keep the dome free of light-blocking droppings.

Yellow paint on the corridor walls did little to widen the hall, or the maze of other tiny halls the detective negotiated to reach his office. Chapell had often speculated that the architect who designed the building was a midget with a self-aggrandizing sense of humor. The facility was much too small for the three-hundred and fifty officers, in addition to the significant civilian staff, who worked there. All of the rooms and halls— even the urinals in the tiny men's rooms—were small. Two of the interrogating rooms were the size of postage stamps, and unlike the movies, there were no one-way mirrors, long tables, and old wooden chairs, along with enough room for three or four men to pace and play good-guy, bad-guy games.

"Gibby."

"Lieutenant."

He walked by the open door of the homicide room, and the detective nearest the door turned. A shift of detectives sat, literally, elbow to elbow in a twenty-by thirty-foot room that would not accommodate the average home's living and dining room. The men worked in minuscule carrels that were separated by commercial office dividers barely three feet high. A head-high shelf that circled the room's perimeter was overloaded with books, boxes, more boxes, and all types of paraphernalia associated with law enforcement. Much of the stuff was obsolete and unusable. A hodgepodge of computers, some as old as fifteen years, was sprinkled around the room. New ones were due any day. In one corner, a six-by-three-foot progress board charted ongoing investigations. Developments were marked on the lined, glossy surface in Magic Marker and erased with a cloth.

Stuffed into one-third of the room was Chapell's own seven-man Murder Squad, which worked the "mystery" murders. The eighteen homicide detectives took the murders when the killer was known, but the Agatha Christie jobs were left to Chapell and his team. Each man might be working on an individual murder, but the eight-man squad, including Chapell, worked as a team.

He had his own tiny office, and its window faced north. He could see that the beltway bridge over the Cumberland was badly distorted with the early morning heat and humidity, along with the exhaust from nearly three thousand vehicles that used it during their drivers' headlong rush to work. It was almost eight-thirty. A couple blocks away, two men were walking across a parking lot toward the Stockyard Restaurant, one of Nashville's finest tourist traps. Chapell wondered if the poor, bloody woman was going to turn out to be another country starlet, and if she was, had she ever done a showcase with the house band in the Bull Pen—the club located in the restaurant's grungy basement? He remembered every one that Gale had done before Columbia signed her. Damn, she was good. The years the girl had struggled ... She was a shoo-in to win the Country Music Association's Female Vocalist of the Year. Last year she'd missed it by a whisker. This new record deal was sure to be the rocket that launched another mega-career like their mom's. Rae Willie still sold over three million records a year, and she had been dead for twenty years.

His mind dissolved the scene of his sister performing on the club's cellar stage, and the small office rematerialized along with the reality of the day. He mumbled softly, "Hell, I'm not sure yet if that poor woman was even a singer. Maybe the maniac has switched M.O.'s."

He called Records on the first floor and asked them to pull the file on the Toy Duck murders. The very first travesty had taken place when Chapell was in high school. The news story had remained plastered to millions of television sets for weeks as worldwide audiences watched in shock, mesmerized by the fact that a live thirteen-year-old girl had been sewn inside a dead horse! Chapell remembered the second case even better. The eighteen-year-old woman had been killed during his rookie year on the force, and every cop in the city had looked at that file. It had been five years between the first and second murders. Unusual for a serial killer to go that long without gratification. Over the years, with the aid of the FBI's Behavioral Science Department, the squad had contacted hundreds of law enforcement agencies in the United States and overseas in an attempt to find similar murders. Any clue would have been a cause for major celebration. The queries had always come back negative. This psycho killed a young female, blond, up-and-coming country star on the average of once every five years whether they needed it or not! This morning had been the fifth victim. Chapell had only just made detective grade when he'd been assigned to the third case.

Without replacing the phone, he dialed another number. A voice laced with coarse steel wool answered, "McCurty." Good. McCurty had already returned.

"Gene, can you come in here a minute?"

"Sure. You want some coffee?"

"Black."

Detective Sergeant Gene McCurty came into the room three minutes later with coffee mugs in each hand. McCurty was punishing his usual wad of gum, chewing it by using just his front teeth. He looked more eastern Mediterranean than Scots-Irish. Curly black hair framed a square face that gave rise to a humped nose that mercifully had been modified by Hibernean-Highland genes before it could spread sideways. Permanent parentheses framed either end of his mouth, and eyes the color of slate in a rainstorm dismissed nothing.

Chapell began, "We've got an appointment with the

captain when he gets back from the governor's break-fast, but I know he'll okay the plan. We'll start on the stitching. Pull Johnson, Tweedy, Ferraro, and Cain off whatever they're doing. I brought several samples, and there are all kinds of pictures, stills and VCR, that will be ready in about an hour. Take a look in the Toy Duck file of the previous murders, and see where we checked the last times to find if the materials had been sold. I remember there was one in Louisville, and another one in Atlanta. There's bound to be a turnover in those kinds of stores, but there can't be very many places that carry that kind of stuff. For one thing, that thread has got to be bloody expensive. Part of the artistry, last two times, was done in spun gold—the real thing. Take a piece to a jewelry store and have it analyzed. Then you can shop for suppliers from there.''

"Check.''

"When we get the necropsy report late this after-noon, we'll have another direction to run—I'm certain the horse was poisoned the same way all the others were. The killer used hydrocyanic acid that was proba-bly mixed in with a pail of feed. Prussic acid is used in all kinds of industrial processes—insecticides, indus-trial cleaning—jewelry, for instance. It's not hard to get.''

"Run down the suppliers.''

"Try. But I don't think we'll find anything. We never have before. This guy is much too careful. He probably bought it a long ways from here and under pretexts that would not leave any suspicion.''

"When will we have the girl's prints?''

"Hopefully within an hour. They're going to do the postmortem right now—slow night. Unless the pattern is changed, she'll have been anesthetized with ether. Tyeson is down there with a kit. He already printed the duck. One partial set. Probably hers. He'll sample her fingernails too, but all he'll find is horse guts. The guy does a good job of putting them to sleep. On the second one we found that damn duck tucked under the woman's right arm. She died before she could thrash around enough to dislodge it. Who knows, maybe this one got to put up a fight before he put her under. There's always a chance that the TBI may have her on file. Maybe she's been arrested for something."

The Tennessee Bureau of Investigation had hundreds of thousands of prints on file. It was here that much of the state's forensic work was done—blood, DNA, fibers. The agency was the state's version of the FBI.

"Have you called the musicians' unions?"

"No. They're not open yet. They won't have a clue unless someone recognizes the photos. I'll wait for the coroner's report and the pictures of her after she's been cleaned up before I phone the label. I'll take them over this afternoon and talk to Reggie." Reggie Mirrow was the soon-to-retire president of Sony. He had been a friend and one of the developers of Rae Willie Rider's career thirty years before. "He may be able to identify the woman's pictures. The last woman belonged to the A.F. of M.; the one before her belonged to AFTRA. The first one didn't belong to either union. However, all three had development deals with Columbia—excuse me, Sony now." The Japanese had bought out CBS several years before. "Columbia" and "Epic" were still displayed on the side of the Sony building on Sixteenth, but the telephone was answered "Sony."

"I remember, they even looked alike, didn't they?"

"And sounded alike. You'll see in the files. I think there are some tapes also. One of the reasons the captain signed me onto the squad for the third one was the fact that all three women looked and sounded like my mother—and all three were on Mom's old label!"

"That's right. I'd forgotten about that connection. Some kind of devoted fan to your mother?"

"Believe me, we tried every angle possible—took the lists of Mom's fan club all the way back to 1961. We also checked the list of IFCO fan members for as far back as the organization has been in existence. We ran thousands of names against several different FBI lists—criminal records, psychiatric hospitals, you name it. We'll have to do it again this time. Get Thompson and Dorfer on it. I'll call the FBI right now. They'll send a consultant from Quantico to sample things firsthand. The captain will be on the hot seat once the woman is identified and the fifth Toy Duck murder hits the media."

The IFCO list had been Gale's idea. The list had been considerably more extensive than their mother's fan club lists. Gale had sung in the backup group for several years at Fanfair's Independent Fan Club Organization show. The show was always on the last night of Fanfair—the week in June when thousands of fans descended on Nashville for the shows and private "fan-appreciation" parties thrown by the stars. Booths were set up in buildings at the fairgrounds where the fans could personally meet, get their picture taken with, and get autographs and souvenirs of, their favorite country artist. There was nothing else like it in the entertainment industry. Chapell had watched his sister sing behind Loretta Lynn, Linda Davis, Hoyt Axton, Johnny Rodriguez, Bill Anderson, and numerous other big names. Some of the older stars had been just breaking in when Rae Willie had been the "Queen of Country" twenty-five years before. Next year perhaps Gale would be featured by herself. She'd certainly paid her dues over the years.

"Why don't you get on the thread and stud angle first? Send Peters and Wilhousky out to River Road. See if any of the surrounding farms heard or saw anything last night. There's a little store out there on the water. Maybe someone unusual stopped in. You know the routine."

"Okay."

"Let's have a team meet at, say, three-thirty."

"I'll tell the guys."

Chapell spun his Rolodex to the R's. Jon Rheinhart was the supervising agent in Nashville for the FBI and an old teammate on the hockey team at Dartmouth. The FBI had only three agents stationed in Nashville. All three were attorneys. The closest they got to most criminals was a computer. SWAT teams handled the dangerous operations. If a man, or woman, wanted a career in the Bureau, then they'd better have a law degree or be an ex-marine.

Let Jon call Quantico. Give him a rest from all the tough and dangerous stuff he's always working on. As usual, the mind vision of his old teammate brought pleasant memories. After graduating, Rheinhart had gone to law school at Yale, while Chapell had gone to graduate school at Harvard to get his master's in criminology. They met each other on the ice in Nashville's Metro League an average of once every couple of weeks. There were other occasions now and then— mostly occupational.

It was almost ten o'clock when Chapell finished his morning calls. In addition to Toy Duck, there were several other ongoing cases, like the thirteen-year-old kid who had shotgunned his childless aunt and uncle with a .410. The murder squad had found evidence that the boy's mother and father were next on his list. With them dead, the kid would be left as sole heir of a three-million-dollar estate. Shades of Lyle and Erik Menendez. The boy had been clever enough to make the shooting look like an interrupted burglary, but he hadn't exactly set himself up for a brilliant career in crime. He had sneaked out of his house in the middle of the night, done the deed, then walked straight home during a light snow. The Murder Squad had caught him by following his tracks, which led down the street about three blocks, up the back steps to the door. Now his mother and father were trying to get him off, and Chapell had a court appearance the next morning and serious plans of nipping that deal in the bud.

It was early afternoon, and he'd been on the phone, or checking off reports for over four hours. The photographer called and said the pictures of the woman were ready—pictures of her after her face and hair had been washed. No one would have recognized her covered in blood.

It was an hour before his appointment with Reggie Mirrow at Sony, so Chapell decided to collect the pictures at the lab in the police station's basement, then drive over to the morgue at General Hospital to take a look at the dead woman. Most of the postmortem should be finished, although results from some of the tissue tests might take a couple of weeks.

"She was a pretty girl, wasn't she?"

Chapell was holding the pictures in his hand, comparing them to the travesty lying on the table in front of him. The tremendous incisions that defiled the poor woman's chest and abdomen always reminded Chapell of a Halloween jack-o'-lantern. Cut open the top, remove the insides. He often wondered if they used a chain saw to do the cutting. They didn't, of course. Slashing such large incisions was simply the fastest and easiest way to remove the organs for biopsies. The viscera would be placed in a plastic bag that lined a five-gallon bucket mounted on wheels. The cop also knew that the skin on the top of her head and forehead would have been excised and folded down over her face in order that the lateral circumference of the skull might be sawed through. The top of her cranium would have been lifted off so that the brain could be removed for study. Then the skull top and skin would be temporarily replaced awaiting the brain's return. The funeral home would punctiliously cover the incision by using heavy makeup and a wash and set of the woman's hair. Chapell knew that some morticians would lovingly stitch every last pervasive wound from a car accident, stabbing, whatever. Others would simply rely on the clothing to cover up any wounds and hope that the embalming fluid wouldn't leak.

His mind wandered even further into the realm of the mortician, visualizing the rivet gun slamming single rivets into her upper and lower gums at the front of the mouth. The jaws were then tied permanently closed by wire wrapped between the upper and lower rivets so that after rigor mortis had completed its cycle, and the body's muscles had relaxed in final peace, the mouth wouldn't unceremoniously drop open. Some morticians used staples instead of rivets, and it wasn't unusual to find that the tongue had been caught between the teeth when the jaws were stapled together. There would be sandpaper cups placed beneath her eyelids to insure they remained closed in the look of rest.

There wasn't any rest for this woman in how she got to look like this. When she was rinsing the sauce from last night's supper plate and scraping stubborn butter from the knife, the fact that she'd be lying on a porcelain table in the morning rather than turning off her clock radio at seven a.m. wouldn't have entered her mind. She was probably thinking about getting the plugs changed in the car; or making the overdue appointment with the dentist to get her teeth cleaned; or writing and mailing the monthly check to the telephone company.

Out loud, Chapell answered, "Yeah, Doc, she was. And probably very talented. We still don't know who she is, but if the pattern holds up, she'll be a singer on the verge of stardom. How about sexually . . . ?"

"No. No semen. No tearing or bruises. Perfectly normal except for a minor yeast infection."

"Thank God for sparing her that. Tests . . . ? Booze, drugs, disease?"

"Tomorrow, late afternoon. They're putting a rush on it. Stomach showed her last meal was probably a TV dinner—a little chicken, sauce, some string beans and corn. He put her to sleep with ether. The organs smelled like it; blood was fluid; viscera darkened significantly, congested."

"She was probably on a draw with the label—wouldn't make much money until they see if her stuff would chart. They're chintzy with their money. Wanna make sure the CEO gets a new limousine every year, not just every other year. If these girls haven't lucked into doing jingles or demos or backup . . ." He let the sentence go when his inner picture wandered.

Gale had struggled for several years to get work. Her mother's name had helped, but she'd had to do it mostly on her own. Thank goodness, none of Rae Willie's kids had ever had money problems. The royalty check from their mother's recorded performances—on records and films—was consistently in excess of a hundred fifty thousand dollars every quarter. Chapell, the oldest, had made sure his younger sister and brother always had everything they needed. Ponder had graduated from veterinarian school debt-free. That reminded Chapell, the vet should have the necropsy report by morning.

Lieutenant, call your brother, the vet, and take him to lunch. You haven't seen him in two weeks.

Reggie Mirrow took one look at the dead woman's picture and blanched into an experimental shade of eggshell-white.

"Oh, God. Oh, no. Oh, God, no . . ."

"Who is she, Reggie?"

The record exec bolted from his desk toward the door to his private bathroom but realized halfway there that it was a losing battle. He barely had time to grab a waste basket, where he deposited a two-martini lunch. Chapell sat and stared dumbly, waiting patiently for the man to ascend from the netherworld. Mirrow sat in one of the office guest chairs with the waste basket between his legs.

"Sorry, Rider."

"Take your time."

Mirrow finally put the basket on the floor, then with a wrinkled nose set it as far from him as he could without getting up.

"Her real name is Belinda Rose Slaven. We gave her the stage name of Bella Rose. She's twenty-three. Looks younger. I just started divorce proceedings against my wife so I could marry her. Oh, God, what a mess. Seeing her like that . . ."

"I'm sorry, Reggie. Can I ask you some questions?"

"Yeah. Rider, what in God's name happened?"

When Chapell left a half hour later, he had the girl's address, the address and number of her parents in Allentown, Pennsylvania, and a list of several of her friends. There were no enemies. Chapell also had several cassettes of the woman singing her own songs. Yes, she did sound like Rae Willie, and, yes, like Rae Willie, she wrote most of the songs herself and was good at it. She had been featured in last month's *Music Row,* and a promising career had been forecast, especially after signing with Columbia for a two-record deal. Reggie had revealed that the company had committed over a million dollars to promotion—the sure road to success. The music industry was like any other industry. The more money invested in advertising, the better the results. Invest megabucks in Phyllis Diller singing "Happy Birthday," and you could have a new star.

The executive had explained that in spite of the tremendous age difference, they really were in love. Most unusual, but it was true. Chapell thought to himself, "Isn't it always?—at least until the bedroom uniqueness wears off—or she's horny, and at sixty years old, you can't get it up three times a day." When asked, Mirrow had left it to the police chaplain to call the parents. Old enough to be the girl's grandfather, the less the family knew about Reggie Mirrow the better.

True love, for sure, old friend.

*   *   *

Chapell called the station and told McCurty to meet
him with the squad and a lab crew at the woman's
luxury apartment on West End. They'd hold the three
o'clock meeting there, more or less. If Bella Rose had
been living in a $1,600-a-month home, why hadn't she
eaten something better than a TV dinner? They'd undoubtedly find that the place was paid for, in one way
or another, by Sony. Even if she was the all-time,
number-one affair of his life, Reggie was too cheap to
take that kind of money out of his own pocket, and
evidently too cheap to see she had enough to eat prop-
erly. Maybe she just liked TV dinners—and maybe
Reggie still had the first dime he ever made.

The squad could get to work that afternoon checking out Bella Rose's neighbors and Reggie's list of her
friends. Tomorrow they'd have the vet's diagnosis of
how the horse was killed. Some kind of cyanide. The
horse's lips and tongue had been burned with the cor-
rosive compound; there was the faint smell of the inside of a peach stone.

*Don't forget to make the lunch date with Ponder
tomorrow.*

The cop had left the Sony Building by the back
entrance, and he had to step out of the way as a large
cartage truck negotiated the narrow alley. There were
several companies in town that delivered the musician's instruments and equipment—drums sets, percus-
sion, including timpani, keyboards, computer racks,
amplifiers, etc. Most of the stuff was packed in foam
inside the large trunks that were on wheels. The cartage company would even set up the equipment. All
the player had to do was walk in, sit down, and play.

Chapell noticed that Ronnie Milsap's studio, across
the street, had just received a new coat of paint. It
was next door to Sound Stage. Years ago, George
Burns had recorded at Sound Stage. Gale had mentioned that a friend of hers had done the scratch vocals on the sessions. Mr. Burns would listen to the

singer on the "work tape" in order to learn the songs and arrangements before doing the session. The record had done extremely well—had put the old vaudevillian on the charts.

Ponder may have some ideas on the poisoning.

His mind drifted between his brother and the case as he got in the car and turned the air conditioning on high. The heat inside the white Ford Crown Victoria, with the blackwall tires and hidden blue strobes and siren inside the front grille, was suffocating. Even if the windows were cracked a couple of inches, Nashville's summer heat turned the inside of automobiles into kilns.

Hell, maybe he'll just go ahead and solve the whole case.

The thought had been framed in sarcasm. The detective lieutenant had always been a little jealous at the deductive reasoning powers that his brother displayed from time to time. He'd often wondered if Ponder wouldn't have made a better cop than a veterinarian.

I'd gladly switch places with him right now, folks.

Chapter Two

Dr. Ponder Chapell swung the car into its customary parking place, locked it, then made his way up the flagstone walk toward the vaulted front entrance of the natural stone building. The extensive flower beds and landscaping shrubs on either side of the walk made a visually striking setting for the building. The doctor had always preferred using the front door of his clinic rather than coming in the back the way the employees did. It gave him a chance to see who and what was waiting. It was also just a pleasing thing to do—something he never got tired of—surveying the grandness of the magnificent facility that was his and his alone. He had envisioned and designed it with only minimal aid from one of the top architectural firms in Nashville.

The building's foyer–waiting room was larger than many veterinarians' entire clinics. Native fieldstone outlined the large open room, which was almost three stories high. Huge twelve-by-twelve oak beams stretched across the skylighted roof expanse, and treated flagstone lined the floor. Greenery abounded, including several trees and a number of potted shrubs that grew from customized stone troughs. The trees and shrubs had not been a great idea. More than one dog had watered them, and several cats had been coaxed down from the twenty-foot trees with difficulty. Ponder had never changed the plants because he liked the way they refracted the light in the room. It brought the outdoors right into your lap.

A number of people sat in the plush chairs that occupied the waiting room section of the hall. Several of them held small dogs on their laps. Some of the cat people had opted to place their animals in the convenient assortment of custom-made cages that lined one wall. It was easier than trying to hold the animals for any length of time. The cages were wiped down with disinfectant after each occupant in order to prevent the spread of respiratory diseases.

"Good afternoon, Dr. Chapell. Good lunch?"

"Very interesting, Remmie. Anything for me?"

"Yes sir." She handed him a small stack of While You Were Out messages.

"Hello, everybody. Be with you in a minute." Ponder had turned, given his most reassuring country doctor smile and addressed the waiting animal owners. Most of the people smiled back.

He perused the messages while walking down the corridor on his way to his office in the back of the building. On either side of the long hall were numerous treatment rooms; two complete surgeries—one with a respirator and a very expensive heart-bypass machine; an X-ray room; an extensive lab containing a chromatograph, a refractometer—for urine analysis—and a full Kodak Ektachem blood-analysis system. There was a room for the ultrasound and another for the MRI—that one hadn't come cheap either. Dr. Chapell's clinic was equipped better than many veterinarian medical school facilities. Little old millionaire widows from Belle Meade expected the best money could buy when it came to saving the life of Fufu or Toto or dozens of other names that always seemed to have at least one letter U or O in them. Patients and their owners came from all over the United States for the services of the tall, taciturn doctor with the dark brown eyes and exceptionally thick, dark hair that cascaded over his shoulders in waves that would delight Fabio himself.

He hung his western-style sports coat on the hall

tree and donned the white smock with DR. CHAPELL
embroidered on the pocket in navy blue. He was tie-
less, as always, shirt open one button farther than de-
cency allowed, revealing a forest of hair. Ponder knew
he was handsome and simply didn't care what effect
he had on women. He did what was comfortable. It
was another part of the arrogance that goes along with
being the best at what one does. A small clump of
black dog hairs covering the D on Dr. disappeared
with a couple of flicks of a finger. "Embroider-eed"
was how many people pronounced it. That's the way
Conway Twitty had sung it in "Middle Age Crazy."
Poor Conway. His ex, his widow, and his children had
spat so vehemently for two years, each refusing to
compromise over the dead singer's multimillion-dollar
estate, that an exasperated judge had finally ordered
that everything be auctioned off and the money split.
The family ended up paying for things Conway had
given them as presents in the first place. The widow
had paid $18,000 for a watch he'd already given her
and the court had taken back.

Helen Towers, the chief surgical nurse, had met him
as he exited his office still buttoning the smock. She
was carrying an armful of files.

"Dr. Chapell, Mrs. Feldman is back with her pug.
Says he's constipated again, and she is not about to
give him the enema herself." She handed him the file.

At six-feet-three, Ponder towered over the nurse.
He took the file, opened it, glanced at when the dog
had last been treated and with what, then said, "Fill
me one of those snouty bottles full of mineral water,
and get ready to hold the back door open so Booboo
can make a beeline for the grass." He was grinning
at her.

Picturing the fat little dog waddling down the hall
to the door as fast as he could go, the nurse smiled
and said, "I'll put them in Two."

Ponder employed two veterinarian nurses—both
surgically qualified—plus the receptionist, plus three

veterinarian assistants who were drawn from the un-
dergraduate ranks of the school at Vanderbilt. There
were also two lab technicians. He ran his practice
without the partnership of another doctor, and it was
not unusual for him to be in various stages of service
for five patients. Surgeries were scheduled on Mon-
days, Wednesdays, and Thursdays unless it was an
emergency. At these times he would use the services
of another doctor to assist if necessary.

"And Mrs. Marinaro is back. She's in number
three."

"Oh, oh. What are we going to do about her?"

The woman brought her poodle in sometimes two
or three times a week, always with imagined symptoms. Most of the time she tried to get the dog oper-
ated on. It was a classic example of Munchausen
syndrome, only instead of using her child, the woman
was using poor little Scobbie to satiate her own hypo-
chondria and garner attention.

With a well heralded arrival at Baptist Hospital,
Ponder Allegro Chapell, Rae Willie's "gonna be my
pride and joy," had been born on Labor Day in 1961.
A twenty-six-hour production, Rae Willie had finally
delivered him at six in the evening, somewhere around
the time when the nation's barbecues were at their
smoking and spitting peak, and the beer was flowing
freely. After a full day of it, the "labor" jokes had
worn vellum-thin. When the mother got her first look
at the squalling newborn, it was all she could do to
hide her disappointment. Ponder favored his father.
Black hair framed a square face, and the baby's eyes
were dark brown. The egomaniacal part of the woman
had never considered the fact that he would not be
the spitting image of his mother—his head flowered
with thick blond hair, his eyes shining sea green. Porcelain doll nose. Using a variety of excuses, she had
refused to breast-feed the boy, and as he grew up,
much of his childhood was spent with nannies and

relatives. In Rae Willie's mind, Ponder was her biggest failure—he didn't look like her. She would have to be satisfied with total and absolute control over him. The megastar would try baby making only twice more, and whether it was sheer determination or blind luck, Gale would be a complete success.

By the time he was in his teens, Ponder had sublimated the obvious lack of his mother's love into sports and the art of self-defense. Her lack of interest had only fueled his devotion to her. Blessed with the dark and foreboding gorgeousness of a George Hamilton or a Warren Beatty, he had commanded an IQ even higher than Rae Willie's, which was rumored to be in the one-fifties. His physique came from his father, who could interrupt the heartbeat of most women by just removing his shirt. For Ponder Chappell there had been few doors he couldn't open. He had excelled in sports. Hockey, basketball, baseball, tennis, swimming, water skiing, karate—he was a natural athlete. He was also a quick study—the kind of person who, to the chagrin of most, does it right the first time. His power of concentration, even as a grade-schooler, had been awesome, whether applied to a game-winning Pop Warner touchdown throw or a crossword puzzle that would stymie most adults. With his mother out of town a great deal of the time, high school had turned him even further inside himself.

"Hey, Ponds, you going to the lake after the game? We got Barboni's houseboat and a keg. Lot of chicks can't wait to go skinny dipping with you."

"Naw, I'm really beat, Rod. I'm going home and get on the living room sofa with half a bottle of aspirin. That left-side linebacker knocked the shit out of me several times tonight because our star right tackle had his head up his ass so far he couldn't see who to block. You're acquainted with the right tackle position, aren't you, Roddy, my boy?"

"Ayeee, I had a bad night. What can I say?"

"Besides, believe it or not, I found this forensic pathology book at a secondhand store, and it is totally fascinating stuff."

"What the hell is forensic pathology?"

"The study of how people died—shooting, stabbing, hanging, all kinds of goodies. Neat pictures—they show this one guy who hasn't got a face—in color! Somebody blew it off with a shotgun to the back of the head."

"You'd rather look at pictures of dead people than the bare bod of Tina Delouggi? Jesus, are you weird, Chapell."

"Yeah, so's your mother, Herr Richter." The name was pronounced with a German accent. The feint at the future cop's head was countered with one to the future veterinarian's stomach.

Ponder was rarely seen in the company of girls. In fact, he was rarely seen with anyone by choice. He seemed to prefer being alone. There were friends, but most of them would have said that the boy seemed bored by people his own age. During the last half of his senior year it was rumored that he'd had an affair with a married woman. Shades of *The Last Picture Show*. If he did, he kept his mouth shut about it, and nothing was ever proven. When he went off to college in New Hampshire, the rumors died a natural death. During the three years it took him to graduate from Dartmouth, he rented a home on the outskirts of a neighboring village, refusing the dorms, fraternities, and even a roommate. During the four years of veterinarian school at Vanderbilt, and two years' residency, he again rented a house, refusing to live at home. He rarely dated, spent most of his time studying or playing sports. There were rumors, however, that the marriages of more than one faculty member had been broken up by the boy's prowess in bed. "Passively predatory" was the term coined by the friend of an economics professor who had discovered his wife in bed with the boy. Ponder never had to go looking for trouble. As in his mother's turbulent life, trouble always seemed to find him. So what? Living on the edge was much more interesting than just living safely and comfortably. The faculty scandal had made the gossip rounds of several university circles, but the fact that the professor had taken a shot at the boy was kept out of the media only because Ponder had refused to press charges—had actually asked the cops to keep it quiet. "Why ruin the man's career? He won't do it again. Leave him alone." Unusual for a twenty-three-year-old.

Six hours after administering the enema to Mrs. Feldman's pug, the doctor was back in the Jaguar and on the way home. He was tired. The day had begun at 4:30 A.M. with an emergency operation on an aging St. Bernard that had fallen down a flight of stairs in the middle of the night. Ponder had told the owner more than once that the dog needed a hip replacement. Hip problems were inherent in a lot of Saints.

Gale's got to be coming in any time now. Damn, it'll be good to have her back again. I'm going home, get on the sofa, turn on the TV to whatever godawful shit is oozing out of the thing, do some serious dozing, and wait for her to ring the phone.

At thirty-eight years old, it got harder every week to keep up with the guys in their twenties with the young legs. The slapshot got a little harder every year, but the wheels and lungs took longer to get the rust scraped off each time he stepped on the ice.

The Metro summer league had been under way for two months. Unlike a lot of facilities—many of them located in the North—Nashville's Ice Centennial used the rink right through the summer, shutting down only three or four weeks in May and June for maintenance on the compressor.

Chapell had been playing since he was six years old. It was a sport he was well adapted to physically—six feet, one eighty-five, muscular legs and enormous arms. He had always been much stronger and faster than he looked. He also had a good sense of balance— it was hard to knock him off his feet. The attributes had come in handy more than once collaring a perp in an alley or running him down through the streets. Excluding Ponder, the cop had never lost a fight and never intended to.

Hockey was a wonderful way to vent frustrations. You could try to kill someone—the goalie—by firing something at him—the puck—as hard as you could, and they couldn't send you to jail! The only casualty was an occasional broken stick. Chapell had been gouging the ice with his slap shot for twenty-five years, and he probably wasn't going to learn how to keep the blade only a fraction of an inch higher now. Hard on sticks, but it felt so good to blast that puck, and the ice, with every fiber of strength he possessed.

Once in a while, if a goalie hadn't quite arrived at the game yet, someone would inadvertently hit him in the cup, which is exactly what Chapell had done with a blistering snap shot from twelve feet. The poor man flopped around the ice vomiting and writhing in agony, and the game stopped for ten minutes while the man came out of serious-pain orbit. The episode of pain didn't particularly bother most of the players—if someone was stupid enough to play goal, then he took his chances. It was the same when the goalie got hit in the neck, or some part of the anatomy that wasn't overstuffed with pads, and there were several of those—back of the calves, back of the arm, back; Chapell had unleashed his slap shot from twenty-five feet one time and caught the goalie in the collarbone. How it had missed the pads, no one ever figured out. The guy lasted another four minutes, then skated to the bench on the verge of fainting. There was a small bleeding wound in the skin that actually looked like a gunshot entrance. Chapell's shot had broken the clavicle, and the goalie took six weeks to heal before he could turn and bend over without pain.

"Slot!"

The game had continued after the goalie had recovered, and Chapell's left wing had picked up a puck from a face-off and carried it, headlong, down the left side of the ice into the offensive zone. As usual, he was preparing to take a poor-angle shot that had a snowball's chance in July of going in. The rebound was sure to ricochet around the curve of the corner boards, then back out across the blue line and out of the offensive zone because the opposing defenseman on that side was still trying to catch up to the play and had only crossed the blue line. Turnborg would shoot the puck if the entire New York Ranger team was standing in front of the goal waiting for a pass and the nearest defenseman was in Smyrna, twenty miles away. He also had the kind of mentality that if he decided he was going to carry the puck behind the net, an Abrams tank could be sitting there, and instead of changing direction, the man would splatter his life away as he ran into the tank.

"Slot, slot. Pass the damn puck, Johnny!" Chapell, the center, was open in front of the net, as was the right wing.

Turnborg shot. And missed the net. The puck hit the far corner and slingshotted out of the offensive zone to fly across the blue line into center ice, where the left wing on the other team picked it up and skated for Chapell's goal. The other team's center and right wing, not having seriously backchecked, joined the man in a three-on-two advantage. They beat Chapell's two defensemen, who hadn't been able to get back quite fast enough, and after two outstanding passes popped the puck by the goalie, upper left.

"Hey, John. Are you blind or just extremely selfish? Exactly when was the last time you scored on one of those?" There had been a line change, and Chapell's first line was sitting on the bench.

"Chapell, fuck off. I had daylight."

"When you've got two men open, why not try something really unique for a change and pass the god-damn thing?"

"And why don't you lick my cup?"

Two shifts later, Chapell got a breakaway, and just as he was about to let his famous howitzer go, the defenseman tripped him from behind. He slid into the net, dislodging it from its pegs. He slowly got to his feet expecting to see the referee signaling a penalty shot, but instead the man was simply skating to the circle for a face-off.

"That's a penalty shot, Baily. What the hell are you doing? He took me down from behind; there was no one else to stop me."

"I'm the ref, Chapell. You just fell down. There wasn't even a penalty, much less a penalty-shot situation."

"I can't believe it. You couldn't see your dick if it was stuffed in your mouth."

"Watch it, Chapell. I don't have to take that."

"Get in the game, Baily. You're being paid to ref, not just drop the puck for face-offs."

The other team put in two more easy goals, while Chapell's team struggled. It was one of those nights when the other team, the Blades, couldn't do anything wrong, and Chapell's team, the Pelicans, couldn't do anything right. He became more and more frustrated. Perhaps an average of four and a half hours of sleep a night had something to do with it.

Once again he was tripped and the ref didn't see it. Halfway through the second period, he took a hard elbow in the chin. Nothing. Blind ref. Another layer of futility seething beneath the surface.

The evening's entertainment culminated when the right wing fed him a quick pass from behind the goal and the goalie was trapped on the wrong side of the net. Half an open net to shoot at and Chapell spent all his frustration on the shot. It hit the cross bar, ricocheted into the top of the glass, and continued all the way to the building's high, vaulted ceiling, where it hit hard, then plopped back to the floor out of play. He had missed an open net with a ninety-mile-per-hour shot.

The detective skated over and slammed the glass with his stick—twice. On the second smash the wooden blade inserted into the state-of-the-art graphite shaft shattered and flew into the air about twenty feet. The sound of the smashes echoed around the building for five seconds.

Both refs blew whistles, and as Baily skated backward toward the timekeeper's box, his hands went to his hips to signal a misconduct penalty, and Chapell went ballistic.

"What da you mean, misconduct, you fucking idiot? That's not even a penalty! Get your eyes out of your ass, Baily. You might actually see a hockey game."

"That'll be two more for zero tolerance, Chapell." The ref signaled another two minutes to the timekeeper on top of the ten-minute misconduct. Referees were not required to take any grief from a player at any time—no back talk on the ice or from the bench, not even a half-hidden lewd gesture from the bench.

"You goddamned moron! If you had another eye, you'd be a fucking cyclops, Baily!" Chapell threw his stick at the boards and skated toward the referee. Two of the players caught him and held him.

"That's the game. You're gone, Chapell. Go get dressed, go home, and cool off. This just isn't your night."

Rider Chapell, captain and team leader, was one of the most level-headed players in the league. It quickly dawned on him that his actions were childish and that he'd overstepped the boundaries. He shut up and headed for the dressing room. Someone would bring the unbroken sixty-five-dollar stick shaft. After the game, he found the ref and apologized.

"Look, Tim, I've had a 'heavy flow' day, and I took it out on you. I've never done that before, and it won't happen again."

"I know. You kind of surprised a lot of people. Not like you—especially in the profession you're in."

"Yeah." *Something about a woman being sewn alive inside a dead horse, and I can't catch the son of a bitch that did it.*

Chapell smiled at the man, patted him on the shoulder, and said, "You reffed a good game, Tim. See ya."

The hockey game had been the culmination of a day that had started badly and gone downhill from there. The detective's appearance that morning in court had not gone well. As the one of the investigating officers, the lieutenant had been called to testify against a young boy who had executed a motel clerk during a robbery. The other members of the gang had stood and laughed as the thirteen-year-old shot the woman in the back of the head three times from a distance of three feet. More and more of the city's murders were being committed by kids who weren't old enough to drive. Perhaps it had been something to do with the fact that much of the time they only received a slap on the wrists. Unfortunately, in this case the prosecuting attorney was a dunce, and the defendant's attorney was as sharp as a tack. Chapell could see the jury visibly embracing the innocent-faced thirteen-year-old who had been temporarily driven insane by everything from sexual abuse to a cut in his allowance, which the prosecutor had failed to bring out had been done because the little bastard was buying drugs with the money.

Not ten minutes after he'd got back to his office from court, Chapell had been called to the chief's office, where the chief had argued with him over his plan of procedure. *Goddamn maniac should have been sewn inside the horse instead of that poor girl.* The chief's family was Nashville "old money." The man had risen through the ranks like a rocket by way of the good ole boy network exerting pressure in the right places. *That buffoon wouldn't know good police work if it was placed in a cocktail glass and shoved up his ass.*

The necropsy on the horse had come in late that morning—twenty-four hours after the woman had been found. But it wouldn't have if Chapell hadn't gone to the lab and raised hell. They'd told him on the phone that it'd be a few days—they were backed up. He didn't have a few days to waste. The reports said that the animal had been poisoned with hydrogen cyanide—Prussic acid—the same method used in the previous murders over the last twenty years. If injected into a human in concentrated form, the stuff was fatal within six seconds—one of the fastest poisons known to man.

Chapell had gone to lunch with his younger brother, Ponder, and the veterinarian had added fuel to the fire by displaying a rather cavalier attitude about how Bella Rose had died and how it was perfectly acceptable for man to routinely extinguish the life of his fellow man by whatever creative means possible.

The lunch had begun well enough. When Chapell mentioned that the Tennessee Walker found with a dead woman inside had been poisoned by Prussic acid, Ponder had launched into a lecture between mouthfuls of avocado salad.

"Hydrocyanic acid occurs naturally in a lot of things—peach and apricot pits, apple seeds. You could get the same result, only a little slower, feeding the horse a branch from a wild cherry tree—preferably one that's been broken off for a few days. The cyanide compounds concentrate in the dead leaves—horse eats, horse dies. There are other ways. Sixty cc's of Sleepaway—sodium pentobarbital—injected would have worked just as well. Sometimes pentobarb will knock the animal over faster than you can jump out of the way. I knew a vet who broke his watch band when a horse fell over so fast it scraped the watch right off his arm. Thirty of Pent and thirty of a disinfectant like Roccal is cheaper—and meaner. Once she's on the ground, you inject the Roccal, it coagulates the blood, and the heart stops. Got to burn like a son of a bitch first, though—if the horse is even slightly awake."

"Yeah, but how are you going to inject a horse in a vein in the middle of the pasture in the middle of the night?"

Ponder had continued with his stream of information. "Of course, the way the pros do it at the racetracks—for insurance? They might stuff pieces of a plastic bag up the animal's nose, or even put the bag over the head and tie it closed. Suffocation. No needle marks, no poison in the necropsy. Then there's a solution of Epsom salts and—"

"Ponder, I don't want to kill a horse, goddamn it! It hurts just to think about it. And that's only a fraction of how much it hurts to consider what that poor woman must have endured before she suffocated. Put yourself inside the body cavity of a dead animal—no air, no light, the stink! No escape! Jesus, I can't think of very many ways to die that would be any more fun than that."

"Hey, Ride, you're sweating it too much. Maybe she got what she deserved. Most of those starlets are sluts. If they don't make it past the producer's choice of motel rooms, they don't make it into the studio. Somebody was probably doing humanity a service. There are too many of them anyway. Too many singers, too many bad songs."

"Sweetis Jesis, listen to you!"

"Maybe they killed her because she couldn't sing in tune. God knows *that* ought to be a capital offense." He giggled.

"Ponder, these women have died horrible deaths. There's nothing funny about it."

"I think it's hilarious. Getting sewn inside a horse? Try to beat that on *America's Funniest Videos.* Good God, Ride, there are too many people on the planet anyway. We're destroying forests and polluting the water at breakneck speed. We need a serious war or a good solid plague to pare back the hordes. Maybe it would stave off the demise of mankind for a few more years. Bubonic plague killed about a third of Europe in the fourteen hundreds. Man, could we use something like that. You can't even drive to the grocery store without someone driving right up your exhaust pipe, ass stuck to their horn because you're not doing sixty-five on a side street."

Chapell was in open-mouthed shock. Over the years he had sensed his brother's growing insouciance from being comfortable in life, while believing no one could take it away. However, he had never seen the side of Ponder that resented others from infringing on his space. Perhaps the man was too inured. Like physicians, Ponder made his living off the misfortune of other people. Like physicians, if there were no patients to treat for a kidney disorder—no diabetes, leukemia, intestinal adhesions, blockages, ruptures, polyps, or cancer—then there would be no hundred sixty grand a year at his Belle Meade practice. A talented vet who specialized in ophthalmology or orthopedics or internal medicine and surgery, which was Ponder's field, made considerably more money than the average general-practice vet. If one was practicing in Nashville's ritziest neighborhood . . .

Although the brothers had always been fairly close, there had always been a perpetual undercurrent of turmoil in the back of Chapell's mind when it came to his relationship with Ponder. Dysfunctional would scarcely begin to describe the family who had grown up with Rae Willie Chapell for a mother. If she wasn't performing or recording, she was drunk or blasted on drugs. Get out of the way if she was coming down from a high. As her career progressed, Jay Jr., Chapell's father, wisely spent more and more time in the woods hunting and fishing than with his wife and kids. The eight-figure yearly income of Rae Willie's career afforded the man the luxury of not having to work.

For years he had played piano in her band, in addition to booking, driving the bus, managing, advertising, and trying to collect the one-nighters' measly hundred bucks—for five pieces, plus singer—from hundreds of smug-faced, anal-retentive club owners who proliferated from coast to coast. Also, with Jay Jr. in Montana hunting, Rae Willie's fame afforded her the luxury of an endless line of one-night stand-ins, and, to the boys' chagrin, their father didn't seem to care. It was as if he'd lost interest in her, and her career, but didn't have the guts to file for divorce. A year after her death, he had been killed in a hunting accident in Wyoming. A friend had mistaken him for a mule deer and shot him in the chest. Like his parents, who had met and fallen in love in an orphanage when they were in their mid teens, Chapell was on his own, and he had just turned eighteen. He had wondered more than once if the family was cursed. He had assumed the role of protector for Ponder and Gale. The incredible income from royalties—over five million a year back then—had solved a lot of problems.

Before the death of their parents, there had been a rivalry among the three kids. Ponder, the largest, and strongest, could get his way by intimidating Rider and Gale. If intimidation didn't work, Ponder wasn't above the use of physical force. However, after the death of their father, the three orphans had grown gradually closer in an all-out defense against the world. Being the siblings of Rae Willie Chapell carried burdens and demands that were beyond the grasp of the average orphan. Survival had turned the kids to each other with an intense loyalty—all for one and one for all. A lot of secrets had been shared.

Ponder's annoying behavior had chewed on Chapell all afternoon and evening until, coupled with the pressures of work, it had erupted on the ice in a most uncharacteristic manner. Like a hyper Pomeranian, Ponder's behavior was still yapping at the back one-third of his mind when he pulled into the half-mile-long driveway to his home.

Gale was on the road. It seemed like she'd been gone forever. The good news was that she was on her way home. *Damn, I miss her.* Gale was three years younger than Ponder, who was two years younger than Rider. Rae Willie's brooding spree, it had been called—three kids in five years.

The next morning the lieutenant was at work early.

"Alicia, did you pull the files on Toy Duck?"

"They're on your desk, darling, right in front of your nose. If you'd clean the thing off once in a while ... I sent them up yesterday afternoon."

"How sweet of you. You're such a treasure."

"And your girlfriend pissed on my face last night."

"If you'll remember, you were responsible for my girlfriend leaving me. Said she couldn't take competing with you. Shameless old harridan, she called you."

"If you'd be so kind as to look up the word harridan in the dictionary, Sweetheart, you'd find that it does not describe a wonderfully full-figured gal like *moi*."

The overweight sixty-four-year-old woman, who was the supervisor of the records department, had been playfully badgering Chapell for twelve years. He was always a little amazed at the woman's imagination.

"I'll be sure to do that before I get on with the day's tasks at hand."

"By the way, your physical is due next week. Your place or mine?"

"I'll call my own doctor, as usual, thank you."

"Well, we're going to need his report for our filey-wilies."

"Of course."

Chapell had always been one of the few cops who used his own family physician to do the annual examination required by the police department rather than using the department's doctor. He always had the doc-

tor do a much more thorough exam than the department required. Another advantage of having money.

He planned to spend the morning reabsorbing the
files of Toy Duck. There were over three hundred
documents in the folders. His mind darted quickly in
and out of the scene at San Antonio Taco with Ponder
the day before.

He had just opened the first file folder when the
phone rang.

"Chapell."

"Lieutenant, this is Ray Robbins. Channels Four,
Two, Five, and Seventeen, in that order, have called
to demand interviews. Also, I've had calls from the
Tennessean and the *Banner,* in addition to four different radio stations—all of this within the last forty-five
minutes. Somebody's gotten on the horn out there,
and they're trying for a new Guinness world record.
Toy Duck fever, at its best—and worst." Robbins was
the head of media relations in the Public Information office.

"We've been expecting it. Actually, I thought they'd
be screaming last night."

"I guess we'd better call a press conference, but
Chief McKinty is adamant about holding off coverage
for as long as possible. The mayor's office has been
all over my ass this morning. The governor's office
called me at home at six-thirty. Holding them off isn't
going to be easy."

"Can the captain handle it? He's good at double-
talk."

"Nope. You've been elected and nailed to the
post."

"Time?"

"What's convenient, early afternoon? Brass said
they didn't care."

"How about one? That'll give me a few hours to
get my act together." Chapell liked Robbins. The man
was not full of himself like a lot of p.r. people, and

he consistently came down on the side of the working man in the department.

"Captain Satterfield will be there, and Chief McKinty will put in his two cents, but you're going to be the guy on the hot seat."

"I can handle it, Ray. As you know, I'm a virtual wizard with words in front of a camera."

It was actually quite the opposite. Chapell and the press played a game whenever he did the press conferences. He would give a statement with only the barest information, and they delighted in trying as hard as they could to pry the details out of him. He'd give them information if they'd ask the right questions, but they knew they'd have to work for every tidbit. The brass liked Chapell to handle the cameras because he did give only minimal information, but did it without pissing off the reporters. He was likable and believable. Above all, he was the son of Rae Willie— Nashville's own, and he was gorgeous. To look at him, he looked like a professional model. Chapell was a fine-looking example of a cop. He had Rae Willie's sea green eyes, complete with their ever present glint of mischief, and curly blond hair, maintained by one of Nashville's more expensive styling shops. He had his father's square face and cleft chin, along with the former lumberjack's hard musculature that had served so well in many situations through the years—situations that the average man would never confront. With the expensive tailored suits and well-manicured hands and face, the cameras loved him the way they had loved his mother.

"Good. One o'clock, then, in the lobby."

He delved into the Toy Duck file and noted, again, that the madness had begun a little over twenty years ago. Interesting, he'd almost forgotten that the first victim—a young girl—had been murdered only a week after the death of his mother. He sorted through the files in utter fascination, losing himself, drinking in the information like a fat man gulping beers while mowing the lawn on a hot Saturday afternoon.

The phone rang.

"Chapell."

"Lieutenant, as long as you're the guest speaker this afternoon, we'd kind of like to hear what you're going to say. Can you come to my office?" It was the chief. Chapell should have called hours ago to see when the "pre-game" meeting was going to be held.

"Certainly. I'm on my way." He had forgotten all about the news conference at one. It was now twelve-fifteen. The brass wanted him to use his charm to get the media to go easy on the department. Fat chance of the bloodsuckers doing that. The first four murders were still unsolved, and everyone knew that little problem was due to the Nashville Police Department's incredible stupidity and perpetual laziness. The reporters would jump on this with more frenzy than an army of yellow jackets on a fresh watermelon half at a Sunday school picnic. It would saturate network news programs from one end of the cable dial to the other unless . . .

One hundred fifteen minutes later, Chapell and his boss, Captain Lou Satterfield, were eating a late lunch at the Gerst Haus. The restaurant had been the city's most famous German restaurant for years. The two men were indulging in the post-game, locker room chatter—analyzing the victory.

"It won't last. They'll fold—as one. They won't be able to keep their hands off this one for a whole twenty-four hours." Chapell wanted a beer, but made it a rule never to drink at lunch with his boss—even when his boss did.

"Probably, but you did a spectacular job gently jerking them off. My guess is it'll hit tomorrow morning. Getting them to hold off today may give us time to turn some leads before the perp is spooked. Maybe we'll find something, and this time we won't look like the bill is due and we've lost our wallet."

The reporters had left the conference grumbling that the department had no right to ask the media to deprive the public of its right to know about good gore when it was available. Chapell's success at getting the reporters to hold off had been no accident. The cop had remained well acquainted with the media over the years; he was the son of country music's biggest, ever, star. The music community regarded him with respect also. He was routinely invited to parties and to the award shows at the Opry House. He was on a first-name basis with the executives of all the important companies and had been privy to a lot of the infighting that had taken place over the years. He also had a sister who had been in the business since she was a kid. If Chapell didn't know someone, chances were that Gale did. With all the contacts, sooner or later he would come up with a solution for the Toy Duck thing, and it would not hurt a thing to have that credit slapped on his proficiency report.

Like most cops, he loved his job—the periodic excitement binges, the camaraderie, the knowledge that you were different than the ordinary citizen—you knew things the average American should never know; you were in possession of power and deadly force that were imparted to only a special few. The biggest drawback with the occupation was that the cop business was a dead-end street as far as providing a man with a serious future as a top-level executive. There was only one commander-in-chief, and getting there usually meant wading through the politics of kissing several square yards of assorted ass, in addition to another fifteen years of time. Even if you did make it to the top spot, you answered directly to the mayor— someone who knew nothing about police work. Being independently wealthy allowed Rider Chapell to step outside himself and look at his career objectively. Most cops didn't have that privilege. They were in it for life and a decent retirement after twenty-five or thirty years. Chapell looked at his career as something he loved and was extremely talented at doing; however, love is, at best, *transient*.

He spent the remainder of the afternoon pencil-whipping the ubiquitous reports and forms that were stacking up. Each time the phone rang he was sure it would be Gale. Each time he was wrong.

By seven-thirty, he was sitting in the chair of his hair stylist. The woman had bought special XXL curlers to perm the light blond hair in large curls. It was a fete of magic to make the long ringlets look short enough to pass police regulations. A manicurist did his nails while the stylist worked on the coiffure. It was a ritual Chapell had endured once every two weeks for years—another necessary evil associated with being the son of a country music legend.

An hour later, as he pulled out of the underground garage in the Universal Tower Building, where the barber shop was located, he popped a new CD of Lorrie Morgan into the Jaguar's player to see if the garage had finally fixed the machine. He'd caught a ride to work that morning so that he could pick the car up from the garage where it had been for four days. Usually, he drove the Jeep to work. The fact that he was wealthy didn't need to be rubbed in. Most cops had to struggle hard to make ends meet, sometimes working one or two extra jobs. The Jag was only two months old, and it had been in the shop four times—twice because the CD player was screwed up. Fortunately, Chapell wouldn't have to worry about the player too much longer. Someone was already working on a new and exciting way to fix it permanently.

Chapter Three

Chapell's car phone began tweeting just as he was leaving the underground garage. It took both hands to negotiate the steep ramp, look for traffic and turn right on the one-way Chet Atkins Place while trying to avoid a cement truck that seemed bent on destroying him. The phone kept ringing. Usually, after the sixth ring his office would hang up and beep him.

Persistent son of a bitch, whoever.

He reached Sixteenth, stopped the car to look for traffic, and picked it up. "Chapell."

"Mr. Chapell, this is Nolan Tyres." Tyres was the author of the unauthorized biography of Rae Willie Rider that had been recently released.

"Tyres, how the hell did you get this number? It's unlisted."

"Hey, what are investigative reporters for, Mr. Chapell?"

"You couldn't investigate your way out of a toilet stall. I told you three times already—you're a blotch of diarrhetic shit, and that's the long and short of it. If I find out that your book was responsible for setting off the Toy Duck killer, I will personally hang you by the balls from the top of the Bat Building." The South Central Bell Building was the tallest building in Nashville. With its two pointed towers on top, it resembled a bat; even before its completion it had been nicknamed the Bat Building.

"You know as well as I, Detective, that I'm not responsible for every Tom, Dick, and Harry who get

their rocks off by sewing women inside dead horses.
I think you ought to reconsider. Just read the book.
What you saw was an early manuscript. Several things
were changed. Your endorsement for the media would
mean a lot."

"I know it would, and as long as you're purporting
the ridiculous theories about my mother, you and I are
in a permanent locked-horns position. Now fuck off!"

He slammed the phone closed and dropped it on
the passenger seat. The man was so utterly disgusting,
Chapell couldn't stand the sight of him. Talk about a
literary mercenary . . . There were a lot of authors who
wrote preposterous things just to make money. Tyres
seemed to delight in ruining lives as well. He had
asked Chapell to read the book well before it went to
print. Chapell had got only to the fifth chapter before
he'd burned the entire manuscript in the fireplace
without so much as a call to Tyres. The bloodsucker
had written that he had proof Rae Willie had a lover
who was fooling around with twelve-year-old Gale,
and Rae Willie was condoning it! It got worse—the
writer said that the fire in Rae Willie's dressing trailer
had been started intentionally—the country superstar
had been murdered! That fire had been investigated
more thoroughly than any fire in the history of mankind. Chapell had read the reports. The investigating
team had determined that the fire started from one of
Rae Willie's ubiquitous cigarettes after she had fallen
asleep on the sofa. She had probably been drunk, as
usual, although that part had been kept from the public. The man who burned to death in the trailer's back
room could have been a lover. If he was, why were
they sleeping in separate rooms? Chapell, who had
been eighteen at the time, had never been certain
about that part. God knows, there wasn't much the
woman hadn't done or almost died trying. But
allowing someone to fool around with Gale was out
of the question. Rae Willie loved her kids. Had Jay
Jr. stayed around a little more, things might have been

different. He'd just seemed to lose interest in it all—
had taken more comfort in the deep woods than his
family.

Nolan Tyres couldn't care less where Jay Jr. had
taken his comfort. Nor could he care less about the
twit who'd been sewn inside a horse, rest her soul. He
had devoted two entire chapters of his new book to
the Toy Duck Murders Connection. With his inside
contact at the police department being well paid for
the work, ongoing files were periodically Xeroxed and
smuggled to the author. He knew exactly where the
police were in their investigation at any given time.
With the other truths he was privy to, it had not been
hard to prove convincingly that Rae Willie was only
the first of the Toy Duck murders. The killer, who
had been viciously spurned by the "Queen"—this psychotic beast, who had been made fun of by her Great
and Almighty Majesty, had then stumbled onto a mar-
velously unique method of killing lookalikes and had
used it whenever the memory of the original bitch
raised its ugly fucking head! It was a great hook!
How opportune that Bella Rose had been sacrificed
with such perfect timing—at the exact moment Bro.
Tyres's excellent literary tome had hit the market. The
blond singer's demise had sent the book streaking toward the top of the best-seller list. A man did what a
man had to do to get the dice in hand, and Nolan
Tyres was on a roll. His last biography, an exposé of
one of the nation's high-profile senators, had been on
the best-seller list for six months. God knows some of
the things the author had done to bring that one off
would easily have been worthy of more than a few
years in federal prison. In near record time, *Rae Willie:
Naked Songs, Naked Nights* was on the brink of making the *New York Times* list; Chapell's endorsement
would have blown it right through the top—instant
number one best seller—millions sold worldwide, and
that's what life was all about.

The author hung up the phone with chagrin and fielded a barrage of wheezing coughs brought on by the stress. He ground his cigar to a bitter death on the desk's glass top, then swept the remains into the waste basket. *Gotta quit smoking that shit. Sure-fire way to kill yourself, Nolan, ole boy—inhaled or not.* There was no reason why, after twenty years, that Chapell couldn't endorse the book. Why try to protect a mother who had hated him and mistreated him until the day she died? Get it out—catharsis—that's the smart thing to do. Get on with life. And, incidentally, make Nolan D. Tyres an icon for the ages. Icon was good. The author already had enough money.

As a kid, Mrs. Tyres's little boy had been the personification of the overbearing loudmouth. Obstreperous, self-centered, indulgent, he had spent most of his life alone because he quickly alienated anyone who had a passing interest in being a friend. It wasn't something he worked at; lack of social skills came entirely naturally. They were the simple by-product of a selfish alcoholic mother who never picked him up and held him and a workaholic father who had never taken the time to throw a baseball with his overweight, ugly little son with the dumbo ears. The boy had learned to make up for his insecurity by expressing himself either loudly, when in the presence of others, or on paper—usually in thoughts wrapped in acerbic vitriol. He had learned how to type on his mother's IBM Selectronic while still in grade school; had paid for his first word processor while a sophomore journalism major at Northwestern by selling the *Tribune* a well documented article about a Chicago's alderman on the take. By his senior year in college, setting the written, scandalous word to paper had become a passion, and with little else in his life that was of interest, other than reading, he had eventually sharpened his skills to a fine, daggered point—a point that made its way through more and more hearts without mercy. After graduating, he'd returned to the city where he'd grown up and got a job as the society reporter for the *Nashville Banner*. It hadn't taken long to discover that as long as no finger was pointed, hands cupped to the sides of their faces, the average Nashvillian sincerely enjoyed telling about the seedy side of his/her friends—especially if the friends were famous. Tyres, the reporter, quickly found that gossip is as much a part of the human psyche as eating and defecating. The journalist made it a hard and fast rule never to reveal his sources, and he gradually established a stellar reputation of never breaking this rule. The result was that the friends and relatives of stars revealed things to him that would otherwise remain in the closet for all time. Little nuggets like the time when two stars mooned each other while they were being driven down one of Hollywood's busiest thoroughfares late at night after finishing the day's work on a movie. Giddy from yet another eighteen-hour day, each had striven to gross the other out as the drivers kept the cars side by side. It had ended when one of the stars stripped to the buff, jumped out of the car at a stoplight, and ran all the way around the car buck naked before getting back in.

The mind picture of her buxom figure running naked in the middle of a Hollywood street had put Nolan Tyres's second unauthorized biography on the national best-seller list. The source of the anecdote had never been revealed.

Tonight he would have his own little soiree. With the kind of pressure he'd been under lately, flying around the country to do all the talk shows and signings, God knows he could use a little release. The entertainment was going to cost five grand, and it had better be as good as his contact had advertised.

Chapell had been using a controlled shout to talk to the author. He was just passing the new BMI building on Sixteenth when the whine of blood coursing through his ears began to drown out the sounds of the road and the Jaguar's quiet engine. He began to concentrate on alpha rhythms to allow pressure to return to some semblance of normal. Tyres was a natural at pissing people off. The man made a career out of it.

The detective's mind briefly skipped across the picture of the poor woman who had been sewn inside the horse. One of the theories proposed during the last murder, five years before, was that the killer's pattern was actually influenced by the release of a major Rae Willie Chapell project. The CBS executives in New York had been brilliant in marketing the dead singer's products. They allowed a major release of material only once every four or five years. They had carefully released projects like *Rae Willie's Greatest Hits* and the movies she had made so that the singer was never overexposed. Streisand had done the same thing her whole career. A minimal number of album releases, movies, and concerts had never allowed the public to get enough of her. She had remained one of the premium draws for well over two decades.

Tyres's biography of the country singer had hit the stores just a couple of weeks before the scheduled network showing of *Night Song*—Rae Willie's third movie. If the killer's urges were triggered by these events, Chapell hoped he would not kill again when the movie was shown next week.

That son of a bitch! I wouldn't put it past Tyres to have killed that last woman just to sell books. And he is much too aware of details that should be known only by the police department. Son of a bitch! Is he good enough to pull it off... ? Why didn't we...?

He grabbed the phone and dialed the squad's number.

"Johnson."

"Rob, what do we know about Nolan Tyres?"

"In which categories? We know he's a degenerate prick."

"Tyres was born and raised in Nashville, wasn't he?"

"True."

"He would have been in his twenties when the first Toy Duck murder went down."

"I suppose. What are you getting at?"

"What do we know about the man? Was he a fan? From the first four chapters of the book I read before I threw it away, I found that he knew a lot more about my mother and especially the Toy Duck murders than the average fan on the street."

"And . . ."

"I'm saying let's do a little digging on brother Nolan Tyres—where he was when Bella Rose was killed. If he doesn't have an alibi, then let's go back to some more of the murders."

"You think he could be Toy Duck?"

"I don't think he's the original, but I wouldn't put it past him to have pulled off this last one for the publicity. I'm not sure if he could do it without screwing something up—leaving something behind—but the more I think about it, the more I need to see the idea disproved. There have been enough pictures of those sutures published that with a little practice someone might be able to pull it off."

"Sounds like a plan to me. I'll get Richy to help me and we'll see what shakes out. Hell, I might even read his book."

"If you can stomach that shit, then you're a better man than I am. Do your digging for as long as you can without him finding out—talk to neighbors, business associates, you know the drill. If he is Toy Duck, we don't want to spook him just yet."

"Understood. Before the week is over, we'll know if he jerks off with his right or left hand, and he'll never be the wiser."

"I'll bet on the right hand—of one of his bisexual friends." The world-famous author had made little attempt to hide the fact that he went either way.

* * *

Actually, Tyres had other ways of releasing his sexual tension besides getting his skin flute fingered by a male or female.

"Where is that damn car?"

It was almost nine p.m. and his patience was growing thin. He had tried to find something to do after Chapell had hung up on him; the man's refusal to cooperate had been upsetting. *I knew better. Stupid bastard won't listen to reason. What he needs is another lesson in humility.* The round- and red-faced overweight author finally had given in to prowling through the front rooms of his half-million-dollar home just off Otter Creek Road, watching for the limo to crawl up the long, steep drive. The car was a half hour late, and for what he was shelling out for the evening's entertainment, late was unacceptable.

"Finally. Asshole."

On the way down the drive, the air in the car turned a dark blue from the stream of invective and vituperation unleashed by an expert.

"I'm sorry, Mr. Tyres. There was an overturned semi on fire on I-65. They were turning traffic around and detouring it onto Harding. What a mess. You could see the flames and smoke from a mile down the road. I'll go back into town on Hillsboro."

Twenty minutes later, the driver let Tyres out at the back of a large, battered brick building that faced Eighth Avenue South. A small neon sign flashed THE QUEEN'S OWN over the front door, but Tyres wasn't going in the front door—not tonight. An extremely large middle-aged man opened the door in the rear of the building for him and said, "Good evening, Mr. T. You won't believe the show tonight."

Tyres grunted gratuitously and quickly stepped inside, where he was ushered down a poorly lit, paint-peeling hall by another large man whose face looked like it had been through a couple of dog fights. They finally arrived at a door that was painted a dark shade of purple. The man opened it and Tyres stepped into a small, darkened private theater.

"Nolan!"

A well groomed man dressed in a tuxedo greeted him with outstretched arms that were never meant to make contact. In spite of the room-wide smile that revealed perfect teeth and crinkled eyes; in spite of the thick mane of expensively cut coal black hair adorned with not one but two narrow strips of white that terminated at the forehead; in spite of the tailored tuxedo, the practiced nonchalance of an old and dear family friend, and many other good proprietary gestures, the man had an oily veneer that would resist being scrubbed away with a hundred showers.

"Evening, John. You said something special tonight."

The theater was nothing like the building or the dirty hall. It was clean, opulent, and equipped with nothing but the best. The host led Tyres the few steps to the front seat and said, "You are going to fall in love tonight. This is one of the finest acts we've ever offered. It's only been in the U.S. for a couple of months—direct from mainland China. Remarkable. Truly remarkable."

"For what you're charging, it had better be."

"You'll agree that it's worth every penny before the evening is over. Please have a seat. We're almost ready to begin."

Tyres sat in the only seat in the front row. He was approximately six feet from the darkened stage. Behind him were two rows of three seats, all like his, theater plush. The theater was not meant to seat numbers. Most acts were for a single or at most a handful of patrons. In front of him, lining the width of the twelve-foot stage, the thickly carpeted floor was covered with soft mats and pillows.

"Would you care to indulge?"

The host presented Tyres with a saucer-sized lead crystal plate that was covered with a matching lid.

Tyres removed the lid and placed it and the plate on the small stand next to his seat. An intricate pattern of geometric white lines decorated the plate's surface. Someone had spent a great deal of time creating the pattern. The host handed him an exquisite cut-glass tube.

"Thank you, John."

"Very good stuff. Direct from Burma."

Tyres put one end of the tube well up his nose, and by carefully following the lines, he sniffed and snorted a quarter of the cocaine on its way into his bloodstream. He replaced the plate's cover and laid the tube next to it. The buzz started quickly.

"Wine? We have an excellent Bordeaux."

"Not tonight. I want my head clear."

The author was surprised to see that a scrim had been erected floor to ceiling at the lip of the stage. About waist high, there appeared to be a small, deliberately hemmed hole in it about the size of a soup can cover. Tyres wondered what it was for. He felt a hint of resentment about the scrim. Most acts were observed without hindrance.

The room darkened even more, and a dozen expensive speakers buried in the room's walls came to life with the sound of oriental instruments. The orchestration was sparse: two drums, a stringed instrument, and a flute interacted with one another. The sounds thickened as more instruments joined the five-note motif, and the lights on the stage slowly came to life. Overhead, animated gels swept a soft yellow light across the stage in patterns. Tyres, aided by the coke, briefly imagined a velvet spring rain dancing in a lazy breeze. The stage and patterns slowly dissolved to blue, then dark-blue, then even darker . . .

There she was. In a frozen curtsy; arms folded across her chest; a single red rose in one hand; eyes, head down; demure.

The lights brightened enough to reveal that she was quite tall. Perhaps five eight or nine. She wore only a

minimum of stage makeup, unlike the caked Japanese
Kabuki dancers. When she slowly raised her head and
unfolded her arms, Tyres could see that she was very
Chinese and stunningly beautiful.

China Doll! My God, how exquisite!

Coal black hair hung shoulder-length in bodied curls
and tresses, not in the ruler-straight sheaths and bangs
worn by the Chinese women depicted on the evening
news or *still another* documentary covering the most
populous and suppressed population on the planet.

Tyres's jaw had slowly dropped open in awed
anticipation.

The music quickly segued into a definite series of
rhythm patterns, and the woman began to dance.
Slowly, seductively. Eyes as bottomless as a deep well
on the darkest night fixed on the imaginary spectators
in the back row of a huge theater, with an occasional
shy flickering at Tyres in his front-row seat to see if
he approved. The sheer ivory gown she was wearing
hugged long legs and perfect hips in intimate out-
lines that belied perfect femininity. With a casual
ingenuousness she combined the grace of the finest
ballet dancer with the sensuousness of a master
temptress.

Tyres did not notice that he was sitting on the very
edge of his seat, hands on his knees in anticipation.
The coke had now scored well in the bull's-eye.

The music crescendoed as more drums were added;
a throbbing was established, and the dancer moved
about the small stage twisting, undulating subtly,
meeting the rhythm's taunts with studied ease. Tyres
was beyond noticing as the oriental instruments
dropped out, one by one, to be replaced with more
and more drums. The beat was gradually and expertly
modified into a commanding chant—a demand for the
body to drive and pulsate before the rhythms.

As if shedding her innocence, the woman threw the
rose to the side of the stage, and her movements became more worldly to complement the pounding

rhythms that had increased in tempo and loudness.
There was a sudden four-beat break of silence. The
rhythm came back in hard, and the complicated ca-
dence began to repeat itself over and over, driving,
driving ... Tyres could see the sheen of perspiration
on the dancer's face. She had been dancing for almost
ten minutes.

She established herself directly in front of him for
a full thirty seconds with her back turned, the easy
bump and exotic arm movements punctuated by
graceful movements of the slippery gown. The music
culminated in two tremendous cymbal crashes, and
Tyres' breathing stopped for ten seconds as she ripped
the gown away and tossed it offstage in one sweep-
ing movement. With his eyes glued to the undulating
muscles of a sweat-glistening back and bare buttocks, he could see that she was wearing only a G-
string, a bra, and ivory high heels. He was impatient
to see how revealing the costume would be in the
front—barely able to control the urge to yell,
"Turn around!"

She did—in a quick spin to land splay-legged, hips
and torso still moving to the mesmerizing beat.

The top of her costume was merely a drape of thin
cloth that allowed the bas-relief of perfect breasts and
nipples. It had flown up at the bottom to reveal the
lower third of her breasts as she had turned. She bent
over backward, and again the bottoms of her breasts
were revealed. Tyres's lecherous scrutiny leaped to the
bottom part of the costume, and he was surprised to
see a three-dimensional, ornately decorated cup covering the pudendum.

She straightened and began once more to dance,
moving around the stage in more seductive movements, breasts flipping the tiny drape up dangerously.
The music darkened and quickened, building, driving
... Legs well apart, she limbo-hopped from her position backstage until she was at the lip of the stage
and, once again, directly in front of the perspiring middle-

aged man in the rumpled suit. Slowly, deliberately, she pulled the cloth top down and away from her body until the string broke. Using the motion of her arm and shoulder, she began to purposely jiggle her breasts in synch with the music, first the right, then the left. Soft pink, erect nipples cut tiny blue-hot swaths through the air as the woman looked the author directly in the eye, in defiance of his obvious tumescence. A low moan escaped from the man's mouth. He unconsciously rose to his feet, sweat pouring down his forehead and cheeks.

The moan turned into a low, guttural scream when she reached down and ripped off the cup. Springing to attention was a ten-inch, fully erect, sweat-glistening penis. The dancer smirked at the astonished man, then turned and began to prance around the stage, totally naked except for high heels. The penis flopped up and down like a branch in a hard breeze. Just when Tyres thought he could stand it no longer, the dancer walked to the edge of the stage and slowly pushed the erection through the "glory hole" in the scrim. He was on it in a second, pouring its head deep into his mouth, his greedy hands kneading the shaft. He barely noticed as two naked Chinese boys entered the room and began to undress him. One of them took his bursting erection into a velvet mouth; the other entered him from behind and began to pump and grind gently. The dancer slowly pulled out of the author's eager mouth, and back through the hole in the scrim. Tyres wanted to cry. He started to protest. Before he could get the words out, the scrim was released from the ceiling and he watched with fascination as it floated to the floor like gossamer. No longer separated, the dancer gave him a saucy pout, turned around, then knelt on hands and knees in one graceful movement to present his naked buttocks to the sweating men. It was then that Tyres saw the folded vulva directly below the anus.

"*Hermaphrodite. Jesus fucking Christ!*"

Now he could see that there was no visible testes *in*

scrotum attached to the erected penis. As with many humans who are born gonochoristic, they were probably inside. The bizarre thought flashed through Tyre's coke-laced brain that because they were not located externally, where the temperature was two or three degrees cooler than the body's internal temperature, they probably would not produce viable sperm. In the male mode this exquisite creature was, most certainly, sterile.

The boy on the floor released the author's cock, and Tyres plunged it into the waiting enchantment before him. The boy behind Tyres stepped in once more and continued to gently pump the author's ass; the other boy lay flat on the stage and began to perform fellatio on the moaning Chinese hermaphrodite while fondling his own erection. When the author finally exploded, the pain from the release was so intense he would have bet the entire $5,000 that he was spurting pure blood!

After the call to the Murder Squad, Chapell had driven the few blocks to Antonio's for dinner. He'd kept to himself, content only to ask the proprietor how *Tony's Lady* was running when the man had made his usual rounds of the dining room. *Tony's Lady* was Antonio's hundred-twelve-foot Hatteras, which had been birthed at one of the local marinas. After receiving a warm invitation to come and see the boat first-hand in the near future, the cop left the restaurant about nine-thirty. He pulled the Jag onto West End and headed downtown toward the entrance to the interstate.

It's still early. I think I'll drop by and see Ponder. See if he's still hosing the world with the yellow liquid by-product he makes between his legs.

Ponder had lived for years in the old family home, which was on a street just off Franklin Road. Chapell never had figured out why his brother stayed there. The house was huge, and it could have been turned

over to the State Historical Society, or the Country
Music Foundation, for a museum. Almost all of the
furniture and personal possessions of their mother's,
and father's, were still in place. Ponder had squawked
high and loud at anything being removed.

Chapell pulled through the granite gateposts, which
were topped with huge iron lions. As a young boy
there had been a period of time when the animals had
scared him, and he would shut his eyes as he passed.
He drove straight to the back of the house on the
long, convoluted driveway. There was a turnoff that
led to a circular drive in front of the house's huge
pillars, but it was rarely used anymore. The antebel-
lum mansion was well lit inside and out, as usual, for
security reasons, but Ponder's car wasn't in the five-
stall garage. No matter, Chapell had a key. He'd go
in and wait. The veterinarian would probably be home
before too long.

Surrounded by its ostentatious colonnades and their
arches, the large Greco-Roman pool glimmered in the
darkness. The underwater lights were turned off. Rae
Willie hadn't been timid about mixing architecture.
Colonial, Greek, Roman, Spanish. Intricate patterns
of tiles decorated the patio that surrounded the pool.
In the daytime it was a rather spectacular backyard.
Pictures had appeared in numerous *Southern Living*
types of magazines, and Chapell had remembered
seeing a color-picture panorama of the backyard in
one of the earlier biographies.

The cop let himself in the back door and made his
way through the mud room into the kitchen.

"Ponder?"

He hollered a couple more times to make sure his
brother wasn't home. It had been almost a year since
Chapell had been in the house. It always brought back
a plethora of memories. He made his way into his
dad's trophy room, which had been a religious experience for the boys when they were growing up—that
is, on the rare occasions they were allowed in there.

Moose, elk, antelope, deer, and even an enormous rhinoceros head decorated the walls, along with dozens of stuffed fish. Scattered about the room were glass cases that housed settings featuring pheasants, partridges, and quail. Chapell's favorite in the room was a large albino wolf with a rabbit in its mouth.

Most of Jay Jr.'s guns were neatly stacked in the huge mahogany case that occupied much of one side of the room.

He wandered out of the room and down the hall toward the stairs. Ponder must have spilled whiskey in the den. The smell was well established throughout the first floor.

Man, I haven't been upstairs in this place in years. I wonder if he's kept Mom's bedroom intact. It'd be just like him.

He climbed the huge circular stairway, pausing long enough to feel the varnished wood of the thick banister. As kids they had spent hours sliding down that banister. One day, after it had just been revarnished, the two boys had spent an hour going over the varnish with beeswax. The varnish cut down on the speed of the slide. He made his way down the long hall, admiring the original art still gracing the walls. A couple Remingtons, a Lovell, and several other local artists had rendered their interpretation of horses in flight. Rae Willie wouldn't buy anything but horses. The graceful animals were for the delight of Gale, who was fanatical over them. She'd had several of her own as a child.

Plank doors rounded at the tops opened to the left and right on the long hall. The house enclosed eleven thousand square feet, including the upstairs. The last room was entered through double, massive mahogany doors. The bedroom suite covered over two thousand square feet and three levels, and to Chapell's recollection, it looked as though it had remained untouched since his mother's death. Well, Ponder wasn't sleeping in here. Probably he still used his own room or one of the guest rooms. Rae Willie's makeup vanity, its mirror lined with lights, was still neatly littered with her brushes and the scores of jars and boxes that held the secrets of her makeup regimen which had been more than considerable.

He picked up a jar, unscrewed the top, and sniffed. *How the hell does he keep this junk from disintegrating with age? It's over twenty years old now.* Chapell had been in the room a couple of times over the years, but he didn't remember everything being kept exactly the way his mother had left it. There wasn't even any dust. Housekeeper probably.

Strange. Very strange.

He left the room and was confronted with the narrow door that led to the attic.

I haven't been up there in almost twenty years.

The door was locked, but he knew the key was kept on top of the lintel. He found it, unlocked the door, then replaced the key. He turned on the lights and started up the narrow stairs. Reaching the top, he was deluged with memories. A whole store full of childhood toys sat quietly as if waiting for someone to return. There were two very large and expensive rocking horses. A couple of sleds hung on one of the walls, although in Nashville there was rarely any use for them. He surveyed the landscape before him, which was made up of old rugs, some water skis, numerous pieces of furniture—bureaus, chests of drawers, a china cabinet; there were six wardrobes that held Rae Willie's old performance costumes; there were dozens of boxes and trunks, and examining a couple of them, he was delighted to find several lead sheets and 45 rpm records of some of his mother's first hits. A half dozen pairs of skates hung from nails on one wall—hockey skates and a pair of Gale's figure skates.

I wonder . . .

At the far end of the room was a door that led to another smaller room. All told, there were seven rooms in the attic. The Opry Room had been the site of many rainy afternoons' entertainment when the shows had ranged from "Houdini's Mighty Magic Show" to the "Great Country Star Countdown," featuring various world-renowned artists lip-syncing to old 78 rpm records on the windup Victrola. There was a makeshift stage, complete with curtains that could be drawn open and closed on a wire stretching from wall to wall across the front of the stage. It had taken them a whole afternoon to make those curtains from several pairs of drapes that had been discarded after one of Rae Willie's redecorating sprees.

Chapell made his way through the rooms, one by one, savoring the memories and secrets of each. In a secluded corner of the final, tiny room that actually topped a sun porch on the first floor, there had been a special place that was located near the angle where the rafters met the floor. The light was dim, but he knew the sequence well enough not to need it. He squatted and duck-walked under the lowering roof line, then finally lay prone on the convenient moth-eaten Persian drop rug that had been purposely laid on the floor. Turning up the rug's end, he removed the loose floorboards. How many times they had hidden cigarettes, *Playboy*s, embarrassing six-grade love notes, an unused rubber they'd found on the floor of the country club locker room, and a dozen other things that would provide mortification beyond belief if discovered by the wrong person. The large tin box came out of the space easily, and retracing the cramped routine, he carried it into the light. The feeling of anticipation at what might be inside rose geometrically. It was like a free trip back in time— a treat rarely afforded a man during a lifetime— a Jules Vernean time machine. Surely, Ponder had forgotten all about the hiding place.

Chapell set the box on a small table, and working carefully, he pried off the stubborn tin top. When he saw what was inside, his heart stopped a full four beats.

"Sweet Jesus!"

Ponder had not forgotten the hiding place!

The box was crammed with long strips of rawhide, elaborate spangles, spools of expensive spun-gold thread, and several open boxes of ornate rhinestones and studs. They were the exact materials that had been used to sew up the slit bellies of five eviscerated Tennessee Walking horses.

Chapell's head reeled in dizziness. He grabbed for the table to steady himself, missed it and tumbled to the floor. The tin box fell, and its contents scattered across the attic floor beside him.

"Get a hold of yourself, Rides. It ain't the end of the world. Maybe there's a good explanation." He pronounced the words methodically, in a low, fuzzy voice.

There was a redeeming factor. When he had first opened the box and seen the stuff, there had been an instant when he'd been washed with a picture of Ponder sitting contentedly at the table on Rae Willie's Silver Eagle bus. On the road, they had always been looking for something to occupy the hundreds of hours of idle time. There was a television on the bus, but the reception was usually lousy. They would just get involved in watching a program when the bus would drive beyond the antenna's ability to pick up the station.

Chapell had a brief glimpse of the summer when Ponder had found a crafts store in Minneapolis where he bought the tools and materials to make leatherwork projects. He had focused his energies into creating original pieces of "Ponder art," as he'd called them, for everyone in the show. Before the summer was over, he had decorated at least a belt and a vest for all the guys in the band, the roadies, the drivers—something for everyone on the two buses and the eighteen-wheeler that carried the sound equipment and props.

After carving and coloring designs in the leather, he'd worked studs and rhinestones into beautiful, original designs that were often further enhanced by his own style of ornate hand stitching. He'd even fastidiously studded several pairs of the jeans with the ornate designs in silver and brass studs. Some of the work was stunning, especially for a thirteen-year-old boy. It showed he definitely had talent.

Perhaps the stuff in the tin box was simply a few remnants of that summer twenty-five years before. Funny how in light of five murders, where the horse was stitched up so ornately, Chapell had completely forgotten about it.

And maybe my subconscious refused to remember my brother's one-summer stitching binge—that I'd seen these kinds of materials before.

In defense, the stitching in the horses was unlike anything Ponder had ever done. *Also, there were so many other fascinating projects that all three of the kids had been into. After the summer was over, Ponder never got back into the leatherworking again.*

He sifted through the stuff. Was the last time it was used twenty-five years ago, or was it used just four nights ago?

The white minidevil that had hopped onto his shoulder finally piped up and said, *He put it in there when you were kids, stupid, so Gale or you wouldn't find it and mess with his stuff. You know Ponder was always hiding his things—hated anyone handling or using them.* The black minidevil on the other shoulder quickly added the con. *No. Something's wrong. There'd be no reason to hide it way back here. It'd be stored in a trunk or a box like all the other old projects. It'd be too easy for you to find it because you both used the hiding place. Ponder is Toy Duck! Toy Duck! Toy Duck! Squawk!*

Out loud, Chapell quietly said, "Shut up!"

More memories broke the surface like large, slow bubbles released from ooze at the bottom of a pond. *Man, when I think of all those radio-controlled airplanes with the gasoline engines we built—most of which crashed shortly after first takeoff; then there were the Revell models of Corvettes and Thunderbirds, of Lamborghinis and Bugattis; the summer of magic and the scores of magic tricks we both did—some of which worked, some of which didn't; two weeks in Chicago, when we built the multilayered box kites from the kits we got through the mail; the period when I went through the electronic wizardry stuff—Jacob's ladder, electromagnets, and Ponder had his slides and the expensive fifteen-hundred-power oil-emersion microscope Mom got him in New York. There were dozens of those wonderful, crazy projects. We were always working on something.*

The white *pro* minidevil chimed in once more and said, *Ponder just hid the stuff and forgot it, Rides, old boy. He forgot about it decades ago, and that's the long and short of it. Give us all a break!*

Con *devil: But he knew that you knew the hiding place, dildo breath. Why would he hide it where you could find it?*

The conscience devils were imaginary, of course. Certain corridors of the cop's mind were lined with doors labeled "Suspicious" and "Cynical;" "How Do You Know?" "Proof Please." Another part of him certainly did not want to suspect flesh and blood. Out loud, he said softly, "Beats the shit out of me." The reasoning continued inside his head. *If I can't understand him today, I sure as hell am not going to come up with what he was thinking twenty-five years ago. Nobody knew what he was going to do half the time anyway.*

The cop carefully put the stuff back in the tin. When he placed the box back into the hole, he heard something fall over. He pulled the tin back out and reached in to see what else was in there.

"Oh, my God!"

When he pulled the object out of the hole and read the label, his heart began beating from inside his throat!

Chapter Four

The cop's mind was reeling badly when he flipped the carpet back over the loose boards and examined the area to make sure there was no evidence of his ever being there—no telltale signs of the dust, nothing moved or out of place. The nauseated feeling reached all the way from his colon to his throat. He quietly and quickly made his way down the narrow stairwell. After locking the attic door he replaced the key meticulously in the exact spot on the overhead sill.

Back in the kitchen, he couldn't believe his relief when he saw that Ponder had not returned home. The cop did not want to confront the awesome talents of his brother until he'd had a chance to consider the possibilities. The back door was relocked quickly, and he caught himself almost tiptoeing to the car. Without turning on the car's lights, in an attempt at being as unobtrusive as possible so that none of the neighbors would see that he'd ever been there, he drove off, willing the car and his face invisible on the street where he'd lived for fifteen years.

He turned onto Franklin Road and drove back toward town. He was looking downward to change a CD in the player when the rear window exploded, followed instantaneously by the windshield disintegrating and a tremendous explosion. He screamed at the sudden terror and wrenched the wheel to the side. The Jaguar went into a slow slide and slammed into a telephone pole. The engine quit, and in the first instant of pregnant silence, Chapell heard the hissing plunks of a bullet perforating sheet metal a nanosecond before the dash erupted. Instantaneously, there was another mind-boggling boom. A howitzer! Although he was dazed from the crash, he'd had enough presence of mind to dive for the floor. The passenger door was blocked by the pole, leaving his door the only exit unless he exposed himself to the shooter by attempting to jump into the backseat in order to jump out the passenger-side back door. Unfortunately, there was a streetlight directly across the street, and spilling onto the blacktop from his side would be Sittingducksville.

He felt around the glass-littered carpet for the cellular and was rewarded by the familiar feeling of hard plastic as he brushed against it. Something wet and sticky was trickling down his face, and he wasn't sure whether it was blood or sweat. When the trickle reached his mouth, the metallic taste removed the doubt.

"Shit!"

He called 911 and was rewarded with a busy signal.

"God damn you sons of bitches!"

In the dim light of the floor he managed to dial the direct number to the police dispatcher.

"Charlie, this is Rider Chapell! I'm under fire. I'm in the forty-six-hundred block on Franklin Road. Somebody's shooting at me close-range with some high-powered stuff. They're knocking the shit out of my car."

"I'll have someone there in two minutes, Rider! Hang on!"

"Charlie, stay on the line!"

"I'm right here!"

Beretta in hand, Chapell turned himself around, staying as close to the floor as possible. He opened the driver's door just in time to hear a car roaring off. He got to a sitting position, then cautiously stepped out, but the shooter had already turned down Curtiswood Lane, cresting the hill to disappear into the night. Chapell visualized the street with Ronnie Milsap's house on one side and the late Webb Pierce's on the other. Ronnie had bought the house from Ray Stevens when Ray got tired of the sight of dozens of daily tour buses unloading at the small parking area Webb had built. Pierce was charging fans $5 a head to go through his house. Milsap actually could see just a little, but not enough to see the buses.

Chapell got back into the car and grabbed the phone.

"Charlie, I couldn't even get a glimpse of him. He's hauling ass west on Curtiswood. Somebody in Green Hills might see something suspicious, but it's my guess he's gone. There are dozens of streets to turn off." The governor's mansion was on Curtiswood—within spitting distance of Minnie Pearl's home.

"I'll do my best, Rider. ETA of the first backup is just a few seconds."

Chapell could hear the sirens of at least two police cruisers, and within twenty seconds the first one had pulled to a stop.

He had holstered the nine millimeter and placed his badge on his coat pocket. Holding a handkerchief to his head, he was inspecting the damage to the Jaguar when the officer got out, gun drawn. Chapell turned to the man and said,

"Mick!" Thankfully, the officer was an old friend.

"Jesus, Rider, what the hell happened? Did he get a piece of you? Let me call an ambulance, and we'll get you to General. I've got a first-aid kit in the back."

"No. it's okay. I hit my face on something—steering wheel, maybe. It opened up a little cut, that's all. Son of a bitch was shooting some kind of cannon. Look, here's where the second round entered the trunk, and I, for shit sure, heard it go over my head into the dash." His arm and shoulder hurt also. He had no idea what he'd done to them.

"Shit, the hole's the size of a cigar, Rider. If it isn't

a twelve-gauge slug, it's got to be a Nitro Express or something."

"It was much too loud even for a shotgun, Mick. You should have heard the thing. Elephant gun of some kind. You could feel the ground shake."

"You sure you don't want me to get the first-aid kit?" Chapell examined the handkerchief and found it soaked in blood.

"Maybe a couple of gauze pads. Wait till the next car gets here to take care of the wreck, then you can take me to Vanderbilt. I have a friend who's a plastic surgeon. I'll call him on the cellular and have him meet me there. If I let some intern sew me up at General, I'll have a scar the size of Chattanooga. I've been through the old stitches game more than once over the years playing hockey—occupational hazard." He flashed the man a grin, and the effect noticeably warmed the officer. Chapell's smile was an awesome weapon.

The other squad car came screaming into sight and quickly slid to a stop next to the first one. Two more cars had joined the meeting within another sixty seconds. The cacophony of red and blue strobes hosed the landscaping of one of Nashville's most expensive neighborhoods like a battery of machine guns on a sure-meltdown fire pattern. With the gauze pads pressed against his cheek, Chapell quickly related to the ranking officer what had happened and which way the shooter had gone. He left directions on where to have the Jag towed, retrieved the cellular, then jumped into the first cruiser. Eight minutes later, he was in an elevator at Vanderbilt Hospital on his way to a third-floor wing where the plastic surgeon had his office. The stitches could be done there with only a topical. There was now a noticeable swelling around the cut on his right cheek. It'd be a bright black and blue in the morning. He'd asked for some ice downstairs but hadn't seen any yet. The trick to not having a noticeable scar was to have a doctor, who really knew skin, sew myriad tiny stitches using very thin silk. The average American couldn't afford to have a plastic surgeon do it.

It was ten forty-five when the squad car dropped him at his home. As usual, he had hidden the fear well, and as hard as he could, he had not been able to stave off the shakes once he was alone. Someone had tried seriously to kill him—with an elephant gun! The sound of the thing alone had been painful. There was no shortage of enemies, plenty of them, scores of whom had come and gone from prisons all over Tennessee. Obviously, he, or they, had been following him, had staked out Ponder's home, and had waited for Chapell to leave. All along Franklin Road the homes were set well back from the road. There would have been no problem in parking a car on the grass in the dark, then lining him up. He ran the replay over and over. The shots had been fired from behind. The shooter had waited until he'd passed by, and try as he would, Chapell couldn't make the picture of a car or a figure appear on the street.

He made his way to the medicine cabinet and found the Dilaudid the doctor had given him a prescription for a few years back. Hopefully, the pills wouldn't have totally lost their potency. Four aspirin went down the hatch for the headache that had plagued him for the past hour, and he wearily climbed into bed. What made him the angriest was the fact that he'd not even glimpsed the car or the shooter.

"Bastard. Wait until he tries it again."

He had the smoke dreams again.

A little after eight in the morning, he was on his third cup of office coffee, but the report he'd been working on lay unfinished on the desk in front of him. His face felt like it had been hit with a puck.

That goddamn shit in the attic last night ... If my little brother has been killing these women ... Oh,

*come on, Lieutenant, you're talking family here. No
way! No fucking way he could have kept something
like that hidden from me all these years. . . .*

Could he?

The mental wrestling continued. The minidevils
were back.

*Rider, this is your brother—flesh and blood. You're
chewing on your own dick here.*

*Sure. But my darling brother's philosophy on life—
hell, on death—ain't exactly mainstream. . . .*

The cop finally straightened in his chair and said to
himself, *All right, Detective, why don't you do a little
detecting? You've got two men looking into the life and
times of Nolan Tyres, and you're not about to assign
two more to do the same thing for your own brother.
Nobody can do this better than you, so play your little
devil's advocate game, and remove any possibility of
your brother's involvement once and for all.*

He picked up a yellow Mongol #2 and began twirling it with his fingers.

*Okay, we believe that there's always been a link to
Mom that has set the killer off—a record, movie, whatever. Count that a given. Probably, this last time it was
that goddamn biography. Maybe we should have seen
this one coming. However, there have been so many
things concerning Mom's career that have hit the media
over the years—and nothing happened at all. Last year
there were two remixed CDs released and no Toy
Duck. The year before that, there was another book.
Not a great one, but it did tell about Mom's life. Not
even the five-year cycle was regular. Sometimes it has
been longer, sometimes shorter.*

*Now, for the sake of this cop's curiosity, how avail-
able was my brother, the veterinarian, when these
women were killed?*

*The summer when Mom died, in Hollywood, I was
at hockey camp in Michigan. I came back for the funeral, then spent the next three weeks with Obie's
mother in Memphis.* Obie Hollenback had been one

of Rae Willie's early producers. He had been as wild
and irresponsible as Rae Willie.

Where the hell was Ponder?

Chapell dropped the pencil onto the desk, leaned
back, propped his feet on one of the open drawers,
and forced his mind back through the years. As the
focus began to close in, forgotten and unwanted memories were dredged up, one by one. The mists cleared,
and the pictures presented themselves in scenarios
that had lain crusted over in fallow earth for a long
time.

*Sixteen-year-old Ponder was in L.A. during the acci-
dent. Then he came home and stayed on the farm in
Homer's Trace with the Dennises for a while. Daddy
took off for Canada, left us high and dry.* Brenda Den-
nis, who was married to a local chemical plant foreman, and Rae Willie had been close friends. They had
been in two orphanages together and had stayed close
over the years. *That old farm is just off River Road
and only a couple of miles from the first murder. Okay.
I knew that. It never meant anything—before.* All five
murders had taken place on River Road—the first one
and the third one had been at the same farm. It had
been a special avenue of investigation ten years before—did the killer have something in common with
the farm or the farmer and his family? Did they use
the same feed store? The same grocery store? Was
there a grudge? Former employees had been interviewed as far away as Arizona. No connection had
ever been established.

What about the second murder?

He leaned forward and quickly leafed through the
second file. Most of the information was already committed to memory, but seeing it on paper helped
him concentrate.

*Okay, the young woman's name was Julia Tibbs.
Eighteen. Jackson, Mississippi. She's six years older
than last victim; killer is six years older than last time.*

What the hell does that mean? No one ever figured it out.

Where was Ponder? Early September. I spent most of the summer at Harvard—I was starting on my master's. I remember well that when Mom's Greatest Hits album was released, there was a big splash in the media. Ponder had been involved in the publicity—talk shows, media blitz.

Chapell grabbed a third folder and turned the reports over, one by one. This one had taken place ten years after the first, four years after the second.

March nineteenth, nineteen eighty-four. Connie Carver. Twenty. So much for a victim who is growing older the same number of years as the elapsed time from the last murder. East Orange, New Jersey. Now, there's a real country music enclave. I had been on the force three years. Where was my little brother, who is acting like the world owes him a royalty check ever quarter? He laid the folder down, tipped the chair back, and once more searched the files in his head. *March nineteenth, nineteen eighty-four! Hell, that was the exact date they inducted Mom into the Hall of Fame, posthumously. Ponder was there—at the ceremony. I remember seeing the tape on the six o'clock news. I would have been there too, but I had to testify that morning at a burglary trial.* Out loud, he said softly, "This may be getting more interesting than I would like it to."

He opened the top drawer of the desk and took out a sheet of typing paper. Using the pencil, he scribbled:

1. Mom dies—August 28, 1974. Victim #1—September 7. *Ponder's staying on River Road.*

2. Mom's album of greatest hits—November, 1980. #2—November 12, 1980. *Ponder's working on the public relations team. Lookalikes?*

3. Mom inducted into Hall of Fame—March 19, 1984. #3—March 20. *Ponder's at the ceremony. Any more starlet lookalikes of our mother?*

He continued the list, using information from the files that he already knew very well.

4. Documentary on Mom's life—released early May, 1990. *Oh, Jesus!* Victim #4—May 12. *Ponder was on the set most of the time; he was the movie's consultant. Stand-ins? Doubles? The actress who played Mom sure looked the spittin' image of Rae Willie Chapell. Shame she couldn't carry a tune.*

5. Mom's exposé autobiography released. #5—Bella Rose. *Dr. Chapell is alive and well. Was he practicing his surgery on a horse in the dark? I wonder if he has an alibi for the night before last? If it hadn't been for finding the suture material—and that goddamn poison!*

Chapell's euphoric reflex was to reach for the phone to call McCurty to tell him, but after picking it up, he said out loud, "Wait a minute, bonehead!" To himself, *This is family. If your brother is doing this, we don't need the Nashville Metro Police Department's dog and pony show on his front doorstep. What if he's not doing it? This is Ponder. I love him and I'm not going to* . . . The thought seeped into the stuffy room's air unfinished. The cop glanced downward and saw the unfinished report in front of him. *Fuck it. Fuck Ponder. I'm going to put my money on a sick fan. I don't think Tyres is smart enough even to have pulled off this last one, much less all of the murders. We're eventually going to find some crackpot who has been killing these poor women for twenty years because God and Bob Wills have told him to.*

A nasty-smelling funk had dribbled onto Chapell's head, and he dialed McCurty to help break its spell.

"Gene, how are we doing on Nolan Tyres?"

"They've got a few things. Johnson's typing a report. You'll have it in a few minutes."

"How about the list of fans?"

"We've been cross-checking the new IFCO fan list by computer that we got from their headquarters in Colorado. There are several leads. Two dozen are from out of state. It'll take some time. Five of them are local."

"Who are they?"

Chapell began to feel more and more confident. They'd find this maniac who had managed to slip through the noose all these times, and he would be right under their noses.

"Three of them are patients who have been in and out of mental institutions. Actually, one of them is already in the Toy Duck files—twice. The other was institutionalized during the last two murders, but he was in minimum security and conceivably could have gone out and come in without being noticed."

"Unlikely. The other two . . . ?"

"John Douchey. He was released from prison two months ago. Murder two. He had been released from prison six months before the last Toy Duck for aggravated assault."

"And the last one . . . ?"

"The last one is the nephew of Hans Trauber."

"Shit! The man who was burned to death in Mom's trailer."

"His name is Robert Lansdown. He's been in and out of a psychiatric ward in Little Rock since he was a kid. Last known address is in Jackson. I phoned their murder squad, and they're going to check on him."

"Do you have addresses for any of these other guys?"

"That's why I was going to call you. John Douchey was staying at a halfway house on Shelby Avenue, but he disappeared two days ago—parole violation. I put an APB out on him an hour ago, and, if you can believe it, a patrol car spotted him on Gallatin Road— Jerry Michelson, old Eagle Eyes."

"He just passed his sergeant test. Good boy."

"Yes. Jerry called for backup, and they're bringing Douchey in as we speak. Care to come to the party?"

"I'm first in line at the son of a bitch!"

One of the reasons the department's interrogation

rooms were so small was the fact that current theory held that a cop could get further with a suspect by working one on one. The old, intimate "Hey, I'm your friend, buddy. I'm here to help you" worked better, as a rule, than two or three cops screaming and yelling at a suspect. With two cops in the room, screaming or not, the suspect tended to feel ganged up on, and he, or she, could easily go on the defensive and clam up.

Nor was there a one-way mirror—same theory: ganging up. The rooms were intimate, to say the least. One room did have a small table. A second had a tiny desk and two chairs. The third had the same desk and two chairs, but a Memorex Telex computer occupied most of the desk. The computer held the program that the police artist used to draw suspects. In the "Ball Room," the largest of the three rooms, four of the detectives took turns grilling the ex-con, one on one, for a total of three hours. Chapell was the first, and he was discouraged after the first ten minutes. Douchey claimed he'd been drunk for two days. He smelled like he'd been steeping in cheap wine for a month. Another patrol car had been sent to check the alibi with some of the man's drinking partners. By four o'clock that afternoon the ex-con had been cleared by three of his companions and two liquor store clerks. He was turned over to the Probation Department, where, in spite of a parole violation, he'd probably get a slap on the wrist and remain free to continue his drinking spree. He'd served less than a third of his second sentence before being paroled. Chapell had heard one judge say that what the entire country needed was a three-year moratorium on the sentencing of repeat offenders. For a period of three years, all criminals convicted for the second or third or fourth, or whatever, time should be executed, regardless of the crime—blue-collar and white-collar criminals included. The prison populations would thin out dramatically, and the court system would become manageable.

By late the following afternoon, Chapell's confidence began to flag even more. The three Rae Willie fan club members who happened to be mental patients had been negatives—two lived with relatives and were so heavily dosed with medication they'd never make it out their front doors; the third, the one who had been investigated for previous Toy Duck murder, had died nine months before. That left the nephew of the burned purported lover. Jackson police called to say that Robert Lansdown had been in court for the last five days and in jail for over six months—he was on trial for raping and murdering a ten-year-old girl.

The lab called to tell the cop that the second megabullet that had entered the XJ-12 through the trunk had then proceeded to plow through the CD player and every device on top of the engine before exiting through the top of the grille. They hadn't been able to pinpoint a caliber, but said it was African safari quality for sure. *Must have been. It killed my Jaguar just when I got the CD player working.*

That afternoon Chapell spent two hours with the chief, the captain, and the FBI agent Jon Rheinhart. The chief was getting pressure from the mayor, and he wanted to know, in detail, what Chapell and his men were doing, other than what was in the reports that Chapell was only two days behind in writing for him. His pressure on the detective was subtle—for now. He offered to give the squad three more men to speed up the out-of-town investigations of the people on the fan list who had turned up cross-referenced with potential customers for studs and expensive thread. Wilhousky had been on the "thread detail," calling shops around the United States, asking about anyone unusual buying the type of materials used to sew up the horse. So far it had been a dead end like everything else.

When Chapell saw the three network news shows, he knew the pressure would no longer be subtle. A

dedicated remote-control finger jockey—sometimes
watching as many as five shows at once—the cop saw
the sensational story about the country starlet who
had been found sewn inside a Tennessee Walking
Horse—and placed there while she was still alive! Included were pictures of the dead horse. So much for
his sway over the media—charm or not. He would
have given a month's pay to know who leaked the
location—maybe the farmer did have his movie deal
already. So the cat was not only out of the bag, it was
dangling in front of every pair of eyes in the United
States that sat gawking at a television set, and the TV
execs would milk it for every percent of the Nielson
ratings possible.

Following the national news, the local stations re-
peated the story in more detail. The cute little red-
headed reporter for Channel Two hinted in her
snapper that because of the incompetence of the
Nashville Police Department, every woman was at risk
of being sewn into a horse at any second. No one
was safe.

Chapell switched to CNN and again was greeted
with the Toy Duck murder in Nashville, Tennessee,
along with a history of the last four murders.

"How the fucking hell did they find out about the
goddamn duck! Somebody's head's gonna roll, by
God!"

The coverage of the murder was unimportant compared to the crime that was sloshed onto the screen
Friday evening, two more times on Saturday, and
again on Sunday—

Nolan Tyres had managed to make appearances
within twenty minutes of each other on two national
talk shows. On the way to the work that morning
Chapell even heard the man on a local radio talk
show. The suppurative boil was everywhere! He was
evangelical about proclaiming that Rae Willie had
been murdered; her twelve-year-old daughter had
been having sex with a thirty-two-year-old man while

the country star watched or slept off her drunkenness; there was an extremely good possibility that the person who had murdered Rae Willie was the Toy Duck murderer.

Chapell had never in his wildest dreams envisioned the little gob of vermin shit getting this kind of exposure. It would now be left up to the public whether or not to believe that Rae Willie Rider was a pimp and a pervert in addition to being a drunk and a dope addict. If there was a person who deserved to be sewn inside a dead horse—alive and kicking!—it was this double asshole.

If the son of a bitch didn't kill that poor woman himself just to garner publicity for his book . . . He'll get his. Mark my words, he'll get a sizable portion. If Toy Duck himself has got even a hint of loyalty to my mother, this cunt fart will wake up clawing horsemeat!

He gave up on the world for this day and went to bed.

Five-twenty the next morning, the phone rang.

"Chapell."

"Rider, we got another one."

"Another what, Gene?"

"Another dead horse with a sutured stomach. Same farm."

"Oh, no . . . On my way."

This time when the M.E. opened the dead animal, the blood-covered face with the unfocused eyes belonged to a balding round- and red-faced middle-aged man.

"Holy shit!"

Nolan Tyres had, indeed, clawed serious horse meat. He had torn his nails down to the quick trying to gain his freedom. This time the incision wasn't decorated with elaborate cords and spangles. Coarse rawhide had sufficed just fine to contain the naked author's terror. The six o'clock news programs had a double whammy—not only had Tyres got the nickel tour of the inside of a dead horse, when the cops examined

Tyres's car, they found a .460 Nitro Express big game rifle in the trunk with Tyres's prints on it.

Well, Rides, I guess that temporarily lets the bastard off the Toy Duck hook. The cop was disappointed. It now left that other distasteful possibility wide open.

The squad had spent half a day trying to track down the slugs that had gone through Chapell's Jaguar. They found one of them at the end of a long furrow in a lawn that was a hundred yards down the street. Unfortunately, it was too badly mangled for a ballistic match, but the weight matched perfectly with the humongous .460 caliber. The other slug was never found.

HEADLINE: "Rae Willie's son allegedly shot at with gun found in biographer's trunk."

The national media went into a frenzy that was not at all unlike the activity in an unearthed anthill. The chief called Detective Lieutenant Chapell to his office for still another "destiny with reality" meeting.

"Chapell, what the hell is going on down there? We're sitting in shit up to our balls, and I don't hear the commode flushing. You guys have got access to computer lists from thirty segs of Internet to the TBI's 'Best of Whores—1975 to Present.' You've got more manpower than the goddamn burglary division. So far this morning I've had calls from the governor, the mayor, two senators, and a dozen other congressmen—local and federal. I'm not even going to mention the fact that the switchboard is on the verge of shorting out from an overload of concerned citizens."

"Chief, it's a slow and tedious search. You know that better than I do. We are doing it as fast as we can. I have doubted from the beginning that this guy would ever be on any kind of list other than for a driver's license—if that. He certainly doesn't fit the profile the FBI gave us—we've cross-referenced every list of perps known to man from country music-loving paraplegics who only rape left-handed catamites to country music-hating Scorpios who have multiple orgasms by sucking the heads off live chickens." The chief stood and walked to the window as if to digest the last sentence. When the man didn't say anything, Chapell continued, "I'll wager he's never been arrested, he's never belonged to an organization, and he works at a job all week long just like you and me. To his next door neighbor he is Mr. Nobody."

"I'm going to assign you five more men. Use them wisely. Check out every weirdo that has ever listened to a country record. My ass is on the line here. We're being ridiculed in the national news every hour on the hour. That goddamn Wolf Blitzer needs to be sewn inside a horse."

"Be careful. That's what I said to myself about Tyres, and some maniac went ahead and did it."

The chief looked at him and grinned.

"Rider, I said exactly the same thing when I saw the son of a bitch in TV. Hey, how'd he do that? Be on two shows at almost the same time?"

Grabbing at the relief of getting off the hot seat. Chapell launched into another lecture.

"It's relatively easy, Chief. They put him in a studio, say, here in Nashville in front of a blue screen. Then they ask him the questions by satellite. The computer in New York fills in the blue screen here in Nashville with the New York set, and the men look like they're sitting side by side."

"Well, he was way out of line about your mother. I knew her, and she'd never do the things he's accusing her of. Why do they let dickheads like him say that kind of stuff?"

"It sells commercial time, sir. That's the bottom line."

"Are there any even minute leads on who stuck him in that horse? I guess we found out who was shooting at you the other night."

"No—to the first question. As usual, there's not a hair, not a thread. As far as the shooting goes, it's really hard to figure. We found a receipt for the gun in his car's glove box. He bought it from a dealer in

New York and had it shipped to Guns Unlimited. Johnson talked with Tyres's shrink and was told that the guy was a walking bomb. A couple of his drinking friends say he threatened to kill more than one person over the years."

"Jesus, an elephant gun ..."

"I guess he was royally pissed off that the family wouldn't endorse his ridiculous book. It would have made a huge difference in his sales if I had. And if I were murdered ... So far we're just as stymied over his murder as we are with the dead women. Poor bastard didn't deserve to die like that, though. We're looking into his personal affairs—enemies he's made with his exposé books over the years. He's had some trouble with a couple of publishers. Family's in Iowa. There are two ex-wives. Could be a copycat killer who's been laying for him."

"Gut feeling, Rider ..."

"I don't believe it was Toy Duck. The stitching wasn't even close—very crude compared to Toy Duck's finesse. And, of course, there was no ornamentation. I think Tyres pissed off an opportunist."

"Well, I'm going to put the pressure on you. I've got it coming at me from a dozen directions. We need to make a break for ourselves—slow down the goddamn media."

Chapell, relieved that once again he had been able to dampen the chief's ire without the old man even realizing it, knew that he was being dismissed, and he got up to leave. He said, "We will. I appreciate the extra men. McCurty's got a long list of wholesalers that bought hydrocyanic acid from the half-dozen companies that make it. We're still checking all the stores that sell ether between Birmingham and Louisville. We can use some help on the phones running down where the stuff was sold. Also, Johnson is fishing for a connection to all of the women over the years—the first young girl excluded. We still don't have an angle on that, but the others—maybe, in addition to

the music angle, they all belonged to the same branch
of the Eastern Star or the same sorority—the same
health club. We've tried it before and come up with
nothing other than the resemblance to my mother, but
who knows?"

"Make something happen, Rider. You're on it because you know the music business better than anyone
here; you're also our best detective."

"Thanks." He turned and walked out the door.

Six days dragged on and useless information piled
up—literally. It had been ten days since Bella Rose's
murder. Chapell was really homesick to see his sister.
She should have been home by now. However, even
if she'd been in town, he wouldn't have had time—
wouldn't even have been able to make time—to see
her. He was buried in work. There were stacks of
Xerox copies on his desk, some of which were eight
inches high. Unfortunately, there was not a single
piece of information that shed the slightest light on
the killer. The poison used to kill the horse had been
traced through manufacturers to two dozen wholesalers, country-wide. Their customers included manufacturers of industrial insecticides and fumicides, along
with scores of jewelry manufacturers and hundreds of
retail shops across the country where Prussic acid was
used as a cleaning agent. Trying to account for every
cubic centimeter of hydrogen cyanide was like trying
to strain fish pee. If someone wanted to badly enough,
they could distill their own. The stuff existed naturally
in all variety of seeds and pits including apples,
peaches, apricots, and plums.

Hundreds of craft stores nationwide that could be
located through chambers of commerce or the Yellow
Pages had been asked to fax copies of receipts for
studs, spangles, and decorative thread if there was an
address or credit card. Two men were tracing these,
but the investigations of customers within a five-
hundred-mile radius of Nashville had already yielded

nothing. Chapell sincerely doubted that the killer would be stupid enough to buy his materials with a credit card.

Ether could be bought over the counter at thousands of hardware and auto-parts stores and chemical-supply companies. It was used for dozens of purposes, from anesthetizing fruit flies in college biology labs to starting car and truck engines in cold weather.

Toy stores had been tapped the same way craft stores had. Nothing of use was turned on the purchase of a yellow toy duck bath toy. Thousands of them were manufactured every year by over two dozen companies.

Dozens of sex offenders, murderers and generic ex-cons had been rousted, and pressured to give up any information that might be even remotely associated with either Tyres's horrible murder or the Toy Duck killings.

Nothing.

It was as if concrete leads had been swallowed by a black hole.

The press would not let the unique and horrifying murders go. Cable kept the thing alive during the day. The network news programs regurgitated them every evening on the regular programs, and then, using "experts"—psychiatrists, psychologists, M.D.s, veterinarians, lawyers—the late-night programs masticated any tiny morsels that had not already been digested. A parade of country music authorities had waxed eloquent, along with an artisan in creating costumes with elaborate stitching, rhinestones, and studs, in addition to several equestrians who were treated as if they alone had the answers to the spectacular travesty that had been served up in Nashville, Tennessee.

Two dozen film crews were wandering the Nashville streets and countryside, shooting anything that might be remotely adaptable for TV. The farm where the two murders had taken place was now as familiar to the average American as the White House. Colorful

computer-generated diagrams on how to get there
were now available at souvenir stands. The farmer had
been besieged with a constant flow of reporters knocking at his front door. He and his wife had become
national celebrities and had appeared on *Oprah* and
Donahue.

Tyres's background had been dug into by investigative reporters, each of whom was working on a sure
Pulitzer. A number of nefarious tidbits had been uncovered, including outright extortion and several years
of serious income tax evasion.

The murders had turned into one of those addictive
phenomena that was so grotesque and invidious—so
unique, so far beyond the imagination of the average
person on the street—that any information, no matter
how remote, was dissected down to molecular levels,
to the delight of the crowd. And in an industry where
far too many people had too little of certain import
to do, the cam crews were sent scurrying from one side
of town to the other at the drop of a hat whenever
a rumor surfaced that something of even the tiniest
relevance had been found. A car dealership on Mur-
freesboro Road had been besieged and its owner cata-
pulted into his fifteen minutes of national fame when
the media found out he had sold Tyres a new Buick
the day before the author's death. A beauty parlor in
West Meade had been deluged with reporters for
three days when they found out it was where Bella
Rose had got her hair done. In spite of the Police
Department seal, the dead woman's apartment had
been broken into so many times the landlord gave up
repairing the lock. Pictures of the woman's hair and
toothbrushes had been sent around the world. One of
Bella Rose's friends had sold a fifteen-minute video-
tape of the pretty little singer, in a leotard, doing her
daily aerobics class. NBC had scooped it up as an
exclusive for a measly $75,000. A tape of the young
woman in a thong bikini at a party on a houseboat
on Percy Priest Lake had sold to a British conglomer-

ate for $135,000. Columbia had quickly mixed ten of the singer's development demos, and the CDs had hit the charts at number seven with a bullet.

Chapell was becoming more and more depressed as the pressure mounted daily on the Metro Police Department. One of Tennessee's senators had called for a Senate investigation—brilliant, that one. If the cops couldn't find anything, how exactly would a bunch of bureaucratic lawyers pull it off? The man had spent a half hour on his speech on the Senate cable channel. *Probably at two in the morning to an empty house. Getting on the record for elections next year, you bastard. I know what you're doing. Then you can charge that you're tough as hell on crime.*

Meanwhile Chapell's engorged murder squad had yet to come up with a single lead on the killer. There was no trail. The man was an evaporated vapor and brilliant at what he did. The chief harangued Chapell on a daily basis to come up with something—anything! Chapell was working twenty hours a day fielding calls and reports, assigning men to investigate new developments and the ever active train of tips phoned in by people who thought they had the information that would solve the case. On some days there was as many as two hundred fifty of these, and except for the totally absurd, they all had to be checked out.

He had spent a total of five evenings hobnobbing with the music industry. There had been two nights of cocktail parties, two showcases at area clubs, and then Friday night, after two shows backstage at the Opry, he had been invited to go along with the group to the Palace for the late show. Each night he'd quizzed old friends, trying to call in favors—anything to produce a lead on some of Bella Rose's friends— or enemies. The FBI had investigated her family and even the remotest acquaintances back home in Pennsylvania. She had been just another all-American girl with the normal circle of friends. She had dropped out

of a community college after six months in order to
concentrate on her music—no enemies. Everybody
was rooting for her.

On Saturday afternoon, Chapell left the office at
five. He'd caught himself dozing a couple of times at
his desk. He was exhausted and knew that if he didn't
get some sleep, he was going to end up in either the
hospital or a loony cell at State. He could take the
pressure of the police work, but it weighed more heavily each day that he didn't call Ponder and Ponder
didn't call him. It had been a week now—since the
lunch, and that was a first. The brothers never went
for more than a couple of days without at least touching base.

What was even worse was the fact that Ponder's
attic could be the most important lead that had turned
up so far, and Chapell had shared it with no one. Had
Ponder found out somehow that his brother had been
up there?

His stomach had been churning all afternoon, and
he'd run out of Tums. Walmart had a sale on a large
plastic jug of them. *At the rate I'm going, it'll last
two days.*

In the bargain aisle immediately in line with the
entrance was a display of remote-controlled toy fire
trucks. He couldn't help buying one. They looked so
real. In the parking lot he called Domino's on the
car phone and ordered an extra large deep-dish, extra
cheese, sausage and mushroom—takeout. The cop
dearly loved pizza and would have eaten it three meals
a day if it weren't so deadly.

*Maybe the cholesterol will do what the Nitro Express
couldn't. Who cares?*

Finally gaining the sanctuary of home, he dropped
the bag with the fire truck on the kitchen counter and
set about putting half the pizza into the microwave
after placing it on a dinner plate. It had cooled on the
drive home. He poured a large tumbler of vodka that
was kept in the freezer and took a long pull. It tasted

like chocolate. He sat the tumbler down and opened the box with the fire truck in it. After popping a total of six batteries into the truck and its remote, he gleefully began to run the toy around the kitchen floor while the pizza warmed on low power in the microwave. There was even a siren. The phone rang and he tossed the control onto a padded place mat on the table, walked to the instrument on the wall, and answered it.

"Welcome home."

It was Gale—finally!

"No, you are welcomed home."

"You sound tired. I've seen on the news what's been going on here. I saw you twice."

"Big deal. I am tired, but I need to talk to you as soon as possible. Have you talked to Ponder?"

"No, I usually call my immediate family in descending order based on their chronology of years."

"Thanks. How kind of you. I'm kind of beat tonight too. How about lunch?"

"Super. About one?"

"Sure. Same old place?"

"Why not? I'll see you there."

Chapell usually took Gale to eat at a barbecue place across the river from the police station. The food was great and so was the beer.

The vodka in his glass was gone, and without thinking, he got the bottle from the fridge and poured another. The stuff was beginning to take hold, and he could feel the kinks let go, one by one. The bell had dinged on the Amana while he'd been talking to his sister. He left the pizza in the microwave and walked outside. The thick night air hung in redolent clumps. There were wafts of honeysuckle; mildew in the eaves troughs that badly needed cleaning; poplars, sumacs, a stand of distant cedar; the musk of two different species of mushrooms growing in the damp loam of the summer woods.

The soothing white noise of the falls began its therapy on the cop, and he stripped off his clothes and walked naked across the vast slate deck to the bordering stone wall. Dark had packed itself into the woods, leaving little room for anything else.

Above, and to the left, was another deck that hugged the second-floor master bedroom and bath. The bedroom was laid out on three different levels. The rambling, free-style, native-stone house sat on top of a substantial spring-fed brook that skipped down a mile-long wooded hill in an elaborate series of pools and falls. When he was twenty years old, he had been totally captivated by a picture of Frank Lloyd Wright's Fallingwater. He had looked for almost a year to find the right land—had bought two hundred acres to assure no one would ever live nearby. The architect had designed the home to straddle the brook at a point where some of the water could be diverted over a sixty-foot-wide, man-made prepuce that had been laboriously built by master stone masons. The falls looked like it had been there for a million years. The uniform white water dropped six feet into a large, deep pool just beyond the deck. The rich aroma of the brook's mist quickly overpowered all the other essences.

Well, Rides, old boy, if you're gonna piss your name, it's better to do it in the snow than in the grass where it'll never be seen.

He topped the wall and dived without hesitating. In spite of the end-of-July heat, the water was still shockingly cold. He swam several laps of the hundred-foot irregular pool where, again, stone masons had contained the water using only natural rock.

He sprinted the last two laps and lay in the shallows panting. Breath regained, he slipped from the water and climbed the flight of stone steps to the deck.

Shunning clothes, he took a bottle of red wine and four pieces of the pizza to the den. On the third click of the remote he was surprised to see his mother's second movie *Sing This One for Me* just beginning on the Chicago channel. The film had swept the country when it was released three years before Rae Willie's death. He would watch it only until he finished the pizza, but was only on the third piece when he realized that the movie was the new version containing several scenes originally edited out. He had never seen them before. In spite of never studying a day, his mother had been a natural actress. Before he knew it, the credits were rolling, and she had made him laugh and cry all over.

You sure as hell had something the rest of them didn't. It's scary—call it charisma, I guess.

He'd meant to be in bed an hour and a half ago, and in spite of being exhausted, sleep would not come. He rolled back and forth, trying to appease the stymied blood flow that insisted the body change position every couple of minutes. Every wrinkle in the bedclothes was magnified. Each click inside the room, an occasional chirp or flutter outside the house—all were reluctantly noticed and filed as significant. The whisper of the air conditioner, either coming on or shutting off, was a major event. He thought of getting a Seconal but decided resting in the bed without sleep was of better-quality repose than the artificial version imposed by the chemical.

At one point there was a great cloud of smoke that snapped viciously at his nose and throat. While trying to get away from it, he plunged headlong into a marsh that was obstructed with underwater obstacles—stones, branches. The bottom was soft mud, and every so often he'd trip and lose his balance, slowly toppling into the murky slime.

When he awakened, at two-thirty, he'd wet the bed again.

Chapter Five

Chapell vaulted out of the bed, furious as usual. He ripped off the sheets, including the rubber sheet, and dragged them down two flights of stairs to the basement laundry room. Some men were cursed with insomnia; some with rafter-rattling snoring; some with apnea, waking each morning totally exhausted from dozens of near deaths regardless of how many hours of sleep. Rider Chapell was cursed with a child's transient disease—periodically wetting the goddamn bed! He'd never married because of it. When women came to the house, they were never allowed to remain through the night. He was too afraid he'd wet while sleeping. Other than rubber pants, the fields of medicine and therapy had never provided a successful solution.

He ran back up the stairs to the kitchen, still swearing and cursing. Another large tumbler was filled with four fingers of freezer-cold vodka. No longer sleepy, he took it into the den and turned on the television set. It was the second time in a week that this had happened.

The vituperation continued, this time directed at the nitwits who had done the television programming for the middle of the night.

"Somebody has got to work extremely hard to come up with forty channels of consistent pureed shit!"

Off went the TV. The new CD of Bella Rose was sitting on the coffee table. Columbia had sent him a comp copy. He put it in the player and was greeted by a wonderful string-section intro. The beautiful little dead woman began singing the torch song at letter A, and the timbre of the low, feathery voice was frighteningly familiar. She not only sounded like Rae Willie Chapell, she was Rae Willie Chapell. Laser-perfect intonation; the not-too-exaggerated scoops and styling licks; the flatted-third blues notes; straight-voice graduating to vibrato on the white notes—the halves, dotted halves, and whole notes. It was all there. The woman had done some homework, that was for sure, and she could flat sing!

She's good. So are a whole bunch of them, but they have a blueprint to follow. Mom is still the original. She established that incredible groove. How could she be so brilliant at getting inside a song and screw her life up so badly everywhere else?

The CD finished, and Chapell took the remote and in the interest of comparison triggered the *Greatest Hits* that was already in the carousel. The vocals had been lifted from the old analog masters, and a new orchestra—recorded in digital—had replaced the old one. God, there was such an incredible difference! The quality of that voice went a thousand layers deep, and the comparison: Ford—Mercedes; Cessna—Lear; K Mart—Nieman Marcus; Garth Brooks—Sinatra. There were a whole series of timbres soaking in that get-deeeeep-under-your-skin patented pathos of Rae Willie's voice that couldn't be duplicated no matter how they tried to imitate her.

The buzzing of a mosquito woke him. The sun was poking through the trees, its sheaves of needle rays methodically climbing the French door panes like a dim-witted, stick-limbed insect. One of the doors onto the deck was standing wide open.

You dumb shit. You didn't even close the door, much less set the alarm. One of these days something will wander in here and bite you on the ass.

He'd slept perhaps a total of three hours after going to bed with the possibility of ten hours of sleep.

"What else is new?"

He was early for lunch. He watched through the window as she rocketed into a parking place going lickety hell as usual. She skidded to a stop in the white whale-tail 911 to leave its front tires not two but one inch from the cement overrun block. On her sixteenth birthday, Chapell had let her drive his Lotus home after they'd gone to get her driving permit. She had slewed the car into the street, guided it expertly around the corners, and by the time they were a mile down Briley Parkway, in West Nashville, she'd had it up to 135 miles an hour when Chapell chickened out and told her to slow down. He'd let her go to that point, because at no time did he feel she was not in control of the car. It was like a gift, a talent. Since she was old enough to reach the pedals he'd seen her do miraculous things with motorcross bikes, bicycles go-carts, off-road motorcycles, farm tractors, dump trucks. The only problem was that in spite of the fact she took meticulous care of her vehicles, it took a mechanical toll on the cars—especially the tires. Gale could go through a sports car suspension in six months, a set of tires in one. And she had never got a speeding ticket. Amazing.

He stood as she came to his booth, grinning. God, she was beautiful. Blond, hazel-eyed. Always up; the beauty queen smile; always with time to stop and talk to the little people.

She hugged him, full-length, long and hard, rubbing herself into him slowly, luxuriously. Had someone not known, they would have appeared as long-lost lovers.

"You're famous, Detective Lieutenant Rider Chapell."

The waitress didn't even bother to take orders. The couple had been eating the same thing for years: barbecue pork plates with extra everything.

"Hardly. The brass like me to handle the press because I don't talk too much. Have you seen Tyres's biography on Mom?"

"Yes, and it's totally disgusting. Where do these people get off? This guy did a whole book of the kind of headlines you read when you're standing in line at Kroger's. However, with this you can't get a good belly laugh out of it because the bastard is serious. Even the people who write 'Eighty-year-old woman gives birth to seven-foot alligator' know it's only in fun. Tyres was a greedy, vindictive blood-letter, and I think he got what he deserved."

"Well, I'm glad you don't have an opinion on him. Hate to think what you'd say if you did." She winked at him, flirting, and as usual the effect quickly filtered down through him, starting at his teeth and ending sharply in the crotch.

The barbecue plates arrived, and while the waitress filled the frosted mugs with beer from the pitcher, Gale asked the woman about her son, who was confined to a wheelchair with multiple sclerosis; and then the daughter, who was in summer school on a three-year bachelor's program for nurses. The woman brightened noticeably as usual at the attention.

Only after she had left did Gale direct her attention to the ritual of dousing her pork in extra sauce and buttering the pancake-style cornbread with two tabs of butter.

Chapell finished the interrupted conversation by saying. "Well, apparently, someone else did too. He never even bothered with the ornate stitching—just sewed Tyres in with crude rawhide. How was the road?"

"The usual. The bus broke down in Durango, Colorado, which is exactly a hundred miles from nowhere. They had to tow it all the way to Santa Fe, and we cancelled two dates. Why doesn't the oil pump ever go when we're in downtown Cincinnati or Chicago?"

"It's a plot."

She grinned and continued. "You know, if we had

a nickel for every equipment and bus breakdown we've been through since we were kids . . ."

Chapell's answering grin finished the sentence.

"We spent a lot of our lives in the bellies of the great, odiferous behemoths, didn't we?"

"I haven't heard that one in twenty years," she laughed. Chapell loved to hear his sister laugh. Something to do with crystal moon bells played by summer's gentlest wind in the high mountains of the Dalai Lama.

She continued, "Otherwise, we played to packed audiences, and the new album is coming out the end of next month. Ronnie told me on the phone that they think it's going to ship gold." Ronnie Light was Gale's producer. He was also an engineer, an arranger, a steel guitar player, and an all-around fine musician, unlike some producers, who didn't know a whole note from a hole in the ground.

"Outstanding. That'll keep you in oil pumps for a year."

"As Larry Gatlin used to say, 'That'll put shoes on the kids for a while.' "

They ate in silence for a couple of minutes, then Gale said, "How's Ponder? I haven't talked to him yet."

A cloud came over Chapell's face. "Here we go," he thought.

"Honey, I need some advice about Ponder. Some serious help, I think."

"You sound like somebody unraveled your favorite cassette. What's wrong?"

He paused for a whole thirty seconds before he began. He finally said, "We have been investigating this last woman's murder—Bella Rose—for a week and a half now. By the way, did you know her?"

"Only slightly. I met her at a BMI party last spring. I knew she sounded a lot like Mom."

"Do you know any of her friends?"

The squad had already found all of the murdered woman's known friends, but it wouldn't hurt to ask.

"If I asked around, we might have some acquaintances in common. She's ten years younger, and that crowd is different from most of the people I know. You're getting off the subject."

"Well, we have come up with absolutely nothing. Not a trace, not a faint hint. This guy has done this thing five times—well, six, if he did Tyres. Considering the tremendous amount of manpower on the case, we still haven't come up with a single, solitary hair, fiber—not even the slightest hint of a lead . . ."

She looked at him quizzingly and waited patiently another ten seconds for him to continue.

". . . except for one. And I haven't told anyone about it."

"Well, you've piqued my curiosity. . . ."

He paused again. She could see he was reluctant.

"Do you remember how we used to play in the attic when we were kids? All the games, the plays, concerts?"

"Certainly. Some of my finest performances came from that makeshift stage."

"Did you know that Ponder and I had a secret hiding place in the room over the sun porch?"

"Sure. That's where you kept the *Playboy*s."

He looked at her in surprise but didn't say anything.

He finally continued, "We have searched the entire United States and Canada for the types of ornaments that were used to sew those poor women inside the horses. They were special studs and spangles and thread that can't be found just anywhere. Some of the stuff isn't even manufactured anymore. We've come up with nothing, as far as anyone remembering someone purchasing those kinds of things. The gold thread is almost a one-of-a-kind thing."

"And . . ."

"Let me digress a little. Ponder and I went to lunch

a week ago and when I mentioned the murder, he acted a little strange."

"How?"

"Well, he got very flippant. Said the girl probably deserved it—that most of those new artists were whores and somebody probably did society a favor— more of less."

"He might have been partly right."

"Gale!"

"Sorry. Go on."

"He said some other real downer things—that we needed a war or a plague to kill off the population of the world; there are too many people."

"Well, I don't entirely disagree with that either. Have you been on the streets on a Friday afternoon lately?"

Chapell could feel the mud at the bottom of the marsh beginning to squish beneath his feet. Exactly when did his brother and sister both have radical surgery on their "love for mankind" lobes?

He pushed on.

"Later on, I went by his place to see if he was all right. I haven't been in the house for a while. He wasn't there, so I got to wandering around; figured he'd be home any minute. I went up into the attic just to, sort of, reminisce. I found the exact materials in the *Playboy* hiding place that were used to sew up those horses. Perfect matches."

"So what? Don't you remember the summer Ponder did the leatherworking thing? It's leftover junk. I'll bet there are fifty people in town that have got the same stuff in their attics."

"Then why did he hide it?"

"Shit, Rider. It's been in there forever. He hid it twenty years ago. God knows why. You could probably find a lot of other stuff we hid around the place that we didn't want Mom and Dad to find. It's a big house. How can you possibly suspect your own brother? You've been a cop too long." She turned sideways in the booth, facing away from him. A familiar gray curtain was slowly lowering on the exquisite face.

"There was something else, Gale."

"Rider, I don't care if you found a signed confession. Ponder is not capable of doing the kind of thing that has been done to these poor women. Very few human beings are. You might remember that we grew up with him—have lived with him for thirty-odd years."

Another layer of curtain.

"There was a bottle of the type of poison used to kill the horses."

"You're going to make a case on your own brother? Jesus, Rider!"

"I wanted to talk to you about it—rationally."

"God damn you! Ponder is not capable of doing this. He cries every time one of his patients dies. He keeps Daddy's bloody fucking trophy room closed because he can't stand the sight of the dead animals. If you found something that is incriminating—and what the hell were you doing snooping in his house—in our house, anyway?—then somebody planted it there."

Animals dying, little sister—animals, not people! You don't know him like I do when it comes to people.

Her voice had risen and begun to carry. There were perhaps a dozen other people in the restaurant, and several of them began to notice.

"What about the poison?"

"He probably has used it in his practice! Who the fuck cares?" She was practically screaming.

"Gale, calm down. I'm not accusing him. I'm asking you how I should approach asking him about what the stuff is doing up there." She was beginning to get under his skin. He hadn't done anything wrong; he had a perfectly legitimate question that needed to be answered by their brother. She was treating him like he was about to yank the "fry the bastard" handle on Old Sparky, and Ponder was strapped blindfolded in the seat with the metal dome on his head. Besides, younger brother Ponder was indeed gentle with his animals. However, people were a totally different matter. That bar in Idaho . . .

She jumped to her feet with a horrified look on her face and half screamed, "You don't need to ask him anything! He's our brother!" Now everyone in the restaurant was looking at them.

"Honey, sit down and help me here."

"You go to hell! If you believe your own flesh and blood is a goddamn psycho, then you don't belong in this family! The three of us have slugged it out arm in arm too long for this bullshit!"

Chapell stood and tried to grab her arm.

"Gale . . ."

"Leave me alone, Rider. You and your cop shit have finally stepped over the bounds. If Momma were here she'd smack you across the face so hard . . ."

She turned and ran for the door. Chapell knew it'd be useless to try to stop her. By the time he'd thrown a twenty-dollar bill on the table and reached the door, the Porsche had already peeled sixty feet of rubber and was accelerating at an ungodly speed down the street toward the interstate ramp.

Chapell drove across the Veteran's Bridge in a daze. He'd never seen Gale act like that. Of course, he'd never accused his little brother of being one of the most diabolical serial killers the world has ever known.

He had switched the radio on for the two o'clock news, and there it was again—the announcer was interviewing a "woman on the street" and she was all over the police department's case for allowing the killer to run free for over twenty years. *Why don't you catch him, then, asshole?* He snapped the radio off with a vengeance and pulled into the garage.

There was a message on his desk to call the chief. *I hope he doesn't want any of the paperwork that's stacked on my desk.*

Once more he was called to the office, interrogated

thoroughly, then reamed out for not producing any leads with a total of fifteen men working full-time in addition to the help of the FBI and the TBI. As far as Chapell was concerned, the Quantico bunch had been next to useless. They had yet to come up with anything other than the fact that the killer was between the ages of twenty-five and forty-five; he was a loner; he had hurt animals when he was a kid. It was the same shit they handed out for every serial killer's profile. They could have Xeroxed it. Chapell was surprised at the chief's change in behavior. The man had lost his understanding of the fact that this killer had no intention of being caught, because so far he had left not even a trace. Nothing! This guy had been thorough twenty years ago; he was thorough now, and every day there was a growing hopelessness that someone would ever phone in a useful tip—a car seen driving away from the scene the morning of the crime—a drunk bragging in a bar that he'd found an empty bottle of Prussic acid. A lot of dead-end cases had been solved by an inconsequential bystander casually observing something that wasn't meant to be seen—pure luck taking over where hard work had swirled in the toilet.

Not in Toy Duck.

Chapell called Gale on her cellular, and she hung up on him. Another first. Why couldn't she just open her mind and think objectively? Maybe blood shouldn't be thicker than water. He was going to have to confront his brother, and he was more than a little afraid that blood was indeed going to flow.

The handsome man with the sharp knives and the well-hidden stash of toy ducks really liked these "quiet" times. No ritual. No pressure to get it right. No heavy responsibility resting on weary shoulders. The others were of such dire necessity—diarrhea with no available john—shit in the woods, use leaves to wipe ... This was a pleasant chore—like the kid who, a few minutes before, had been riding the buggies down the slight hill in the parking lot. Collecting the carts was a bag boy's bona fide excuse to goof off— to temporarily duck the demeaning responsibilities imposed by clerks and supervisors inside.

Without these little recreational soirees, the other serious ones might have been a chore. "Use it or lose it, kid. But you knock her up and she'll ruin your life." That's what Daddy said. "I ain't gonna knock her up tonight, Pop. She ain't gonna live that long!"

So, here he was waiting in the car for her to show up at the consensual rendezvous.

"Ah, this one's on time."

She wheeled into the auxiliary lot next to the large, mostly empty parking lot and parked the white Cadillac out of the influence of the streetlights.

No wonder people get mugged and killed all the time. Stupid whore didn't park in the light. Maybe she's expecting we're gonna do it in the backseat.

He saw her examine the area for her customer. Seeing nothing, she sat quietly, waiting for her john to join the party. He sat back in the seat and watched, savoring her impatience, saw the flame as she lit a cigarette. For a promised five hundred bucks, cash, she'd wait.

"Gonna make you happier than a two-donged donkey at a Tijuana whore convention, baby." He had mumbled the sentence to himself softly and continued the line of thought inside his head. *Ought to have some bumper stickers printed up that say that*. Well, happiness was snatched and grabbed where one could get it. Tonight's version would come from wetting the widdle wang in miss meet-in-the-Kroger-lot's personal honey pot. Pure fun! Shoot the cervix with the liquid stream of life. Hit the target, hit it good, and you get the kewpie doll with the anatomically correct crotch. This adventure should be shared with the whole world too, but, unfortunately, these girls really ought to remain anonymous. So it's one more soul for the pile, boys/One more soul for the pile. Good country song in there some place.

The nice thing about these exercises was that the participants didn't have to be meticulously hand-picked. A call, the promise of big-bucks employment, a little casual recreation for the employer. Hell, what was the difference between twanging the prong and a Monday night at the bar with Frank and Al and Alex? Or a beautiful Saturday afternoon with friends on the lake. "Relax, enjoy the weekend, y'all." Only it wasn't the weekend—it was a too-horney night almost two weeks later; it was almost midnight; some sweet young thing was about to become a fucking fish feast!

Goddamn cops were so stupid. After all these years, all the missing women—they still hadn't come up with the fact that one of Nashville's favorite celebrities entertained in two totally different circles—one that was all work; one that was all play.

Ah . . . That's it. You were told to get out of the car. Stand there so I'll know who you are, baby.

Because the dumb twit had parked in the dark, he'd decided to have a little extra fun. *Double coupons tonight, Chicky.* He left his truck and quietly made his way through the small thicket bordering the lot. One of the nicer things about the human body is the fact that it can be turned off like a light in regard to making noise—screams, cries, whatever. A good stout pop to the solar plexus and, *poof!*—no noise. He was wearing his special shoes—the ones with the crepe-gum soles. He stepped from the hiding place in silence and put a hand on her shoulder. Before she could scream, he'd spun her around and socked her in the diaphragm. She folded, gasping quietly. He grabbed her under the arm before she could hit the pavement and thwacked her on the mastoid process with the sap—not too hard, not too soft. Now she was out until he revived her with the ammonia capsule. Who cares if her head was a little damaged? The chick was destined for a marine burial in the sea of death.

Get the truck . . .
Car lights.
Shout.
What the . . . Is he serious?
Car door opening.
Flashlight.
Goddamn stupid son of a good Samaritan bitch?
Muffled shots.
Car rolling down hill.
Over embankment. Into deep dark.
No attention attracted—too late at night.
Toodle-loo. Wrong place, wrong guy, you fool!
Should have minded your own business.

Back at the ranch, he took great pleasure stripping
her slowly. "Now, this is what fun's all about, folks."
When she was naked, he licked her in several places,
savoring the different tastes. When the ammonia returned her to "Our Wonderful World," she was already tied in the famous "assume the position" that
draped her over a special two-by-four railing he'd con-
structed about a yard off the cement floor. Legs nicely
spread, her feet were anchored to cement blocks on
the floor, wrists tied to ankles. He had taped the
mouth of a couple of the early ones, but after trying
it without the tape, he'd quickly come to the conclusion that the entertainment factor was much more intense when they could squeal. The basement was
seriously soundproofed, so they could scream and
grunt and fart all they wanted.

He'd already been hard for a half hour. God, he
loved this. All the years of not being able to bring the
women home to a quiet night of, say, some cheese
popcorn, Thunderbird wine, and a little quality fucking; a before- and after-breakfast *boink* on a Sunday
morning; her going to work with a smirk on a weekday
in yesterday's rumpled clothes—more proud than
embarrassed. . . .

She groaned and opened her eyes.
He straightened, quivered, and carefully entered the

first of her available orifices. God had been so kind—had gone right ahead and designed all the holes in just the right assortment of sizes.

An hour later, after his third "come" he was wasted. Unfortunately, she'd had the bad taste to die, so the fun was over. Blackened and flayed skin was drenched in blood in spite of the cauterizing of hundreds of surface blood vessels. Using the fancy professional cutlery in this manner was such a treat. The average American male would never know that the third orgasm of the evening can be an eye-blower if you've worked up a solid coat of the chick's blood, not only on your dick, but all over your body. You don't even have to be inside the bitch! "Slippery" is all you need. And this new innovation ... Why hadn't he thought of it before now? The crowning glory—Mr. Coleman's propane blow-dry, blow-job, blow torch!

"Well, folks, I've certainly found it to be the fastest, no-nonsense method to get a girl hot down there. And don't you just *love* the smell of barbecued pussy?"

Chapell had to know if Gale had told Ponder about their lunch. It had been driving him crazy all morning, and he'd been unable to concentrate. On impulse he grabbed the phone and called Ponder at the clinic. He was relieved at his brother's friendly voice—no indication of anything being wrong. They made small talk, then agreed to meet for pizza that evening at Chapell's home.

Maybe I just imagined everything. Maybe there really was no tin box in the attic hiding place.

"Seven?"

"Great. See you then."

In spite of his strength, and all the police training Chapell had undergone over the years, if his younger brother had a mind to, he could beat the shit out of the cop as easily as he had when they were kids. Ponder was three inches taller and had always outweighed his older brother by at least forty pounds. In high school Ponder had been recruited heavily by a half dozen major-college football teams. He'd chosen to follow his older brother to Dartmouth and had made the starting lineup as quarterback his freshman year. He was quick, brutally strong, and as gentle as a snail unless somebody riled him.

Chapell tipped back in his chair, greatly relieved. He looked at his watch. "One-fifteen, Jesus!" If he wasn't interrupted too many times, he might make a sizable dent in the paperwork that was clogging his desk. Part of it consisted of summary reports that had to be written from scratch. Everybody had to be kept apprised—Metro, the FBI, the TBI, Davidson County Sheriff Department; the report for the state legislature and another for the governor's office—he'd been working on those for three days; the Senate committee on crime also wanted an in-detail summery of exactly how the investigation was progressing.

The phone rang.

"Chapell."

"Lieutenant, this is McLenden in Personnel. Have you finished with last week's overtime vouchers?"

"I'm trying to, Bob. I've got a foot of paperwork staring at me."

"Rider, if I don't have them by four this afternoon, we can't put in for the overtime the men have drawn."

"It'll be there."

An hour later, he had made considerable progress. The phone had left him alone for most of the time. He needed to ask McCurty a technical question for one of the TBI reports and decided to take a stretch by walking next door to the Murder Squad's office.

"Seen Gene?"

The board had the detective signed out, but there was no way of telling when he'd be back or where he'd gone without calling the dispatcher.

"He's at the railroad bridge in Bordeaux, working a murder."

"Why isn't Homicide doing it?"

"The woman was found floating in the Cumberland. She was wrapped in a rubber raincoat that was secured by twine. She'd been cut up pretty badly before she died, and it looks like she'd been badly burned in places—deliberately!"

"Why the hell didn't somebody tell me?"

"The call just came in. Gene was already in Bordeaux checking a pawnshop for a gun used in a shooting last week."

"Shit."

"There's a helluva fire up there too. Got traffic backed up all over that side of town."

"Fire?"

"Yeah. Six-alarm. Tank farm near Tennessee State. You can see the smoke all over the city."

"Gene's going to need some help. I'd better go give him a hand."

"It's okay, Bobby's with him and the lab crew's on its ..."

Chapell was already gone.

"... way."

He rushed back to his office, grabbed his summer suit coat, and hurried to the garage. This sounded like a new twist in man's continual search for creative murder, and the cop wanted to see it firsthand. Jesus, cutting and burning? With the grille strobes and siren he was able to get onto 265 within three minutes. The exit for Eighth Avenue and Metro Center was a little harder. Even from two miles away, flames could be seen rising hundreds of feet into the air. An enormous display of firelit smoke fumed and roiled upward to disappear in a layer of altocumulus. Traffic was backed up because cop cars were blocking the four-lane boulevard while the officers slowly turned the traffic around or shuttled it onto side streets. He flashed his badge and they let him through. Fountain Square flew by, followed by the Metro golf course. He was doing almost eighty, and it was jarring his teeth. The whole area had been built on an old landfill, and the road bedding had sunk in some places and risen in others. The street was like a roller coaster, and there had never been enough money to smooth it out.

He slowed for Clarksville Pike, where the traffic division had again cleared all the cars from sight. One of the officers parked in the middle of the intersection recognized Chapell.

"Tanks may blow, Lieutenant. Civil Defense is evacuating both sides of the river."

"I need to get over there, Dave. There's a murder at the railroad bridge. I'll take responsibility."

"You got it."

He accelerated across four lanes and shot between McDonald's and Mrs. Winners to bear right on Ed Temple Boulevard—Temple had been a coach at Tennessee State, which was a mile up the road. At the first right, a short street that ended in the petroleum tank farm that straddled the river, he saw the dozens of fire trucks. They were obviously losing the battle with flames that were shooting into the low-lying clouds. He turned onto the street to get a better look, and when he lowered the car's window, a rolling wall of fireplace warmth hit him in the face. The deafening roar of the burning fuel sounded like a jet engine. All thoughts of the murder left his mind. He parked the car behind the last fire truck in line and ran the remainder of the distance to the stormy conflagration.

Later, when it was finally under control, he looked at his watch.

"Damn, I'd better get out of here. I'm supposed to meet Ponder in twenty minutes."

The pizza fest in Chapell's kitchen was cordial enough on the surface, but the cop could see that Ponder was preoccupied. His sentences were curt. When he smiled, the smile never left his lower face. Chapell was sure that his younger brother was playing with him. In spite of the merciless pressure at work, in spite of the fact that the evidence in the attic was damning, it was still too circumstantial to get a warrant. Even a mediocre lawyer could get an arrest thrown out and then file lawsuits for all kinds of things. They could question Ponder, but they couldn't charge him without a confession. Chapell decided that until he had further evidence, the little cat-and-mouse game Ponder was playing would have to continue. He decided to keep his mouth shut about the attic.

After Ponder had left, Chapell spent the half hour before bed in deep thought.

I need a plan and I don't see any good ones on display at the plan market.

There was only one thing he could think of to do, and if caught, there'd be hell to pay. Sleep once more came slowly, arriving in a bedraggled state some time in the middle of the night.

The next morning at work, Chapell fielded questions, got politely bawled out again by the captain because the squad had still not turned any leads, and tried to make a dent in the paperwork, which he was beginning to seriously loathe. It seemed every time he finished ten sets of forms, twenty more took their place.

Lunch was skipped in favor of putting an even larger stack of paperwork in the out box. The phone rang, and it was a voice Chapell was beginning to dread—the chief's secretary. If they increased the calls demanding his presence any more, he was going to hand out numbers to wait in line.

Jesus, they've already stuck a dick up my ass once today. Are we moving to a twice-a-day schedule?

In the chief's office the older man was somber. He said, "Rider, you knew Richter well, didn't you?"

Joey Richter was the cop who had been killed in a Kroger parking lot two nights before. They had found him lying in some brush a few feet from his car, which had been rolled down an embankment. No prints, no witnesses. His car and body were found only a stone's throw from the Cadillac that belonged to the woman who had been pulled from the river in North Nashville during the tank farm fire. A convicted habitual prostitute, her fingerprints had been on file. The current theory was that Richter had seen the kidnapping and had tried to prevent it. The cop had been shot in the face repeatedly. He was Chapell's age and had three kids.

He was also considerably overweight, and had he been in shape, he might not have botched what should have been a by-the-book arrest of a perpetrator.

Richter's demise was one of three priority "mystery" murders the squad was trying to investigate at the moment—in addition to Toy Duck. A Tennessee congressman was the third case. He'd been found naked in a motel room on Lebanon Road. There was a single small-caliber hole in the back of his head. None of the force would lose any sleep over that one.

"Very well. We went through high school together. One of his kids is named after me. Lucy and I used to go out before Joey started dating her. Nothing romantic—just good friends."

"I'd like you to present the flag at the funeral tomorrow."

"Chief, that's asking a lot. I'll pass, thank you."

"Why?"

"Too close, I guess. It hits too close to home. Hurts a lot and I don't know if I can stand up."

"I think you'll do just fine, Lieutenant. You were by far the closest; it always falls to the men who knew the cop the best."

"Sir, I really would appreciate letting someone else do it. Rob Burris knew Joey almost as well as I did."

"Lieutenant, there are times when you have to do things for God and country you don't want to do, especially if God and country want you to do the same thing *I* want you to do. And God knows, you manipulate this department enough as it is. You give the fucking flag to the lady, and that's a direct order!" The man was glowering intensely at Chapell.

That's totally uncalled for and way off the mark, old man. If I could manipulate this department, we'd have someone sitting in your chair that knew what the hell he was doing rather than forty ways to kiss the mayor's ass and make him giggle. Out loud, he answered, "As you wish, sir." His voice was totally without contention. He was just too tired to argue. He turned and walked out the door.

It was late when he approached Ponder's clinic on Harding Road. He parked the Cherokee in the back alley and made his way to the side door. After using his own key to open it, he punched the correct buttons on the alarm, then walked down the dark hall to his brother's office.

Let's just see if by some wild chance you're hiding something, brother of mine.

The cop took an hour to search the building systematically, omitting most of the obvious places in favor of air-conditioning ducts, the top side of the suspended ceiling, the motor compartment of three refrigerators. Along with ether and hydrocyanic acid, he was looking for anything else that might be out of place, suspicious. There might be other things too—a pail that smelled like apricot pits, a flashlight with a spot of molasses on it. Chances were slim. Ponder was thorough. However, the clinic was more or less out of bounds, and the doctor wouldn't expect anyone to be conducting an in-depth search.

Chapell was extremely careful to put everything back in its place exactly the way it was, in spite of the fact that one of the nurses or assistants could have moved it. Ponder was by nature suspicious. If the veterinarian suspected that his own brother had proof, Chapell wasn't at all sure if Ponder night not try to kill him. The cop had seen the cool, efficient machine in action—had seen it land three guys in the hospital one time when he was in college and Ponder was still in high school. That mugger in downtown Cleveland whom the brothers had left bleeding in an alley ...

For as long as Rider could remember, his brother had been studying the martial arts, and any other kind of arts that had to do with fighting and killing whenever he could get into a class. Even in grade school he'd wanted to make a career out of the military.

"Warrior. Ponder Allegro Chapell, warrior."

Unfortunately, the military wouldn't take him because of a little problem he had. It was nothing that shouldn't easily have been remedied, but for some reason the little malady had stubbornly resisted drugs and other treatment. Over a period of years the man had slowly learned to sublimate his fighting urges into other activities. However, he'd never stopped studying the military arts. His library contained hundreds of manuals on everything from edible plants in the average backyard to booby traps and bullets—exploding or nonexploding—to field surgery—how to amputate a leg with a jackknife and a cigarette lighter.

After finding absolutely nothing, Chapell rearmed the sentry and locked the door. He was careful to make sure no one had seen him enter or leave the clinic. He'd just started the Cherokee when the Jeep's back window shattered in a subdued *crunch*. A feathered, short arrow smashed into the windshield just below the rearview mirror. It lacked the energy to punch through the glass and rattled onto the top of the dash before dropping harmlessly to the floor. Because the Cherokee hadn't been started, the quiet was unnerving—no resounding boom echoing off the trees and houses like with the gun.

"*Crossbow*! God damn you, Ponder."

The cop snapped off the ceiling light of the Cherokee, opened the door, and darted for the bushes. He drew the Beretta and racked a round into the chamber. He had parked the Jeep in the dark behind a row of stores that were adjacent to Ponder's clinic. On the far side of the alley there was cover in a row of bushes that delineated someone's back lawn from the commercial area of the stores. Ponder would initially expect him to run for the stores. In the deep black he squatted and waited. A car with a half-shot muffler slogged noisily down Harding—probably a young couple coming home after a late date or a middle-aged manager working long hours to protect his job. Somewhere in the night two cats were howling at each other with studied ferocity. The echoes of their screams careened off hundreds of rigid structures, giving the sounds an eerie, unfocused effect.

Chapell was tempted to run down the lawn next to the row of high bushes and then cut back into the alley, but he wouldn't be able to keep the alley in sight.

From a dog's-eye level he could see that the bolt had probably been shot from about thirty yards down the alley. There was a small cement cutout that had been designed to hold a dumpster. He straightened and ran to the side of one of the buildings along the alley. Nothing. No sounds. No movement. He darted back across the alley and dived into the bushes again. The dumpster was now only fifteen yards away. Two more zigs and he was there, confronting what he knew he'd find all along—nothing. The shooter had slipped away as quietly as a snake on a fur rug.

You bastard.

There were no other ambush spots that would support a crossbow. He never had believed that it was Tyres who'd been shooting at him with the elephant gun. It would be just like Ponder to obtain the man's credit card number and then order the gun from New York. Once Tyres was under the ether, slap his hands all over the gun to print it. Ponder hated Tyres as much as Chapell did. Setting the man up, then killing him was brilliant. But this . . . his own brother . . . this way . . . and how the hell was Ponder so on top of things? The guy must be watching Chapell's every move. He had to sleep sometime.

The alarm went off much too soon at six-thirty.

His first thought was, "I don't remember spilling whiskey in here last night. But then, after four o'clock I don't remember much of anything. Smells awful. Must have been the better part of a bottle."

He'd taken three Anaprox when he'd got home, which had been about one. They took the edge off any hangover in the morning. Sleep had plunged down its evasive track again like a runaway locomotive. At least he hadn't wet the bed.

The auto glass garage answered the phone at three minutes after seven, and Chapell told them he needed an emergency repair—police business. He did not want to explain the hole in the window to anyone he worked with.

"Two-hundred-sixty-foot-per-second tree stab. Sucker came through the back window—went right through the damn glass clean as a dipped dick. Helluva thing."

By eight-fifteen, he was on his way to work. No one had to know that Cain was out hunting again, and Abel was not about to tell. He turned on the radio and was not surprised to hear that all three country stations were having Rae Willie Rider days.

Wonder whose brilliant idea that was.

He turned the air conditioner on full and aimed a vent at his face.

God, I'm tired. Got to get some good sleep. It was a term Rae Willie had often used—"good sleep."

When did she ever get any "good sleep"? She thrived on going without sleep for days, unless she was passed out.

By ten-thirty, he'd already been to the scene of a double murder in West Meade, had placed three reports in the out bin, and had fielded a dozen calls. He hadn't done anything in two weeks except sit at his desk and write reports, it seemed. The fingers fooled him, and he saw them punching up the number of Gale's home phone. It wouldn't ring. He dialed her cellular. It wouldn't ring either. There was a chance that she had cooled down, and he desperately wanted to talk to her about what he believed Ponder was trying to do to him. *I mean, fratricide is still taboo in most families, isn't it?* There was simply no one else to talk to. Spilling the beans could mean Ponder's arrest, and if younger brother was innocent, Gale would never speak to him again. That much he knew he could take to the bank. The family came before anything. To breach the trust . . .

He tried both numbers again, and both refused to ring. Strange. The panicky feeling of losing her started at his hairline and drifted down to the tops of his legs. On the way down it made him sick to his stomach.

At least her phone ought to ring. She'd never leave town. Where would she go? Besides, I'm sure she'd call first, regardless of how mad she was. And the phone company would have a 'no longer in service' or 'change of number' message on the line.

He called Ma Bell and asked if the phones were out of order. Quite a coincidence—both of them at once.

"We have no listing for a Gale Chapell, sir."

"I know. Both numbers are unlisted. Check that page."

"No, I'm sorry, sir. There is no listing for that name or those numbers at all."

"Have they recently been disconnected?"

"I don't show it."

"Well, the numbers were working a few days ago. What could have happened?"

"I have no way of knowing, sir. Perhaps customer service could tell you."

"Could they have been inadvertently deleted from the computer?"

"No. If they are a working number, they have to be in the computer or they won't ring."

He could see he wasn't going anywhere here. He called customer service and was put on the holding list. Every few seconds the bad music would be interrupted by a voice that said, "Please do not hang up. Your call will be answered in the order it was made." Five minutes later, it was answered by a real person who, after checking, told him that there was no listing for a Gale Chapell, and as far as the computer was concerned, there never had been.

Fuck you and your entire horse herd, shithead.

After the funeral he'd simply drive to her house and see what the problem was. The uneasy feelings in his stomach began a new round of roller derby. He reached for the jar of Tums and downed six.

If she's pulling that shit again, I'm going to personally throttle her and not look back.

After the funeral . . . The goddamn funeral! Goddamn Joey Richter, who ever since high school had never wanted to be anything but a cop. How had the poor fool managed to turn up in the right place at the wrong time?

Chapell did not want to present that flag to Lucy Richter. To have to look into her eyes was more than he wanted to handle right now. It was more than he should *have* to handle right now. The brass were on his case. They had all but accused him of stonewalling on Toy Duck—

"Seventeen men, and you haven't come up with a single, solitary lead, Lieutenant. That's some kind of a world record, isn't it?"

"We're investigating every possible angle and a few impossible ones, sir. This guy just doesn't leave any pieces of himself lying around."

"Lieutenant, nobody's that good. I don't think you're applying the resources in the proper channels." The chief had a fire blazing in his eyes. Probably he'd got another call from his friend the governor that morning. "I think you're dissipating your assets. Somewhere this nut has left a trace of himself. You're not concentrating on where to look. Focus your assets, Lieutenant!" Chapell knew that the department's top executive had just come back from another seminar for high-level supervisors. Evidently, he'd picked up some new jargon, and the buzz word was *assets*.

Chapell had one answer on his lips that had to do with finding out how far up his hemorrhoidic *ass* the old man's head could *set,* but he swallowed it.

"Sir, if you'll read the personnel dispersement reports, you'll see that we are working this case from at least six different angles, all of which require hundreds of phone calls."

"I'd love to read the goddamn PDR's, Chapell, but you're five days behind on them."

"You should have them by this afternoon."

"I'll look forward to it."

These bastards were beginning to get to him. they needed him a lot more than he needed this job. Let them push much more and he'd . . .

It was another muggy summer day in Nashville. Chapell had been to this cemetery too many times. The first time was when they buried Rae Willie. In fact, her grave and Jay Jr.'s, with the life-size statue of an angel, were only a stone's throw from where the detective stood in full dress blues. It was a stop many of the tourists made on the circuit. It was also part of the reason Chapell didn't want to be here—those memories, as old as they were, hurt.

The police chaplain droned on, broadcasting his platitudes in neat formations like the rows of gravestones that stretched across the hills. The last time Chapell had been here was six months ago—at the other end of the cemetery. A detective had tried to swallow a bullet faster than it could go through the back of his head. He'd lost the same way all the other cops in the world had whenever they had played the same macabre game.

There was something drastically wrong with Chapell's stomach, arms, and legs. As the ceremony drew closer to the twenty-one-gun salute, taps, and the folding of the coffin flag into the familiar triangle, anxiety welled ever stronger in nauseating waves. Muscles had turned to rubber, and he was certain his legs were shaking. He could not do this.

B-b-brack!

He jumped noticeably, drawing the attention of the men on either side of him, as the M-16's spoke once, twice, three times. Somewhere in the distance a hidden bugler played taps. Chapell had seen many funerals where the family had been able to hold back the tears until taps. There was something about the timbre of the horn that broke the shock spell and said, "Yes, it's for real. He will no longer lie next to you during the cold December rains; he will never again leave his egg-coated breakfast plate in the sink without rinsing it off. He's actually inside that box, and they are putting him down there in the ground. When you come to visit, he'll be just a few short feet away, but he definitely will not be coming through the front door again to say, 'What's for supper, babe?' "

Chapell glanced downward and saw that he had sweated through the summer blues under his arms. The landscape danced in front of him, and he felt himself swaying.

"Pre-sent arms!"

The four-man detail lifted the flag from the coffin; one man on each end presented his corner to his partner, who folded it again lengthwise; after four inches were tucked under at each end, the laborious task of folding the entire length into tight triangles began. If the folds were done precisely, the final triangle showed only red and white stripes.

Richter's mother continued to sob. Lucy had remained ashen and stone-faced throughout. Perhaps the fact that she knew, as did Chapell, that Joey had sported several recent affairs with other women helped. The three children—four, six, and eight—fidgeted continuously, heads twisting this way and that as they examined the funereal sights and sounds that would not be burned into the memories of most humans until they were considerably older.

The detail sergeant held the triangle point out as a patrolman tucked in the loose ends of a not-so-hot folding job. He did a brisk right-face and walked toward Chapell until he stood directly in front of the lieutenant, where he turned the point of the triangle to himself and saluted.

Chapell wheeled and bolted for his car.

He hardly felt the tongue-lashing the chief and Captain Satterfield gave him two hours later in the chief's office. The roils of aversion had subsided considerably, but the roils of questions in his own mind kept coming at him like north Hawaiian surf on a bad hair day.

"I don't give a rat's tit if you've been working eighteen-hour days, Lieutenant. We've all worked those kinds of hours or we wouldn't be here. You were given a direct order and you disobeyed—in front of a battery of television cameras, for God sake! We needed a little help from you, and you went over the wall."

"This is going to play in homes from coast to coast, Chapell, and it will reflect like shined shit on this department. I won't have it, Chief McKinty won't have it, and as of this minute, you're on three days' suspension. I don't want to see your face around here until you get some rest and your head's bolted on straight. I would suggest you take a look at your booze list and reevaluate a few things. That's just a start."

The headline at the bottom of page one in the Tennessean the following morning read: "Rae Willie's son gets suspension." Chapell didn't see it, he was sleeping. He'd gone to bed at six-thirty that evening and finally awakened at noon two days later. On the night table next to his bed, there was a single golden spangle that hadn't been there when he'd gone to sleep.

Chapter Six

Slater Howe coughed and rolled onto his back. He lay still for a minute, then reached for the remote and touched a series of numbers. The transparent sound of *soli* muted cellos floated close to the right-side bank of Bose speakers. As the other muted strings were added, the lugubrious melody line soared higher and higher, its harmonies pealing off in geometric progressions as the sound blossomed and unfolded. By the end of the intro, the arrangement's orchestration was spread over five octaves, and it saturated every crack and cranny in the room with the writer/singer's forthcoming pain.

> No one to love this evening . . .
> No one to kiss hello . . .
> Now that I've lost my pretty baby . . .
>   my baby, ooh . . .
> I ain't got no place to go . . .

The burnt-whiskey voice rendered the opulent textures and overtones of the huge $3,000/song string section insignificant. Cold chills feathered from Slater's neck down his back and onto the tops of his legs. No matter how many times he played Rae Willie singing "I Ain't Got No Place to Go," it always set him afire with chills. Her "torch" voice was totally mesmerizing. It blistered souls.

> I know a place in New York . . .

I know the seeds to sow . . .
But here I sit and watch the rain
                    rollin' down my window . . .
Without my man, ain't got *no* place to go.

The strings and harp began the staggered sweep into the chorus, and Rae Willie belted the lyrics mercilessly while Slater writhed on the floor in empathetic pain.

"Oh, God, baby! Why'd they burn you? I miss you so much!" Such magnificent pain.

A copy of *For You,* Nolan Tyres's version of Rae Willie's life, had been pushed beneath an end table. The fifty-six-year-old balding man had finished the last chapter—the fourth time he'd read the book—in tears, as revulsive as it was. He'd not been able to help himself, hungrily licking every sentence for the thinnest essence of flavor like the last ort of a delicious dessert.

Still strapping big—six-three, two-fifteen—he'd had little trouble exacting his due payment from the son of a bitch who had stiffed him. He'd read in a trade that Tyres was working on an autobiography of Rae Willie Chapell. With tabloid news paying up to $150,000 for succulent bits of scandal, what harm could there be in biting off a little retirement chunk for something that had remained a secret for over two decades? Everybody else was doing it—maids, bodyguards. He'd certainly paid for the privilege of getting something from all the years he'd spent driving her bus. Him with a master's degree in electrical engineering—driving a bus for a country music singer? And then the fire. God, how he'd tried.

That voice . . .

She had been a slut, screwing everything that wasn't tied down. How many times had *they* done it? Her and him. The back of the bus. Back of the plane. Back of the trailer. Backstage. Jesus, she had been good, too. Tight as sin; moves that would make a queer come.

It had hurt when he'd seen her with the other men. No doubt what she was going to do. She'd even laughed at him a couple of times when he'd petulantly mentioned it. And Jay Jr.—the man couldn't have cared less. He'd had his own little "piece" of mind in Montana, and the age and sex of that little gem would have stunned the world. Why the two had never got a divorce had always been a total enigma. Slater Howe was probably the only man who had ever been seriously in prolonged love—and hate—with Rae Willie Chapell. The love part kept him driving the bus; the hate part made him do other things.

"I've got something that will put your book on the charts for a long time, Mr. Tyres. You wouldn't believe the things I can tell you, and I've got proof—pictures, for instance." There had been times when Rae Willie was so drunk she didn't know what she was doing. A man in love-hate will take pictures an ordinary man, who was just in love, wouldn't. He hadn't been a complete fool—it wasn't all fanatical desperation. If the feeling became just hate, the pictures might come in handy someday. Fortunately, they'd been hidden in a place where no one had found them until his memory returned. The joy at finding them intact had been one of the highlights of his life.

He'd given the ugly little fat man all the details and some of the less revealing pictures, but he had stubbornly withheld the name. The elaborate dressing trailer had been parked on a back lot at Twentieth-Century Fox, in Hollywood. Rae Willie was starring in her fourth film. Some nights she was too tired, or too stoned to go all the way downtown to the hotel. He'd been watching the trailer that night for some time, and he knew exactly what was going on inside—had seen it twice with his own eyes when he'd sneaked up to the back window, then the front window—one, two in the morning—no one around—they thought. God damn, how could she do that! Her own twelve-year-old daughter making it with that gigolo. Gale certainly didn't seem to mind—like mother, like daughter—but by God, that was perverted!

He'd seen the dark figure sneak into the trailer. A few minutes later there was a soft explosion, and the guy fell out the trailer door, smoke and flames blasting out behind him. Panic-stricken, Slater Howe, decorated Korean War hero, raced to the rescue. Someone had to save her life, and no one else was available. "Oh, I couldn't sleep; was out walking around; just happened to see the flames; had to try, Officer." Forget how he happened to be so close to her trailer at three a.m. This woman could not be allowed to die.

The fire starter had taken off like a bat out of Hades, and Slater Howe was sure the man had never seen him—had looked right at him in stark terror, clothes smoking from the heat, little wisps curling up from his hair. But he had never seen Slater Howe lurking in the dark!

So the bus driver dives into the blast furnace, useless as it is to drag the blackened corpse out. It had cost him a year and a half in the hospital. The disfigurement was so bad from the third-degree burns that even after he'd been able to walk again, he couldn't be seen in public. It had taken fifteen years before technology had produced the prosthetics and the synthetic skin that could make him look like a normal man again. It had taken almost seventeen years before he'd been able to remember everything. It had come agonizingly slow, in microscopic pieces over all those years. It had been ten years before he'd even remembered the fire. The foundation had paid his medical bills and continued his salary, but they had steadfastly refused to give him a lump-sum consideration for bravery above and beyond the call of duty. The unsaid voices said, "You went into that inferno on your own, Mr. Howe. It was a damn dumb thing, for sure, and we ain't payin' a dime for your Mississippi stupidity."

Would he do it all over again if the chance to save

her life presented itself to him? Yes. She meant that much to him.

Not a minute of all the years had been without pain, in spite of the plethora of painkillers. If he forgot to take them just once, out of the four or more times a day ... with all those operations, and the amount of burning of his larynx ... After he'd been made presentable enough so that the average American on the street wouldn't scream at seeing him, the foundation had rewarded his years of suffering with a plum—curator of the goddamned museum! He quickly grew bored with the job. With $200,000 for the information that would make the biography the greatest explosion on the literary scene since Hamlet, he could quit, invest the money, and live the way he wanted for the rest of his life.

Who'd have thought that Bro. Prick Tyres would stiff him? They'd agreed on the price and signed the contract. However, when Slater Howe had refused to give up the name, Tyres said, "Sorry, fuck you," and printed what he had. When Howe confronted him with the contract, the little cocksucker had showed him the fine print. No name, no bread. Slater Howe had lost his retirement fund and Nolan Tyres had lost his useless little faggot life. It'd taken some time to set up, but No-lan No-Dick had bit the horse's tit. If the little prick had only had the patience to wait a little longer....

Giving up that name wasn't worth $200,000 until Slater Taft Howe carried out what he had in mind for the lucky fellow who had started the fire in Rae Willie's trailer. Now that his memory was intact, he knew whose balls needed the liberal application of blue flame. All that was left was getting the proper funds.

Plan B. It hadn't taken long to find out that his conscience had also burned in that fire. He'd staked out a couple of drug dealers in East Nashville—that certainly wasn't hard to do. It had taken a month of working late evenings, but he'd managed to follow both of them to their sources, then follow the sources to their sources. Imagine the surprise when the money couriers for both wholesalers got popped in one night. It was cash, and it would have to be handled very carefully to avoid drawing suspicion, but after counting the total, he found he had over a half million dollars. He found a place to hide it and began to pursue the get-even business with a deep and abiding vengeance.

By two p.m., the thick, sticky cobwebs that had been stubbornly stretched across the inside of Chapell's head had still not cleared. He sloughed off the spangle on the table next to the bed.

"You probably left the goddamned door open again, stupid, and Ponder decided to let you know he's in the game. I'm surprised he didn't play 'Pretend to kill your brother' again. Bastard. I'll get to him later. I want to find out what little sister is up to, whether she likes it or not! 'God, I'm tired—and what a screwed up family we make.' "

An hour later, he was driving down her street in Brentwood, fighting the fatigue that just wouldn't quit.
Stress, my boy. The old-high-wire act without a net. Just trudge through it, Rider, my boy.

It had been a long time since he had been here. Whenever the family got together, it was always at Chapell's place in the woods. They could swim, cook out, whatever. There had been some radical changes in Gale's neighborhood: new houses, a new condo complex. The houses all looked the same to the cop.

"Goddamn builders have got as much originality as a family of frogs."

He drove down the street and was simply unable to discern which house was hers. He'd never written down the number. You don't write down the number of your own sister's home. This was ridiculous. The changes were substantial, and the area looked totally

alien compared to the last time he'd been here, which
had been five years at least.

"Am I on the right street?"

He tried the streets on either side. A mailman in a
right-side-drive Jeep was making his way down the
row of mailboxes stuck on posts next to the curb.
Chapell pulled up next to him and hollered, "Can you
tell me which one belongs to Gale Chapell?"

"Chapell?"

"Gale Chapell."

"Nobody like that around here."

"Maple Pointe . . ."

"No. Nobody like that on Maple."

"You positive? She's lived here for ten years."

"I've been on this route for six, and there's no Gale
Chapell listed as primary resident anywhere in this
area—or anywhere else that I know of."

"Thanks."

What the hell was going on here? First, she eighty-
sixes the phone company files; now this. How? Why?
This was the kind of thing the federal government was
good at doing—making people disappear. He was too
far behind the power curve for this—too exhausted to
contend with something that involved exotic sources—
Uncle Sam?

Way back in the uttermost recesses of his mind the
familiar little chrysalis was breaking open much too
soon. As he drove back toward home, the ugly bug
slowly emerged, and Rider Chapell knew what had to
be done, and quickly, if he was going to beat them at
their own game.

Snowy Lockhart sat cross-legged on the sofa wearing nothing but a Martin guitar. A yellow legal pad
lay beside her. She picked the guitar thumb-and-
fingers, and it *spronged* and *twanged* filthy funk.

I ain't leavin' lovin leavin' lovin' you.

> Goin' out that door's the hardest thang I'll
> probably ever do.

Flecked liberally with acid brown, the husky voice
growled and spat, tearing at the words like a hungry
mountain lion at a freshly killed deer....

> You been waterin' your horse all over town,
> This drinking trough is done shut down;
> I ain't leavin' lovin' leavin' lovin' you.

The little blond singer paused and giggled.

"That's utterly terrible. But maybe the hook will
work."

She reached for the silver Alpheus Music Writer
with the enlarged eraser, and scratched down the
stanza anyway. The pencil needed sharpening badly,
and she had to exaggerate the size of the writing to
compensate for the thick lines. Finishing, she glanced
at the battery-powered clock on the wall.

"Oh, dear, it's almost ten. I'm gonna be late."

She laid the Martin on the couch and ran for the
bedroom and clothes.

Seven minutes later, wearing white shorts and a
green halter top, she stepped from her doorway into
the dark, guitar case in hand, notebook held to her
chest.

A chill scooted up her back like a hurried spider.

That light is out again.

The chill had been initiated by the dark rather than
the muggy-night temperature. she walked briskly toward the white CRX at the end of the apartment-
complex parking lot. Beyond the blacktop was a
nasty—at night, anyway—woods which swept up a hill
too steep for dwellings.

As she struggled to get the key into a lock that was
invisible in the dark, she heard a slight rustling behind
her. Another chill blasted across hairline and forehead. Before she could turn, a dish towel soaked in
ether slammed roughly into her face as an unrelenting

hairy arm grabbed her around the chest, knocking the wind out of her. She gasped hard to catch her breath and was rewarded with the decrescendoing sound of an obnoxious eighteen-wheeler flatulating its way up a low-grade hill on the nearby interstate. Struggling arms and legs went limp in utter frustration as pungent fumes tore up her nose and down a throat that was attempting to breathe and, at the same time, expel this abomination that was making a perfectly fine world go dizzy black. Sight and sound turned inward, where ears were already screaming loudly in a high-pitched turbine whine. The young woman's bare legs convulsed in a last-ditch throe compelled by the primordial fear that possess a drowning victim whose hands will later be found clenching mud and grass from the bottom. The terror of the just-before-death bolt of panic causes the victim to grasp, literally, at straws for salvation, because there is nothing else.

Lose the towel, dickhead, or she'll die.

The woman was totally limp.

Forty-five minutes later, he walked boldly into the dark pasture carrying a bucket. There were the feelings of *déjà vu* and *jamais vu*—the feeling of having done this before and of having been in an unfamiliar setting before. The three horses eyed him cautiously, but the sweetfeed was too much to resist. They trotted, slowed, and walked up to him boldly. He gently pushed aside the head of a gelding. A mare took his place and plunged her snout into the bucket. The crunching sound of specialized molars at work resounded around the inside of the large head. She ate for a half minute before she pulled her nose out of the bucket sharply. He barely had time to step out of the way as she fell and began to convulse.

A half hour later . . .

He chanted the clichés, sotto voce, with intense concentration, constantly visualizing the glorious birth of the healthy, familiar girl. As he sang, the wound in the animal's belly was stitched closed with remarkable quickness, the ornateness developing as if by magic as the elements were selected and introduced into the sutures.

"May you be born strong and healthy, wizened for the world we must live in. May your birth be an easy one. May you know love and peace all the days of your life."

Finishing the task, he replaced the tools and materials in the small case. Then he kneeled, head and forearms to the ground, and chanted for another five minutes, increasing the concentration to even further levels.

It is granted.

The voice was soft and pure. Had there ever been any doubt?

He picked up the box, stood, and surveyed the scene with a smile. She would be born beautiful, healthy.

When he turned and began walking to the gate, the muffled shrieks of terror fell on totally deaf ears. The outline of kicking knees and scratching nails marking the skin was as implausible as a fully operational Burger King on Mars. The only sounds that came to his ears were crickets, a bullfrog in a shallow pond, and a barn owl sitting in a tree at the edge of the nearby thicket.

"Can you sing?" he had asked. Slater Howe was sitting at a booth across from the young lady with chicory hair that had been highlighted with amber streaks.

"That's what I do."

"Well, you probably won't have to. We may need to color your hair, though. And change the makeup a little."

She had wanted to balk at destroying a $75 hair job, but kept quiet.

She had given him a voice-over demo tape when they'd first met. Just talking to her Slater could hear

how close her speaking voice was. He'd have to work
with her on the accent and the inflections of certain
syllables, but if she could take direction, she could pull
it off.

Before the fortuitous meeting with Jeni, pronounced
with a French J that sounded like the beginning of
Zsa in Zsa Zsa Gabor, Slater Howe had first called
both the Los Angeles Screen Actors Guild and
AFTRA, the American Federation of Television and
Radio Artists, to ask for suggestions to cast a specific
type for an acting part. He had flown to L.A. and
interviewed over twenty women. He might have found
the lookalike actress in Nashville, but he didn't want
to raise any flags that might be remembered sticking
into the top of the mountain later if the shit hit the
fan. None of the L.A. women filled the bill. A couple
of them were close and might have passed with the
right makeup and hair, but they just didn't feel right
in his gut. His instincts had never let him down, and
he wasn't about to push it now. He had flown back
to Nashville discouraged about probably having to fly
to New York to do the same thing all over again. The
evening he'd arrived back home, he had been picking
over heads of lettuce at a grocery store. There she
was. The hair was the wrong color, but other than the
fact that she was an inch taller, the resemblance was
closer than he'd ever seen. Voice? Could she act?
Would she do the job? Was she nefarious enough to
be tempted, by big bucks, into doing something that
would not take place on a stage or in front of a camera
or microphone? He struck up a conversation. Her
voice was right. He then brought the topic around to
the fact that he was a producer looking for a certain
"type," to do a very special acting job. If she was
interested in making an easy $5,000 cash, she should
call him. Forget the fact that she was local. He handed
her one of the special cards he'd had printed just for
the occasion. Once he had completed her training,

he'd deal with the bizarre acting job that he wanted
her to do. She had called early the next day.

Her full name was Jeni St. Azzure; she was di-
vorced, no kids; her father was a Wesleyan minister
in Montreal; she spoke fluent French; she had been in
Nashville for seven months; had come to make one
last attempt at stardom—at thirty-four years of age;
she hadn't had any luck; her money was running out;
no, she wasn't savvy enough to know that if a "producer" hands you a card and wants to meet you at
the Demonbreun Street Shoney's instead of his office,
there's a good chance he's a rip-off artist. Anyone in
the business who isn't established and successful
enough to have an office is usually trouble. The trades
are full of them—phone numbers connected to answering machines. "We want your songs." Sure they
do—just pay them $500 each, and they'll cut them just
as fast as you can write them. And some of them do
a good job of it. However, legitimate producers and
publishing companies pay the songwriters and the artists for the music, not vice versa.

Slater debated whether to just level with her. This
gig was so far off the wall, he wasn't sure the cover
story would hold up.

*No. What if she gets pissed at something and goes to
the cops before it's over? What if she gets a conscience
attack and backs out at the last minute?*

He gave her a thousand-dollar advance and they
began work. He rented an office in Berry Hill, and
they held the accent sessions there. Sometimes they
would drive to one of the parks and walk and work.
It had taken only a few days to see that he'd have to
level to a certain extent with her. He would fill her in
on family details, show her the films, let her listen to
the records. The more he worked with her, the more
pleased he became. Another month, maybe less, and
the "set" would be ready. He'd had trouble locating
the right studio couch. Curtains he'd ordered from a
small company in Connecticut had just come in, and

they were perfect. When the fire starter got to finally
see this production, he was going to go into "sponta-
neous combustion" mode. If not, maybe Slater Howe
could provide a little assistance.

The "fire starter" badly needed relief from the
splendid case of blue balls he was sporting.

"Hornier'n a porcupine in a briar patch. Best you
find a little taste, my boy, or you're going to 'splode.
Last time you waited way too long, sweetie."

There had been a chance encounter with a young
woman at the grocery store who had been behind him
in the checkout line. When the line got backed up
because of a lack of baggers, she had left her cart,
told him to shove it along in the line, and had begun
bagging groceries for the clerk. He'd piddled around
until the clerk had finished checking her out, then he'd
walked to the lot, wheeling his cart next to her. He
told her thanks; that was a special thing to do; she
told him thanks for moving her cart along; they both
remarked about the weather, and within five minutes
both cars were loaded and she was gone. Following
her directly home left too much chance of being spotted. Fire starter called Motor Vehicles with the story
that he'd dinged her car in a parking lot—he had the
plates and he needed the driver's address for his insurance company. Even though they were no longer supposed to, they gave him the address. Later that
evening . . .

. . . the little fool had left her patio door open, and
no one heard or saw him leave, carrying her over his
shoulder like an in-need-of-cleaning rug.

In the smallest hours of the night, he used her up,
managing to come twice in an hour. Finished, he practiced on her with his tools for a while, but the third
time wouldn't materialize. The woman kept passing
out when she should have been screaming. And the
damn torch . . . The urge to singe some serious muff
was there, but the torch had picked the most inoppor-

tune time to run out of propane, and he didn't have a spare. How stupid!

"Shit and God damn! You never can rely on the little things in life that make it all worthwhile."

After he'd made very nice bracelets for each arm out of a section of her large intestine, the woman finally went into convulsions and quit breathing for good. He wrapped her and threw her in the trunk. Three seconds after she'd gone over the side of the bridge, at one a.m., he'd forgotten about her. Just another piece of flotsam on the river of death.

By two a.m. he was back home and not sleepy.

"Take a swim."

Naked, he walked to the edge of the swimming pool and pissed in it. He liked that. It always reminded him of his mother giving him a bath when he was three, four years old.

"Mommy, I've got to pee."

"Well, go, then."

Something about the warm yellow stuff in the bath water made him feel cozy, comfortable.

Diving into the pool, he was totally unaware of the piece of dark that was leaning against a large hackberry tree about fifty feet away. There was very little light, but when the fire starter passed through a sliver from a house window on the way to the pool, the former bus driver turned museum curator turned acting director had a quick glimpse of the face he loved to hate. The look was serene—totally unlike the visage of panic after setting fire to a dressing trailer on the back lot of a movie company. The prissy look would be changed soon enough. It had taken over three years of planning and hard work, but the lure was now almost ready and the trap was on the verge of being sprung.

Chapell awakened again to the sound of a couple of angry jays. A farm cat was wandering through the woods looking for lunch, and the birds were thoroughly pissed off.

"God damn it, I know I closed that door! You'd better get your head out of your ass, good buddy, or you're going to pay dearly." The door to the deck was wide open again. The clock radio said it was a little after eleven o'clock.

It was his last "day off" and he intended to use it wisely.

The phone rang.

"Hi."

"Gale!"

"How are you doing? I heard about your suspension."

"Where the hell have you been? Do you know what I've been through trying to find you?"

"Well, it's not like you haven't been through it before, is it?"

"If you're going to fade into the woodwork, how about letting me know beforehand? You almost cost me a heart attack."

"Sorry. Want to have lunch?" Evidently, her anger had dissipated from the last luncheon outing. It always did. Gale did not hold grudges.

"Sure. Same place?"

"None better. Twelve-thirty?"

"Fine. You've got some explaining to do."

"In due time, sweetie. How about if I ask Ponder to join us?"

For some reason Chapell's heart skipped two whole beats.

"Darling?"

The cop recovered from the pregnant pause and said, "Do you think he'd come? He's always so busy during the day."

"I'm sure I can get him to come—a little finessing, a few small promises . . ."

"Good luck. I'll see you in a while, then."

Well, that took care of how he had planned to

spend the day—feuding with some faceless high-level asshole in a government office building. *My sister has disappeared; the phone company has deleted her records; the post office has done the same. I want to know who she's working for and what you've done with her.* He had been sure that she did something for Uncle Sam when she pulled this stunt. Why they'd want to use a country singer, a musician, totally baffled him, but then a lot of the clandestine shit was baffling. Try as he would, he'd never been able to pry what she'd done for them out of her. On top of that, it pissed him off when they told him they had no idea what had happened to her. He could almost hear them sniggering.

Except for seeing his beloved, gorgeous sister alive, grinning and well, lunch was not fun. Ponder was late, but after joining the "welcome home" party Chapell quickly found out that his brother was still acting like a glans penis. Smug, heartless, aloof, he played up Chapell's cracking up and getting suspended; he played down Gale's disappearance, about which she wouldn't talk. The thought went through Chapell's mind that they might be in it together.

As a cop, Chapell wanted vehemently to confront Ponder with what he believed the veterinarian was doing to these young women, but he still couldn't prove it; and the brother part of him just refused to believe it. It didn't help matters any that he possessed an extremely empirical sense of logic. He believed very little he couldn't see or prove. Had someone shot a rifle straight into the air and a man died from a bullet wound on the other side of a hill a few seconds later, Chapell would want to see the ballistics report to match bullets and the autopsy report to see the angle and direction of the trajectory. In his mind, there was always the chance that someone else had fired a gun at precisely the same instant and killed the man. More than once he'd seen guilt-ridden suspects own up to a crime because they believed they'd committed it. Later, scientific evidence would show that they hadn't. To accuse his brother and be wrong would be a mortal, unforgivable sin. He would have to catch Ponder in the act or hear a confession—one that could be proved—from Ponder's own lips. Knowing Ponder as he did, Chapell knew there would probably never be a confession. Ponder was one of those rare individuals whom the Russians could have tortured with beatings, electricity to the genitals, drugs, and execution of family members right before his eyes. If Ponder made up his mind he wasn't going to tell, he'd go to his grave in silence.

Had Gale told Ponder about her cop brother's suspicions? To his surprise, Chapell found his little sister sticking up for the doctor. It was if the two of them had conspired to gang up on their older brother.

"Well, Rides, you think the cops will ever find the guy who's doing the music and horse businesses these magnanimous favors? It's only been, what, twenty years now?" Ponder looked him in the eye and took a huge bite of barbecue.

"We'll get him. Sooner or later he'll screw up." Chapell held the gaze, took another swig of beer, another bite of barbecue.

"Sounds to me like it's lions five hundred eighty-two, Christians nothing." Gale glanced from one to the other and turned another tub of butter upside down on the cornbread.

"What happens if the bastard decides to sew our little sister in the next available dead horse, Ponder? How would you feel then?" More beer, a forkful of beans.

Gale answered, with half a mouthful of coleslaw, "Rider, I'm not in the 'deserving of punishment' category. He's not after someone like me. I didn't establish my credentials the way most of these sweet young *thangs* do today. The bitch who gives the best Friday afternoon under-the-desk blowjob in the producer's office gets the gig. Believe me, it's the way things work, and the industry is better off without them."

Chapell didn't do a good job of hiding his shock. He managed to weakly answer, "I find that hard to believe, little sister. I still think it's done with talent and being in the right place at the right time."

"Well, what you don't know won't kill any horses." She giggled and so did Ponder.

Chapell was relieved when Ponder said he had to go. "I've got a date with a poodle at two o'clock— kidney transplant. I *love* this business."

"Where did the donor come from?" Chapell asked curiously.

Ponder looked at Chapell with contempt and said, "Where all the donor organs come from, Rider. Where do you think? From one of the sacrificial dogs we keep for blood transfusions and operations just like this."

Chapell was beginning to not like his younger brother more and more. This was not the Ponder he'd grown up with.

A few minutes later, he kissed Gale good-bye at the restaurant doorway and headed toward the john. The pitcher of beer was manifesting itself already.

Where does that bastard get off, demeaning me that way? Who the hell put the spike up his ass?

As usual, he was unconsciously peeing on the toilet's ramp that led into the pool. A man's stream pouring directly into the toilet's water was one of the most repulsive sounds he knew. The sound of a woman taking a piss was even more disgusting. It had taken years of practice and dedication to hit the tiny band of porcelain just above the water if the toilet had no ramp. If you peed directly into the water, people could hear you, especially if the rest rooms were adjacent. There would be no doubt about what you were doing in there.

Remaining invisible carried over into other parts of Chapell's life. He had a serious aversion to anyone knowing where he was or what he was doing when he was by himself. If he was outside—in the woods, in an alley or parking lot at night, around the grounds of the house—he took pains to move quietly, to close the car door with a *click,* not a *thunk.* If he was inside, he was careful to close doors silently and not to clatter across bare floors or scuff the soles of his shoes on the carpet. It was simply good survival technique, and it was instinctive for most of God's creatures with the exception of man. If you were silent and invisible, you couldn't be killed and eaten.

When he'd finished in the john and finally got to the Cherokee, he found that two of his tires had been slit.

Chapter Seven

We were typical bored high school boys—sixteen and eighteen, in a strange town while on summer vacation. Mom was performing in the field house at a small university in Alva, Oklahoma. The promoter was an old friend of Dad's, and he offered to let us borrow his new Eldorado convertible. It took all of one second to say yes to that deal.

I bought the beer. No hassle in a town where they open a kid's mouth on his eighth birthday and shove a wad of tobacco into it. We drank a little, drove around the town square a dozen times, listened to the radio, and honked and whistled at anything with two lumps under a blouse—young or old.

We finally got hungry and found a Sonic drive-in. It was one of those places with the diagonal stalls and the roof overhead—menu boards and phones by each parking place—cherry limeades, chili cheese coneys—good American stuff. We figured the waitresses were college, but with a new Cadillac convertible and a free concert as bait, there was no stopping us. There's no greater summum bonum for two high school boys than to score with older, more "sophisticated" chicks. And it wasn't hard. The enticement of a Rae Willie Chapell concert usually worked getting chicks anywhere in the United States—and most of Canada. If we were lucky enough to borrow a car, probably five out of ten times we ended up in the boondocks somewhere with two sets of clothes on the front-seat floor and two sets on the back-seat floor. If we didn't have a car, no problem.

We'd just scour the audience, pick the victims before the concert began, go and offer to let them come backstage and watch. It's amazing what an aphrodisiac it is to have access to a star. There were a couple of chicks that followed one of the guys in the band all the way across the country. Groupies are one of the "great American" giveaways.

Anyway, at the carhop we got lucky. The waitress said she had a friend, and they would love to go to the eight o'clock show and meet the star. We got names and directions to the house, and we believed it was a foregone conclusion that the wicks would get dipped— or was it the dicks would get whipped?—before the night was over.

They got off work at seven, so we couldn't go get them until seven-thirty. I can still remember the brassy look the town had from the sun dropping toward the horizon that time of day. Lot of wheat fields, red dirt. There were several cars parked in front of the house, but I found a place for the Caddy down the street. We could see from the sidewalk that there were four guys sitting in lawn chairs on the house's front veranda. I figured they were harmless, were probably waiting for their dates to go to the concert.

I'd almost reached the door when one of them says, "Who the hell're you?"

No "Howdy. How ya doin', strangers? Fine night. Where y'all from? Think it'll rain? Are you outatowners here to fuck our very own personal ejaculating machines?"

Another guy says—nasty voice—"Hey, teeny boppers, he asked you a question."

Even at sixteen Ponder was big. Six-one, two-ten. He'd been into the martial arts thing for several years, had a seventh-degree black belt, and as a sophomore made the all-state team as the first-string quarterback. I wasn't so big, but I was a lot stronger and faster than I looked. They put the radar gun on my slapshot that following fall, and it was in the low nineties. The bot-

tom line is that we weren't anywhere near as afraid of
these college boys as they thought we should be.

Funny, it was almost old hat—we'd been through it
before—several times, in fact—different places around
the country. Horny intruder comes sniffing around
looking to mate. Bull moose or head-of-the-harem go-
rilla or chief-stud mustang charges to scare the stranger
off and keep all the ladies.

Ponder, God love him, says too calmly, "Why don't
you boys act your age? You're supposed to be into the
mature, Joe College role by now, aren't you?"

That starts to piss them off. Second guy barks—high
voice—I'll never forget that little-boy voice—anyway,
he says, "And why don't you teeny boppers play with
kindergarten kids your own age instead sniffing ass
where you're not wanted?" I thought his voice was
gonna crack from puberty stress fractures.

Ponder looks at me and says, "Jeez, Rides, I thought
we were wanted—loved, even cherished. We have our
invitations . . . right . . . here . . ." He pretends to search
in his pockets, finally pulls out his hand like he's holding up an invitation. He looks at his hand with this
funny face, and his index finger slowly extends in a
bird. I wanted to laugh. God, I wanted roll on the floor
and laugh.

I says, "No doubt about that, Ponds. We were definitely invited. Don't see the problem."

All four of the college guys are on their feet.

First guy says, "Why, you wise-ass prick," and he
charges. Ponds doesn't move a muscle until the guy is
four feet away. The idiot's gonna hit Ponds with a
cross-body block—you could see it like he was carrying
a sign. Ponds steps to the side at the last second and
kicks the guy so hard in the nuts, you figured the kid'll
never father children. The guy folds on the porch into
the fetal position. He's holding his gans and puking his
last three meals down the side of his face onto the floor.

"Uh-uh, boys. Don't do it. It's gonna hurt."

A waste of breath. Two more come at him—they're

gonna gang-tackle him together. Football mentality against Chuck Norris—what's wrong with this picture?

Last second, Ponds drops to the floor. They trip and go over the top of him, over the railing at the end of the porch, and into some kind of thorn hedge. You could have heard them screaming all the way to Dallas. How he knew that hedge was there, and that it was all thorns, beats the hell out of me. But he always knew that kind of shit. He was two years younger physically, but mentally he was a thousand years old.

Left alone, the other guy backs off.

We get the girls, go to the gig, get laid, and at two a.m. we bring them home. Nobody's gonna hang out until two a.m., right? Just to get even? Well, these cowboy kids had heads with nothing in them but little piles of red dirt. The girls go inside, we start for the car, and all of sudden there are ten of them—including three of the originals.

To make a long story short, Ponder gets three of them without a scratch on him. He just kicks them in the gut with that spin-blur kung fu thing. Heel spin, I think they call it. Meanwhile, two of them are at me, I punch the first guy's nose across his face. Blood, he's gone. The second guy, I get his shirt up over his head so he can't see, and then set a few on his face. If the fourth one hadn't come at Ponder with a bat, he'd probably just ended up with a stomach ache like the rest. I get a glimpse of Ponder and the kid with the bat. Kid swings, Ponder sidesteps. At the guy's backswing, Ponder—so fast, so unbelievably fast—pile-drives the kid in the forehead with the middle row of knuckles on his hand, and I could hear the whack ten feet away. Kid goes down like a bag of cement, blood all over everything. The other guys see all the blood and back off. Ponder pulls out his handkerchief, kneels down, and presses it against the cut. "Here, put some pressure on it, and it'll stop bleeding," he says. Kid takes the handkerchief and does it.

We hear sirens—all hell breaks loose with red and blue lights.

Cops take three of them to the hospital. The other guys admit that they started it—at least they had some character. In the car on the way home Ponder says, "You want a guy to bleed, Rides, forget the nose shit— that's expensive surgery in case you and your insurance company ever end up having to pay for it. Open up his forehead. Bleeds like a stuck pig but doesn't do any permanent damage. Good way to make the rest of them quit." Now, how the hell did he know that? He could have killed any one of those stupid kids. Instead, he puts them on the ground, one by one, then stops the fight with the blood thing. Me, I hurt my guys. Probably ten, twelve stitches each.

Chapell did some grocery shopping on the way home from the lunch and pulled into the four-stall garage at three o'clock. He was still tired. Even with three days away from the stress of work, the fatigue had let up very little. The fact that he'd have even more paperwork to catch up on when he got back didn't help any.

He put the groceries away, put a load of sheets, underwear, and socks in the Maytag and turned it to the maximum-length cycle. Shirts and pants were always done by the laundry, but underwear, socks, and the like were easier to do at home. He went back upstairs, filled the CD carousel with some old recordings that had been recently remixed for CD— Lambert, Hendricks and Ross, Maynard Ferguson, George Shearing, the Hi Los—turned the volume to low, then lay down on the twelve-foot sofa.

"Rest or die, Detective Chapell. You're going back to the front lines tomorrow, and it won't be easy."

Gale ran several errands after lunch. Having been out of town most of the last couple of months, she needed the time to catch up on the kinds of things that can't be done over the phone. At two sharp, she had a meeting with her investment broker and got caught up on several things that she had lost track of; she made a trip through the drive-in teller at First American to deposit several jingle residual checks she'd picked up at the AFTRA office; there was a quick run to the Taiwanese tailor's shop to collect some costume alterations that had been there for two weeks; and by four o'clock she was in the promotion office of the label on Sixteenth to make some scheduled long-distance calls to several dozen radio stations sprinkled through the Midwest. After a six-thirty appointment to get her hair cut and highlighted, her last stop was at H.G. Hills to buy enough groceries to stock the larder.

She finally walked into the house at quarter to eight. Tom Oliver was on the private-line Codephone. They usually communicated by Codephone because one or the other were frequently out of town or out of cellular reach. Tom was tall, good looking—had even done some part-time modeling at one point in his life. He'd gone to Vanderbilt on a baseball scholarship, had majored in business. A week after graduation, he had begun work in his father's construction company as a common laborer. Three days after his twenty-seventh birthday, the young man's father had died from a heart attack. Having worked his way up to foreman, Tom had taken over the operation of the company, which was one of the largest in the state. Under his leadership the business had thrived with new and ongoing projects in Nashville, Chattanooga, Memphis, and Knoxville. Tom flew his own Beech King Air and lived by himself in a fabulous country home that had its own paved and lighted landing strip.

Fucking friends, Gale called them. Neither he nor Gale had time for a full-time partner, or wanted one. Both were far too selfish with their time and careers. For years they had got together once every week, or two, or three, or four, eaten a pizza, drunk a bottle of wine, then screwed each other's brains out. It had been a long two months since the last time they'd been able to connect. The arrangement was much more efficient than having to spend the unnecessary time it took to maintain a relationship which included all the temperamental give and take that came with a full-time commitment. It also eliminated the possibility of contracting several serious, or even deadly, diseases that came with dating and sleeping around.

"Call me when you get time. I'm in Memphis and should be home by nine. I'm horny as hell—may have to jerk off in the plane a couple times before I get there. Will that cost me my membership in the two-mile-high club?" He and Gale had done it in the plane a couple of times—two and a half miles of altitude and no oxygen. Tom had filed his flight plan after they were airborne, and after programming several way points into the computer, he had put the King Air on autopilot for a flight to Kansas City. Gale had climbed onto his lap after she'd stripped him and herself. Flying over twelve thousand feet without oxygen was dangerous and illegal as hell, but the result was worth it to the couple. When the brain is starved for O^2 the sex sensation is heightened significantly. It's the same principle used by the deviants who temporarily strangle themselves with a cord while masturbating—auto eroticism—starving the brain of oxygen while having sex.

She grinned and said out loud, "You'd better save all the jism for me, Tommy O. I want to feel the delivery vehicle in at least two of my body orifices tonight. I may even let you play Ass Bandit." She called his machine and told him to bring a loaded pizza, she had the wine.

Nine-thirty, the doorbell rang, and there was Tom balancing a large pizza box in one hand like a waiter and holding a large bottle of Lambrusco in the other.

The automatic timer turned out the lights on his Mark VIII just as he said, "I brought more wine."

Instead of stepping aside in the doorway and letting him in, Gale snapped off the porch light, kneeled, undid his jeans and pulled them, along with his underpants, to the ground.

"Now, this is definitely one way to welcome company, Gale Marie."

She said nothing and took the already swelling "vehicle" in both hands. Tickling the scrotum lightly at the stem with the fingertips from one hand, while "spidering" the growing "Pinocchio's nose" with fingernails from the other, she teased him rock hard within ninety seconds.

"Ooooh. In front of the neighbors. I love it."

In full view of the street and an occasional passing car, she took him into her mouth all the way to the testes, lingering deliciously, pressing him home gently with both hands that gripped the swollen shaft at its root. Whenever she pulled him out—slowly—she would scrub the bottom of the bulb in short strokes with the full width and length of the tongue's surface while two fingers lightly pinched their way along the underside, starting at the base. The effort efficiently milked the lubricant into her mouth. After teasing him to the brink and backing off three separate times, she finally relented. Deliberately pumping the pipe between sphinctered lips in several quick, full strokes, which were followed up and down the shaft by both hands, she allowed him to explode. He dropped the pizza and barely held on to the wine. It had taken her a little over three minutes.

His knees bucking and shaking from the orgasm, he managed to say, "My God, woman! Are you trying to give me a heart attack?"

Gale looked up at him and grinned. "You managed to drop it right side up, so I guess we still eat. Sorry, but I just swallowed all the hors d'oeuvres."

"Holy mother of shit! I'm still shaking like a leaf."

She picked up the pizza, took the wine from him, and said, "What are you doing with your pants down on my front doorstep? What will the neighbors think?" The saucy grin followed her into the house. Tom labored through the ricocheting frissons to pull his pants up. He finally made it through the door, which he closed and locked behind him. It had always been this way. He had done the same thing to her on his front porch, although there were no neighbors in viewing distance. He had taken her jeans entirely off, and as usual she wasn't wearing any underwear. She had casually stripped away the rest of her clothes, and her orgasm had come while he stood holding her on his shoulders. She had maintained their balance by holding on to the inverted gingerbread railing that bordered the veranda's ceiling.

Fifteen years to the day when he and Loretta Schwunn had been caught in bed by her gun-waving husband, Dr. Ponder Chapell, D.V.M., Diplomate, American College of Veterinary Internists, stood on the back deck of his home and sniffed the wonderful scent of the stalker who was, without a doubt, now out for blood. The memory of the woman and her tear-stricken spouse had floated across his mind, perhaps pried loose by an errant electrical impulse or a slightly off-balance enzyme. He disposed of the picture and returned to the problem at hand. With his life in tangible jeopardy, now there was something to sink steel teeth into. The danger and the intrigue were welcomed. Talents that the ordinary man had no use for could now be brought to bear. How unusual it was that a slightly moody, mild-mannered animal doctor should be so steeped in the mental disciplines of the Far East—disciplines that eagerly battled the mind's depraved desire for danger and combat. In addition, there were all those years, including thousands of hours of practice, in the martial arts. And how many veterinarians could make a booby trap out of a half dozen shotgun shells, a couple of springs, two boards, two bolts, and a handful of nails? Step on it and the shells would render a man unrecognizable. Not many middle-aged men knew how to pack a Hydra-Shok .45 bullet with the right kind of easily accessible explosive, so that when the round hit a manhole cover, the iron would be blown into pieces so small there would nothing left that was heavy enough to use as a paperweight. Hit a human with one of them?—thank you— guaranteed no survivors!

A veterinarian? You got to be kidding! Ponder Allegro Chapell, you cunning fox—you belong in the SEALS or Delta Force. The CIA should have scarfed you up. Dealing with the blue-haired ladies who pamper three-thousand-dollar birds and spoil four-thousand-dollar dogs is a pathetically menial test for your abilities.

Fuck them all. He had his fun, and no one had come even remotely close to catching him yet. There was no greater thrill in life than to pull off an intricate mission—one that would baffle the authorities for years—and leave behind no clues, no chance of capture. It drove them crazy.

Ecuador had been like that—more or less.

He had read about the drug in a veterinarian medical journal. The compound had been used with great success on renal and hepatic cancer in a number of animals. Unfortunately, it would not work on humans. It was called Kellcilon heptoxy-122, and the Ecuadorians were not sharing the details of the discovery with anyone. Distilled from the sap of an extremely rare tree found only in the mountains, the compound had proven to be nothing less than miraculous in dissolving specific kinds of cancer cells. Unfortunately, because it took so much sap, which had to be collected over a period of months from so few trees, the tiny bit that was produced was outrageously expensive. It was estimated that an ounce was worth in the neighborhood of fifty thousand dollars. The molecules were large and complicated, and the compound had resisted all efforts to be synthesized in the Ecuadorian university's lab. In fact, it probably wouldn't be synthesized for years. Scientists around the world had pleaded with the South Americans to allow them to try—the cure was just too precious not to share. The Ecuadorian government had selfishly and steadfastly resisted. They would do it themselves, register the patents, and get all the royalties.

If you're as good at disease research as you are at cooking the other shit you and your Colombian neighbors are so famous for, it should be on the market within a week.

For some reason, reading that Ecuador had no plans to share the compound, or the research, pissed Ponder off. The doctor was first and foremost a healer. Anything that could prevent suffering and save lives deserved to be available as soon as possible. Animals were a lot more loyal than humans; they returned love for love; they never stabbed you in the back; they deserved the best.

A man could walk through customs with an ingeniously adapted squeeze bottle that was only partly full of Dristan nasal mist, spraying his nose for the damnable allergies that bugged him so badly at the ungodly altitude. He could even carry a second bottle in his pocket—the entire supply of Ecuador's Kellcilon heptoxy-122. Wouldn't it serve the selfish bastards right?

Through the efforts of a colleague whose wife belonged to the Ecuadorian upper class, Dr. Ponder Chapell, fluent in Spanish since grade school, had made arrangements to do some lecturing at the country's largest veterinarian school. Over a period of one-week stints spread over a six-month period, he had taught the Ecuadorian veterinarian surgeons techniques that could be used to save the lives of the bloody expensive thoroughbred horses stabled by the country's elite. These people took their horses seriously. They didn't hesitate to spend ten, twenty thousand on an animal if it meant saving it from certain death. Dr. Chapell had taught their finest doctors how to transplant lungs, kidneys, and livers; how to resection bowels, maximizing resistance to infection; how to repair heart problems. In America, the owners preferred to collect insurance on a million-dollar animal rather than to spend money experimenting on lifesaving techniques. Ecuadorians, many of whom had made their fortunes exporting cocaine, had no insurance programs, and they had embraced Ponder's techniques wholeheartedly.

Whenever he made his trips to Quito, he had asked carefully disguised questions while casing and planning the robbery. He had even wrangled a tour of the research wing that produced the compound, although his questions never touched on the substance. Any curiosity on his part about Kellcilon would be remembered after the researchers discovered it was gone. As far as they knew, he wasn't aware that it existed. They showed him the antiquated lab, told him the stuff was miraculous. Had he read anything about it? "No. Sorry. What is it used for?" They even jokingly showed him the old cement and iron safe where they kept the compound. It didn't need refrigeration. Ponder did a superb job of acting like he was not paying attention, wasn't in the slightest interested.

It was on his fifth trip when he had finally gone after the stuff. At two o'clock in the morning he'd left the rented apartment by the back door and quietly made his way through back alleys and narrow streets the ten blocks to the university's perimeter. Security was nonexistent, except for a couple of night watchmen who punched old-fashioned security clocks on their rounds. Dressed in black and carrying his "tools" in a small backpack, he'd made his way unseen to a side door of the research wing. It had been locked, but a thin sheet of aluminum had wedged the crash bar's latch open. From here on, he must not be seen.

He could not simply throttle a guard or late-night re-
searcher who had worked through the night. His presence must not be detected; the lab could not know
the compound had been switched until Dr. Ponder
Chapell had returned to the United States for good,
and that flight left just before noon. Distance pur-
ports innocence.

If one can gain the distance ...

He had almost made it to the locked lab door when
he heard someone coming—from two different
staircases!

Sweet Jesus, is this a goddamn convention or what?

He backed into a workroom across the hall from
the lab and left the door open a crack so he could
see what was going on. Three men appeared,
dressed in black as he was. One of them went to
work on the lab door, and within seconds they
were inside.

They were either too cocky or too dumb to post a
guard. Ponder made his way across the hall, went to
his hands and knees, and crawled into the room on
his stomach. He had already unholstered the high-
powered .22 pellet gun. The gun was all but noiseless.
However, placed right, the pellets were as deadly as
a .44 Magnum.

*Those bastards are here to steal the Kellcilon. I don't
believe this!*

The lab was dimly lit by a streetlight on the university's quad, outside the building, and the American
could see the thieves at the back of the lab as they
worked on picking the lock to the small room where
the safe was kept. Their whispering arguments covered
any noise Ponder made as he crawled along the floor
behind a long lab counter. When he finally reached
the end of the room, the men were about twenty feet
away. The lock submitted, and two of them entered
the small room with the safe.

Ponder's shot hit the man directly through the left
eye. The thief never made a sound; he just collapsed

on the floor in a heap, unnoticed by the two men
inside, who were busily preparing to get into the safe.
If they were stupid enough to blow it, they could easily
destroy everything inside. The flash heat alone could
render the compound useless. Ponder rose to his feet
and stepped over the dead man. Peering into the
room, he could see by the light of the flashlights that
they were on their knees before the safe, and they
were indeed rigging charges to blow the door off.

Dumb, boys. Really dumb.

Ponder shot the nearest man in the ear, and as
the thief was falling, the second man jumped to his
feet and swung the light into the veterinarian's eyes.
There had not been enough time to reload the pellet
gun. Shots had to be extremely well placed for it to
be effective anyway. Ponder had already dropped it,
and while shielding his eyes from the light, he drew
his dagger. The thief dropped the light and sprang
with his own knife. Rae Willie Chapell boy quickly
found out that the thief knew how to use it.

In the near dark it was hit and miss. The American
took a superficial slice on the forearm, and he missed
the thief's throat with a backhand. The man was
warming up to the task, sensing an easy victory. Ponder forced his mind to jettison the panic, and he
slipped into his martial arts mode—all the years of
practicing, all the matches, the fights as a kid where
he'd pulled punches.

Not today.

The thief faked several lunges, then made a light-
ning-quick stab for the veterinarian's throat.

It was too easy. Instincts took over as though he
did this a dozen times a day, seven days a week. With
lightning reflexes that were much too fast to be en-
trusted to a man so large, Ponder parried the attack-
er's arm to the side with his left arm. Using the man's
own momentum, the doctor buried his six-inch dagger
in the thief's heart and instantly twisted it to open a
hole. The thrust had been angled up and under the

rib cage. The throat would have been quicker, but too messy. It was just too easy to get soaked with spraying blood if the knife was off only a little.

"Ooof . . ." It knocked the wind out of the man.

It had not knocked him down. The thief turned quickly and took another swipe at Ponder's throat. Ponder knew he'd struck the vital organ, and now it was just a matter of seconds. More than one victim has taken a direct bullet, or knife, in the heart, then walked to the car, got in, started the motor, and even driven off before dying. It didn't always happen like in the movies. This man could still kill him. Ponder jumped back, out of reach of the knife, quietly waiting to see what the man was going to do next. In the reflection of the dim streetlight, the vet could see the glistening spot of pulsing liquid that was slowly growing on the front of the man's shirt. The thief, sensing his plight, charged. Ponder again stepped out of the way. Weakened, the man was not able to pull up his charge, and Ponder chopped him behind the ear with the handle of the knife as he lunged by. The thief finally fell and went into convulsions. Ponder left him, went to the safe, and from his pack he took out his finest stethoscope. With a safe this old, a safecracker really could hear the tumblers drop. Within three minutes, he had the door open. With three men to take the rap, there was now no need to replace the compound with a ringer. The cops would believe that the men had been double-crossed by a fourth colleague who had escaped with the Kellcilon. Forty-five minutes later, he was back in his apartment, and no one was the wiser. A few hours later, he'd gone through customs as he had planned, sniffing the Dristan.

A few days later, the head of Vanderbilt's cancer-research department had received a mysterious package which included a vial labeled KELLCILON HEP-TOXY-122. There was a one-page brief explaining that the sample had been donated to a private party, and the party was now donating it to the school. The school's qualitative analysis researchers did not try very hard to find the source.

Chapter Eight

When Chapell awoke, he could see through the bedroom's wall of fan windows and French doors that a thick fleece of clouds coated the heavens. It was six-fifteen. He lay on his back for a few minutes, trying to organize the day, but his mind resisted. It felt tired, sodden, fused; his head felt too big for his hair.

"Gotta cut down on the nightcaps, old fella."

He had played hockey the night before. Usually, the only thing that interfered with making the games was work. However, one of the disadvantages of playing regularly in the men's league was that the games didn't begin until nine-thirty or ten at night, and they lasted for an hour and a half. The Pelicans had played against the team that agent Jon Rheinhart played on. Whenever Chapell played against his old college teammate, he had to crank things up a few notches. The rivalry had been going on for three years now—since Rheinhart had been stationed in Nashville. After the game, in spite of the hour, many of the players always went to one of the local pubs to down a few glasses of liquid bread. Chapell had been waiting for Rheinhart outside the locker rooms, and the FBI agent had asked Chapell to join the crowd. As usual, the cop had turned him down; he preferred to drink alone. In spite of the mandatory parties that he attended in some of the music circles, Rae Willie's boy didn't enjoy socializing. The music-industry events were endured like a root canal. Most of them he attended only for Gale's benefit.

When the two men were out of earshot, the detective had asked, "Jon, we haven't heard much from our brothers in the federal employ. What's going on over there?"

Rheinhart knew Chapell was talking about Toy Duck. He paused too long before answering. The detective's sense of suspicion leaped to attention.

"Well, we've been looking at one guy who looks pretty good for it. We've had him under surveillance for a while now."

"Whoa! I thought this was a joint venture. You want to tell me about it?"

"Well, we're not sure. Guy's name is Howard Peretti."

"Oh, shit. I thought you were going to be of some help here. Peretti's harmless, Jon. We went up one side of him and down the other. He's just an old kook. Neighbors down the road from him call to complain sometimes when the old fart gets drunk because he walks around the fields and woods without any clothes on—even in the winter. You've got to do better than this."

"Well, he fits the profile."

"Profile? The old bugger's over sixty. That's a far cry from Quantico's famous *profile.* He's practically an invalid. He's been a loudmouth all his life. He's always had more mouth than brains. I'm disappointed in your friends in Virginia, Jon. Maybe they ought to change the letters after the B and the S on the Behavioral Science signs to what we call the fecal material generated by male bovines."

"They think he looks good."

"Take it to the bank, Jon. He's not our boy."

Chapell watched the sky through an opening in the trees as a hole opened and sunlight tumbled through. The deck was soon mottled with faint shadows.

"Shit!"

He sat up in the bed and looked at the end of his

finger. It was coated with a thin layer of blood. While he'd been procrastinating his exit from the bed's cocoon, he'd been mining his scalp for alien bumps with his fingernail. Sweat pimples, some called them—the product of strenuous activity—hockey, in this case. They were noticeable on the buttocks of a lot of athletes in the locker rooms, regardless of how many showers were taken. Chapell got them on his scalp. He had unconsciously popped the scab off a pimple that had festered and died unceremoniously, perhaps, aided by the fact that he'd just switched shampoos. Cursed with a digital fixation, busy fingers were always busy doing something mischievous—picking scabs, winding curls, pulling out the incongruent grays, whatever. He wiped the tiny bit of blood on the sheet.

"Can't put it off, Rides, ole fellow."

He finally got out of bed and lumbered off to the bathroom. Returning to work was met with mixed emotions. His bizarre behavior had been chalked up to overwork by everyone, including himself, but after three days of rest he didn't feel rested. The responsibility of catching the crazy bastard who was murdering the poor young women was still yoked across his shoulders. The vision of a staggering canoeist carrying his vessel around a long series of bad water flitted through his head like a bird with a bad wing. The fact that more and more it looked like his own dear brother could be that exact crazy bastard was a weight that would have brought most men to their knees.

He needed a strategy to trap Ponder. Rifling his brother's office had been a mistake. Ponder had caught him, and had shown his displeasure by putting an arrow through the back window of the Cherokee. One thing was for sure: little brother would turn up the heat with the cat and mouse game, although Chapell didn't believe Ponder would actually kill him—yet!

He arrived at his office an hour early, and while walking through the maze of narrow halls, he was greeted politely by several of the cops and civilians.

"How you feeling, Lieutenant?"

"Better, thanks."

"Hey, don't sweat it. You'll get the guy."

"Thanks."

McCurty found him poring over the paperwork. The sergeant knocked on the doorway.

"Come in, Gene. You want to bring me up to speed on this last one?"

"Yeah. He broke the pattern. Two in less than two weeks—unprecedented in twenty years."

"I called the captain when I heard it on the news. He told me they were handling it. Any progress?"

"Good joke—progress, with this bastard? Girl's name was Snowy Lockhart. We're still waiting to get tapes of her from the publishing company she worked for."

"What company? Maybe I can hurry them along."

"Legacy."

"Charlie Previn. I'll call him. Our boy must have been hurried. The woman doesn't fit the pattern of the last twenty years at all."

"Yeah. This one's definitely different. She was blond, but she didn't have the look of the other girls. She wasn't artist material, just another song writer. My guess is she won't sound like the others either. I got the impression that this was an emergency job. He took who he could get. The sutures had his signature—quality stuff—but they were nowhere near as elaborate or intricate—just the bare minimum. It looks like he didn't get to spend as much time on them as usual."

"I wonder if he was spooked. Has the team covered River Road? Sooner or later somebody's going to see something that looks suspicious. Where the hell does he park his car?"

"Lot of questions like that. How's he carry the women up to half a mile into the pasture? Does he take his supplies at the same time or make two trips? I've got John and Terry covering River Road again."

"You look at the girl after they cleaned her up?"

"No. I haven't had a chance. I've been on the woman we found last night in the river. Perp must have kept her around for a while. She'd been tied up. Ligature marks had bled some. Bruise marks say rape, although there was no semen."

"Used a rubber."

"Yeah."

"Who was she?"

"Don't know. My guess is a high-priced hooker. Just a feeling. Killer cut her while he was banging her, M.E. thinks."

"Jesus!"

"Surgical tool. Very sharp, definite technique with the cuts. Like he was exploring anatomy."

"One of Jeffery Dahmer's little curious sidelines."

"Yeah. It looks like we now have two maniacs on our hands."

"What about leads on Toy Duck?"

"We've exhausted all the sources for the suture materials that we can find in the country. We're now starting overseas—Europe, Far East."

"That sounds like a hopeless job."

"Tell me. Nothing's been turned on the Prussic acid or for the ether—long shots anyway. We keep checking the street to see if anybody's heard anything. This perp doesn't associate with his kind or else he really knows how to keep his mouth shut."

"You check the trash of the last Toy Duck women?"

"Yeah. Nothing out of the ordinary. We've questioned hundreds of people even remotely linked to these women and are still at it. It's totally abnormal not to pick up a single lead. It's like this guy doesn't exist. We're certain he's choosing them because they resemble your mother, but there are a lot of serious pretenders to your mom's throne who are not killed. Right now we know of six women, industry-wide, who look significantly and sound significantly like your mom."

"Interesting. I had no idea there were more."

"Some have never been to Nashville. Some only work live gigs on the road. Trust me, there have been a bunch over the years. Remember, your mom was as influential as Elvis. A lot of women have imitated her."

"Some have come close."

McCurty, who had always been a big Rae Willie Chapell fan, frowned and answered, "I don't think so. No one's ever had that kind of charisma, to say nothing of the voice, the pathos, the . . ."

"Okay, okay . . ." Chapell smiled and held up his hands in submission. "What about the cycle?"

"It has totally baffled us. Until Snowy Lockhart he was only killing someone every five years, more or less; we have no idea why."

"And there's been no line of investigation that's linked all these women together?

"No. All they have in common is favoring your mother, and until this last one, they've been signed to her label."

"We've checked out all the personnel who worked for the label in the past?"

"With a fine-tooth comb. We're still working on some of the employees who have transferred, gone to other companies, or retired. Several have moved to other states. There's a lot of transferring back and forth between Nashville and New York. There have been a few without alibis, but they aren't really candidates. Too crippled; too old; women who are too frail; too young. This isn't the kind of copycat murder that a wannabe could make work."

"You're positive this last one was our boy?"

"Yeah. M.E. said there was no doubt about the quality of stitching. God, I'd like to know what makes him tick."

"You and every cop in America."

"Has the FBI checked in?"

"We haven't heard anything from Rheinhart in four days. If they had something, they'd have let us know so they could gloat."

"I played hockey against Jon last night. Quantico thinks Howard Peretti fits the profile."

"Are they insane?" McCurty was looking at Chapell in total disbelief.

"Desperate is the operative word, my boy. Hell on 'em. They've been useless for twenty years. Why change now? Listen, I'd like to take a look at Snowy Lockhart. Want to ride over to General with me?"

"Yeah, I need to look too."

Chapell stood and took his coat from the rack. He and McCurty made their way out of the building, down the sidewalk to the garage.

"You know, Gene, if these poor women had been men, I'd say sooner or later we would find some jealous whacko bastard who was eliminating his competition. He'd be over the hill by now, after twenty years of it. But these artists are women, and a jealous woman wouldn't have the strength to carry out these murders unless she'd spent her entire life in a Russian gym."

"I have little doubt but what it's a longtime fan of your mother's. He resents the intrusion of the imitators. He's never been arrested, he's probably the president of a fan club, a Mr. Super Normal in some small town not far from here. You know, a real estate salesman or a CPA or a commercial artist. He could even be a Sunday school teacher or a Boy Scout leader. He's got some kind of access to screening the up-and-coming talent—trade magazines probably. We're running different profiles through the computer subscription lists for a dozen music-trade magazines. I think that's our best avenue of investigation. So far we've come up blank, but eventually we'll find the bastard, if it takes checking out those lists for the next year."

"That works until you ask, 'Why the horse and those incredibly beautiful sutures?' He could kill the competition with a lot less bother."

"God only knows how the heads of some of the world's greatest whackos work. When you've got some of them who've admitted on national TV that they just wanted to keep the bodies around as long as possible for companionship . . . So, they go and bury them in the cellar, or backyard; they cut off the heads, and nuts, and store them in metal and wood boxes, or even worse, the refrigerator . . ."

"Or eat them."

"This guy gets to keep them by this elaborate ritual, and we've yet to find a shrink, or one of the 'brilliant ones' at Quantico, to come up with exactly how."

McCurty pulled across 2nd Avenue and onto Gay Street. He followed it under the Veterans' Memorial Bridge, then the Woodland Street Bridge and continued along the cliff above the river until Gay ran into 1st Avenue. The air conditioner wasn't working, and all of Chapell's dinking with the dash controls didn't bring it back. His head ached fiercely from the late-night-early-morning booze.

"It's been coming and going. I just haven't had time to put the car in the garage."

They rolled down the windows, and the early morning August heat, humidity, and street smells hit like an all-pro linebacker on a blitz. The men made small talk as Riverfront Park and the city's enormous incinerator complex, which was adjacent to the park, slipped by on the left. A left on Hermitage brought them quickly to General Hospital. The hospital was set on a high cliff overlooking the Cumberland and an enormous scrap-metal junkyard on the other side of the river. The junkyard had been featured in the movie *Nashville*. With all the gorgeous sites that were available in one of America's most beautiful cities, no one had ever figured out why. The Forensic Sciences

Center was located at the far end of the hospital's southeast parking lot.

The sergeant quizzed Chapell in depth about how he was feeling. Chapell told him he was tired, he still felt the pressure, he wouldn't mind hanging it all up and going to the Bahamas for a year.

"Rider, don't let it get to you. We do what we can. They didn't get this guy the last four times either. The brass and the media are farts in a fast wind—they're harmless. It'll eventually blow over. We've all been on the toilet when the seat broke. You get your ass a little wet, but the only thing hurt is your pride. If this guy can be got, we'll get him. If he can't, it ain't the end of the world, and I don't think they're going to fire you for it." He grinned.

It was extremely difficult to fire a police officer—especially a lieutenant—unless he had broken the law or had blatantly disregarded regulations.

"Thanks, Gene. I appreciate it."

In death, Snowy Lockhart wore her nakedness like a starched uniform. The attendant had known which of the four bodies in the forty-degree stainless steel vault was hers, but he'd checked the toe tag to make sure. The stainless steel cooler was about the size of a small bedroom. It resembled a walk-in refrigerator in a large hotel, and it smelled, badly, of rotten meat in spite of the customized venting system. If necessary, it could hold as many as forty-eight corpses, and more than once it had been filled. Metro's morgue didn't have pull-out "file-cabinet" trays as in the movies. If relatives needed to identify a body, they did it through a one-foot-square window in the large stainless steel door that opened into the room. The gurney with the victim would be wheeled to the window, the victim's face uncovered. Then the small steel door covering the window on the inside would be opened for viewing. Under no circumstances were the relatives allowed anywhere near the body. More than once ugly scenes with guns and knives had erupted. In fact, the building, only a dozen or so years old, had actually been designed to withstand an attack. The double doors to the front offices weighed ninety pounds each and were set with bulletproof glass.

"She's definitely not in the same race as the other women."

The dead woman's face was long and thin. Her complexion showed present and past effects of acne. The skin on her chest was blotchy. Chapell could picture her as the kind of woman who might not even bother wearing makeup, figuring it was a lost cause. She had long, stringy blond hair of uneven lengths and split ends. The pinched effect of death exaggerated ears that were too large, eyelashes that were too short, a mouth that was too narrow, and a chin that was too long and pointed. She was thin—too thin for five-four; she probably weighed less than a hundred pounds. She certainly wasn't in the glamour category with the killer's other victims. Like Rae Willie, they had filled their bodies to the prescribed limits—the kind of lines that constantly turned heads. They had flaunted alabaster-cloud skin and had spent a minimum of a hundred dollars a month on hair care and makeup. There were a few women who achieved stardom without dynamite looks and bodies, but they had to have a mesmerizing charisma and a super tanker full of talent that made up for it. John Q. Public, who plugged the majority of quarters into the jukebox in Joe's Bar and Grill and occupied the majority of parking spaces at Tower Records and Video, preferred the titillation of a low neckline and a high hemline that could break a sweat. The year Reba McIntyre had worn *that* evening dress on national television for the Country Music Awards—the one that was cut to the navel and showed a full two-fifths of her breasts, complete with jiggle—as she sang "Does He Love You" with Linda Davis, had pushed the envelope. The girls needed to fill paint-tight spandex pants in perfect proportions, and show at least two inches of cleavage, or they had better be able to sing and write like K. T. Oslin and Mary Chapin Carpenter. In a couple of hours, when Chapell would listen to one of her demo tapes, he would find that she wasn't even very good at writing. She was just another of thousands who came to town each year figuring on staying only long enough to make a few million before returning to the hometown ticker parade in triumph. Her bank account would reveal she had another month, at the most, before she'd have to give up the dream and either take a steady job, as 99.9 percent of them did, or return home to the one she'd left in the first place. Nevertheless, there was a lot to be said for the Snowy Lockharts of the world. They were the ones who had the guts to try. They were the ones who kept the boss's wife from finding out that he was spending Wednesday afternoon in a motel room three towns down the line with the dental hygienist who worked across the street. They made the office coffee in the morning; they birthed the kids who would never go to Harvard or jail for drugs or DUI—the kids who would one day become the backbone of the country's labor force; they bought the majority of products in the grocery store; they kept their husband's belly full and his seminal vesicle empty. Snowy Lockhart, as unglamorous as she was, lying on that steel gurney, had not deserved to die the hideous death forced upon her.

"We find this son of a bitch, Gene. We need to make sure he doesn't get to make his sales pitch to a jury—the one that says, 'Hey, so I'm crazy. Gimme the seventy-five grand that's due me for my TV movie and put me in the loony bin for a little while. I couldn't help myself—it's my father's fault for abusing me when I was a kid. I'll just become another productive jailbird selling his made-for-TV-movie while you pay my thirty-thousand-dollar-a-year tab, not including a million-five for all the defense lawyers and appeals.' "

Chapell pulled the sheet over the woman's face and

turned toward the door. He continued, "This bastard's skin needs to be nailed to a tree in the deep woods, and he doesn't need to be in it."

"I won't tell if you won't, Lieutenant.."

Neither man meant it, but killing a repeat killer was the kind of thing that never left the back of a good cop's mind. There was too much chance the murderer would be presented with the opportunity to do it again. Massachusetts governor Dukakis had found that one out the hard way.

They closed the door, and for the first time Chapell noticed the vertical line of dents located at the exact height of a gurney's leading edge. *"Careless lack of respect."* The thought nettled through his mind that the thousand-dollar piece of stainless steel ought to be replaced. Snowy Lockhart didn't deserve to lie in a morgue that looked like the hell had been beat out of it by indifferent orderlies.

So, was it Ponder? Was the inimical surgeon responsible for the sacrilege lying under the sheet? Was Rae Willie's progeny capable of creating this kind of travesty just to protect the memory of his mother? Protect—why? The woman didn't need protection—not from anybody or anything in this life.

In the interest of everything that was decent, it was left for the head of the Murder Squad to set a trap for his own little brother in order to find out. If it worked, Ponder would end up in a mental hospital, or death row, and neither he nor Gale would ever speak to Rider Capable Chapell again. If the trap backfired, Ponder might kill him. If he didn't and younger brother told Gale what the cop had done, and he most certainly would—neither the veterinarian nor Gale would ever speak to Rider Capable Chapell again. If the detective sprang the trap and the perp was caught, and it wasn't Ponder—neither he nor Gale would ever speak to Rider Capable Chapell again. So much for grace in this family. For some reason the cop felt like crying. He fought, with the greatest difficulty, the desire to go home and sleep.

He had just sat down at his desk when the phone rang. The chief wanted to see him immediately in his office.

"Are the pricks going to start on me already?"

The captain, as usual, was at McKinty's side to assist and protect, and the chief's face was a new and unusual shade of red that Chapell could never remember seeing before. Evidently, the feces links were about to hit the fan in a gout that would display force and volume as of yet unmeasured. The voice was subdued, but the words crackled with undisguised malice.

"Ten minutes ago, the FBI gave me a courtesy call to say that they are on the way to arrest the Toy Duck killer. They've had him under surveillance for some time at a cabin outside Homer's Trace—Homer's Trace, Lieutenant—that's where most of these murders took place, isn't it? The perp's name is Peretti. We have been extended the privilege of watching then bring him in. That makes us about as useful as a nun at a *Hustler* staff meeting, doesn't it?" If the intensity of disgust on McKinty's face could have been harnessed to a stove, it would have boiled water.

"Sir, I can't believe they went ahead with this. Rheinhart told me last night they might try to arrest this guy. I thought I had talked him out of it. The man's name is Howard Peretti. He's harmless. We checked him out A to Z. The fyebyes are up the wrong tree on this one, and you can take that to the bank." This man was beginning to seriously annoy Chapell. The chief's contempt of what had been good police work revealed how incompetent he really was. Had he bothered to read the reports, he would have seen that Peretti was a joke.

"Lieutenant, they don't fly SWAT teams around the country if they're not sure what they're doing."

"They flew a SWAT team in here? Are they totally insane? Did they say what their evidence is?" Chapell threw up his hands in disgust and turned away from the chief.

He turned back when the chief answered, "They traced a hate letter. Said they'd brief you at the scene."

"Well, they kept the letter to themselves, then. We never saw a letter. I still don't believe this guy would be capable of following through. He's crippled from arthritis. He's poor, he's—"

"I don't give an airborne mayonnaise jar of goat shit what you believe, Lieutenant. The truth is, we're going to look like amateurs on the six o'clock news tonight." The decibel level had risen noticeably. The man consciously lowered his voice and continued, "The Federal Bureau of Investigation in all its wisdom, be it as it may, would not put all their eggs into this basket if they were not in possession of cocksure evidence. Now, I think you'd better get out there and watch the show. *Their* show. And when you come back, we need to have a little talk." The boiling water would have all turned to steam by now.

Chapell was on the verge of telling the stupid son of a bitch to shove his job and the entire Federal Bureau of Investigation up his ass, but his curiosity quelled the urge. He said, "All right. We'll go. We'll watch and we'll laugh."

He quickly returned to the squad room, collected the three men who were there, had the dispatcher call the other four, and McCurty, who had gone to the bank.

Homer's Trace was a twenty-minute drive from the station at full siren. Rheinhart was waiting for the cops at the two vans that were parked at the bottom of a small hill. The vehicles had been parked so that they blocked the dead-end dirt road. Chapell knew the cabin was in a clearing just beyond the top of the hill. There was thick woods on either side of the road all the way there. There was also a uniformed SWAT team member standing next to a portable satellite uplink dish. He was wearing a headset and talking into a hand-held radio.

"What's Rheinhart doing back here? I'd think he'd want to be in on this with a news cam behind him."

"Jon's not a bad guy. Gotta helluva wrist shot. Let's see what he has to say."

Chapell and the two men with him got out of the car. McCurty and the other cops hadn't arrived yet, but according to the radio, they were only five minutes behind.

Rheinhart approached Chapell as the cop got out of the car and said, "Glad you're here, Rider."

"Jon, I can't believe you're going to try to hang this on Peretti."

"Well, it's Quantico's shot. They developed the evidence."

"What evidence?"

"They've got some hate mail that they traced to him. We tried to pick him up early this morning for questioning, and he started shooting. I called the office to get them to call you for backup and somebody called D.C. I guess the brass are looking for some favorable press to counteract the fiasco in Florida last month, so they sent the SWAT team. Overkill, if you ask me. You and I could have handled it." The FBI had raided a commune much like the Branch Davidians in Waco. They hadn't burned the place down, but a dozen women and children had been killed in the crossfire. "They want this guy bad, and with all the press Toy Duck has got, they figured to do it totally within the department and take all the glory. Personally, I think it stinks. They don't care that you and I have got to work in the same town together."

"And that I have to kick your ass all over the rink every couple of weeks." Chapell grinned at the agent. He continued, more seriously, "I appreciate that, Jon, but I'll stake my badge on the fact that you're wrong."

"We'll see, Judson, how close are they?" The agent

had called to the man who was monitoring the team by radio.

"Two minutes."

"We'd better get down there. I, for one, don't want to miss the show. There's plenty of cover in case he starts shooting again. Let the boys with the charcoal-colored suits dodge the bullets."

Privately, Chapell would rather have been in on the actual arrest, but it was too late now. Peretti was a loose cannon—unpredictable—if he was drinking ... He'd done time for attempted murder. If the fyebyes wanted to risk their necks, fine. Cops were a much more pragmatic lot than television gave them credit for. If someone else wanted to take a chance on getting shot, any sane cop would be a fool to argue with him.

Chapell turned to the agent with the radio and said, "There are two more cars of cops right behind me. Brief them and send them down the road, will you?"

"Check, sir."

The five men began trotting down the dirt road toward the cabin.

Chapell said softly, "Jon, I still think you've got the wrong guy. Peretti is a nutcase, granted, but I told you, we wrung him out and that's all he is. We picked him up on the computer—he was on a couple of fan lists, and he's got a record. What's this hate mail?"

"We traced a letter to the Columbia Record Company back to him—no signature. He left prints. Fool. We also sampled the DNA in the saliva on the envelope, then got a court order to intercept one of the outgoing letters in his mailbox to compare it with. Perfect match."

"How come we didn't know about the letter?"

"CBS sent it to the New York office, and they sent it to Quantico. I saw a copy. It contained threats against Bella Rose for imitating your mother—fanatical old boy about his country music."

"I can't believe this old fart is capable of killing

time, much less those poor women." *Maybe Ponder's off the hook!*

The FBI agent continued, "We've spent the last week investigating his past, including his family, his old grade-school classmates, his former jobs—he worked for the phone company for fifteen years. He was fired because he was making obscene phone calls from the tops of telephone poles and in his spare time was taping his boss's conversations with a mistress. They see him walking around without any clothes on. He poured gas on a farmer's cow and set it on fire."

Chapell interjected, "He told us it was because the cow kept breaking down his fence and shitting on his front yard. Jon, he gets drunk and does funny things. Felt horrible about the cow when he'd sobered up. Okay, he's a pervert about the obscene calls, but that was almost twenty years ago."

The agent continued, "There have been complaints that he's been picking up stray animals in town, bringing them home and torturing them."

"Then he's probably a sick bastard, but son, we grilled this old boy for the better part of a whole half hour—that's how long it took to make us believe he couldn't have done it if he'd wanted to."

"What makes you so sure?"

"Have you talked to him?"

"No. That's what we were going to try to do this morning."

"He's had a rare form of arthritis since he was a kid. It's so bad now, he can barely move his fingers, much less overpower a woman, gut a horse, and sew up those sutures. It doesn't show—his fingers aren't gnarled or anything."

"We know about that. The brass decided he was using painkillers."

"It's possible, I suppose. He does use some powerful stuff, but I'll give you some more reasons why we didn't bust him. He's almost sixty years old, and the neighbors say he hasn't left Homer's Trace in ten years. He only drives his truck to the market and back when the pain will let him. Most of the time he sits in his living room, watches television, and drinks beer."

"He could be going out at night. There are ways of getting around that."

The remainder of the Murder Squad had caught up to them just as the dirt road started up a hill.

Chapell turned and with his voice very low said, "Gene, did they brief you?"

"Yeah. We're okay. Just gonna watch."

"Good." He turned back to the FBI agent and, still speaking softly, said, "Okay, but what about this? Peretti had nothing in the bank—we checked—and he makes five hundred sixty-five dollars a month on Social Security disability. He certainly couldn't afford the bloody expensive materials it took to sew those horses up. They estimated the gold thread alone was worth, what, Gene, twenty-five hundred?"

"Closer to three thousand, including all six murders it was used in."

"Here's another one—unless it was stored in laboratory conditions, keeping hydrocyanic acid around for twenty years would be a tricky proposition. We know he'd have a hard time getting away from his house far enough and for long enough to buy any. And where's he going to get ether? The little hardware store in Homer's Trace doesn't carry it."

"If he wanted it badly enough, he would have managed to get it."

The party of men had topped the hill, and one of the SWAT team was standing behind a tree next to the road. He waved for the men to get into the woods for cover. The old log cabin was now visible. It was set in a clearing about fifty yards down the road where it made a curve to the left. Behind the house were a couple of outbuildings; behind them the men could see open pasture stretching up a long, wide valley. The ten cops stepped into the woods and began to fan out. Chapell and Rheinhart finally reached the edge of the clearing and squatted behind two large walnut trees.

Rheinhart spoke only one word into his radio. "Go." To Chapell, he said softly, "They've got a 'no knock' warrant."

Four of the SWAT team members materialized from the woods and slipped quietly onto the front porch. One of them tried the door. It was apparently locked. Two of the men used the standard-issue battering ram to smash the door. It was solid enough so that after three hits it still hadn't caved in. The onlookers were shocked to hear a muffled shot inside the cabin while the door simultaneously blew apart, taking both of the men with it.

"Shotgun. Son of a bitch!"

"He was ready."

They could hear shooting but couldn't make out what was being said.

The two men lay squirming in pain on the porch. Body armor hadn't taken all the lead shot from the shotgun. Two members of the team materialized and dragged the wounded men off the porch toward the woods. Chapell saw four more men appear and take cover in the backyard behind the outbuildings. They would cover any retreat from the back door. The men at the front door would make the assault.

One of the men on the front porch hollered, "FBI, Peretti. Give it up. You're surrounded."

Another shotgun blast chewed more pieces out of the front door. One of the four men on the porch tossed a concussion grenade through the hole that had been shot through the door. There was a loud *fumph* inside, followed by another shotgun blast through the front door. This one blew the door open and took it off one of its hinges. Three of the men on the porch stuck the barrels of their M-16's through the door and, on full auto, emptied sixty rounds of .223 bullets into the house in the space of six seconds. They quickly reloaded and in a carefully choreographed procedure entered the house one after another. There were no more shotgun blasts. Rheinhart, who had the earpiece to the radio in his ear, said, "He's dead."

Peretti lay crumpled on the floor of the kitchen in the four-room cabin. He was indeed dead; there were a number of blood spots on his clothes where he'd been hit with the barrage. How he had survived the concussion grenade to fire the last shot was anybody's guess—perhaps orneriness and reflexes. Their work finished, the SWAT team left the cabin as quickly as possible.

"Peters, Tweedy, take a quick look in the buildings out back, will you?"

Chapell and Rheinhart did a walk-through with their hands in their pockets. Nothing could be touched—everything would be left as it was for a lab crew to piece together. If the entire Murder Squad was turned loose on the place, valuable evidence could be lost in spite of the fact that the men were all professionals.

As they began the tour, Chapell said, "Well, Jon, your boys or mine? A lab crew needs to take the place apart log by log. If he's our boy, we'll find the suturing material and maybe some of the other stuff."

"It's ours. Washington's orders. The lab crew's already on its way in a Lear. If it was up to me, I'd turn it over to you. Judson just told me over the radio that he's already called for the county M.E. and an ambulance."

In a couple of minutes, McCurty appeared driving a squad car. He drove into the driveway, got out and began stringing the yellow tape that said, POLICE CRIME SCENE DO NOT ENTER around the trees in the yard to seal the place off.

"Media's going to go into a feeding frenzy."

"They'll film this place until it's as familiar as Madonna's ass over the next few days."

"Lieutenant!"

Tweedy had appeared at the back door.

"Yeah."

"You need to see this."

He led the two men to the larger of the two sheds behind the house. They entered what appeared to be a cluttered workshop. Peters was standing in front of an ornate, varnished wooden box that was decorated with painted golden scrolling and golden studs. The box was about a foot square and four inches deep. Using his pencil, he opened the top. Inside were half a dozen spangles, a spool of rawhide, and a small tin of studs. There was also a small bottle of a clear liquid.

"I'll be goddamned."

"I'll bet it's Prussic acid."

"That old bastard—who would have thought . . . ?"

A chill bounced up and down Chapell's back at least a dozen times within the first second he laid eyes on the box. The last time he'd seen it had been on Rae Willie's dressing table the night he'd been in Ponder's house. It had been lying open, had been full of their mother's face creams and ointments.

It was several days before the media was allowed near Howard Peretti's rural cabin. When they did move in, it was without enthusiasm for the Toy Duck murders. That morning Maudry Evans—number seven—had been found sewn inside another Tennessee Walker. The sutures were as wonderful as ever.

Chapter Nine

Not reporting that the wooden box full of incriminating evidence was a one-of-a-kind gift that had been made and given to Rae Willie Chapell by an amorous miner from the northern Yukon sealed Chapell's fate as far as coming clean about his brother. He had now passed the point of no return. Without even looking, he could have told the FBI that any prints found on the box would be smudged and unreadable. The fyebyes would take it for granted that the prints were Howard Peretti's. Ponder would not have left the box wiped clean—too suspicious. The question of the century was: how did Ponder know the fyebyes were going to raid Peretti's place? Ponder did play racquetball with Rheinhart—occasionally. Ponder had entered Dartmouth when Rheinhart and Chapell were juniors. The three of them had done a few bars together. They were still friends, and Ponder did treat Rheinhart's hybrid wolves. Maybe Rheinhart had let something slip.

When Maudry Evans was discovered in a pasture two miles down the road from where Snowy Lockhart had been found, Chapell would have given a year's pay to have been a fly on the wall in the director's office in Washington, D.C. The FBI had made megamedia mileage out of the bust and the fact that they, and no one else, had caught the Toy Duck murderer after twenty years; that the brilliant work of the Behavorial Science Department at Quantico was unsurpassed anywhere in the world; that the country could sleep safe knowing that Uncle Sam had a firm rein on maniacs who went around sewing women into dead horses. Two made-for-television movies were already in production, and both scripts were still being written. The Federal Bureau of Investigation had serious egg on its face.

Just before he received the call from the department to tell him there was another Toy Duck murder, Gale had awakened him at six a.m.

"Hi."

"Where the hell have you been, damn it!"

"Oh, that's nice. Nashville's most eligible bachelor is awakened by a sexy woman, and he spews scurrilities all over her." He could hear her giggle.

She'd done another one of her disappearing acts. Chapell had quizzed her before—mercilessly—on exactly how, and why, she did this. Was she working for the FBI, the CIA?

"I want to know, damn it. I've got a right to know how it is they make you disappear off the face of the earth as if you never existed and why the hell you let them do it!"

"Have you talked to Ponder?"

"No. I've been busy. Have you?"

"No. He told me he was going to Guatemala for a seminar for three or four days."

Maybe that's what he told you, little sister. If he was in Guatemala, then he managed to squeeze in a side trip to Homer's Trace. He desperately wanted to tell her that he had evidence that Ponder was killing these women—their mother's box from her dresser. However, he knew beyond a shadow of a doubt that she'd twist it around, deny, get mad, accuse him of attempted fratricide, then hang up. Gale's sense of loyalty far outweighed her sense of logic. The only way she'd believe would be if she witnessed Ponder sewing a woman into a dead horse!

Chapell had little doubt that this last murder was Ponder's way of showing utter contempt for the FBI, letting them know how powerless they were against a genius who'd worked for over twenty years with impunity. What a travesty—to kill a beautiful young woman who had the potential of an entire successful life ahead of her just to stroke an ego. *God damn the son of a bitch! And now I can't even bring him in and put him on trial if I catch him red-handed. It'll mean my career, my reputation—I'll spend the rest of my life in some remote corner of wilderness trying to escape the press and the mortification—that is, when they let me out of prison after ten years for aiding and abetting— withholding evidence as a police officer. I'll give him every benefit of every last ounce of doubt. But if I do trap him, then I've got the problem of murdering my own brother and not getting caught for that! It had better be a perfect murder. Jesus, what a mess. God damn you, Ponder! How in the hell could you change so much from when we were kids?*

"Did you watch Mom's movie?"

"What?"

"Hey, wake up, big brother. I said, have you seen *Last Song* yet?"

"Sorry. Yes. I taped it and watched it a couple nights ago. They've been running it for a while. I watched *Sing This One for Me* last week. First time I'd seen it with the new scenes in it."

"She was good, wasn't she?"

"Yes, very. You're changing the subject. I want to know about this vanishing act."

"I've got to leave again."

"What? Jesus Christ, Gale! This really is not fair! What happens if you get hurt or in trouble? I have no idea how to get hold of you. We're supposed to be a family. God knows, we're screwed up enough as it is. I don't need to lose you when I no sooner get you back. I have a right to know what's going on. I want you to . . . Gale?"

She was gone. All that remained of her was a dial tone. He dialed her number and got the recording that said "We're sorry. The number you have dialed is no longer in service."

"Those goddamn sons of bitches!"

Chapell bolted out of bed, threw on a pair of jeans, a T-shirt, and a pair of sneaks, then ran for the Jeep. "I'm going over there and find out what the hell is going on."

It wasn't until after he'd started the engine that he realized the only place he knew where to look for her was the place he'd gone last time. He still didn't know how to find her house.

"Well, Rides, you asshole, it serves you right for never going over there to see her all the times she asked you to."

He turned the engine off and went back into the house.

The media blitz covering the life and times of Rae Willie Chapell continued at full tilt. The tube had been saturated with everything you ever wanted to know about the country star and weren't afraid to watch. The radio stations had pulled out every cut she'd ever made and were playing them twenty-four hours a day. *Sixty Minutes* had done an in-depth piece on her life, then another piece, immediately following, on the Toy Duck murders in Nashville. Somebody was killing young women who looked and sounded like the dead megastar. They had been doing it successfully for twenty years, but now, for whatever reason, they had suddenly gone ballistic, killing three in less than a month, sewing them alive inside dead horses.

The farmers, who had lost prize animals, had been interviewed extensively. The Metro Police Media Relations Department had been driven crazy by the frenzy of requests for information and interviews. Ray Robbins had been working twelve-hour days. His face was becoming familiar to households across the country. *Hard Copy, Entertainment Tonight, Prime Time, Day One,* CNN, TNN—they were all in line, jumping up and down for attention like a bunch of third-graders who had the answer to a teacher's question. *Forty-eight Hours* had wanted to follow one of the detectives assigned to the case full-time for a period of two days. When Robbins explained, in detail, how utterly uninteresting it would be listening to the man spend hours on the telephone, and if leads did pan out, the television crew would not be privy to them anyway. They backed off. To his credit, Robbins rarely let the reporters at anyone outside his public relations department, sparing the officers the wasted time. However, the press had quickly learned the faces of most of the men working the case, and it was not unusual to have to run the gauntlet just to get into the building.

Chapell had quickly returned to the eighteen-hour-day routine. The work took his mind off any other problems, and all thoughts of resigning were once again put on the back burner. He simply loved the job and loved being at the center of the universe too much to walk away. He threw himself into the work, analyzing and writing reports, making personal requests of other police departments around the country when a possible suspect was turned.

Maudry Evans had come from a wealthy family in Chicago. Her father had been successful in applying pressure all the way from the Illinois governor to the office of the president of the United States. The call to the chief from an aide in the White House had prompted a trip to McKinty's office, where Chapell was once again accused of everything from laziness to ineptness to stonewalling. Chapell never did understand how the chief could say he was stonewalling— the Murder Squad and its supplemental help was investigating twenty-five hours a day. They had interviewed even the most remote acquaintances of these women. Chapell had approved voucher after voucher for the detectives to fly all over the United States to interview anyone who had even the faintest connection with one of the dead women. he also knew the killer would not be caught by police investigation. If the killer really was Ponder, the doctor was far too smart to leave any trace of himself. If left up to the police department, the killer would never be caught. As far as the Chapell family was concerned, once proven guilty beyond a shred of doubt, Dr. Ponder Chapell would turn up missing—probably buried in the deep jungle, the victim of violence or a botched kidnapping carried out by a South American criminal element.

While he and McCurty had been looking at Maudry Evans's nude body, Chapell had a brainstorm. A chill of excitement had rippled through him, head to foot. *What if the poor women sewn into the horses aren't my brother's only work?* What if there was another avenue of investigation that proved Ponder Allegro Chapell was the maniac presently in the spotlight? Maybe younger brother hadn't been quite so careful in his avocation.

The nude woman found floating in the Cumberland, whose corpse looked like what was left of a medical student's cadaver at the end of the semester, had been identified from her fingerprints. The blackened burn areas on her face and in the pubic and anal regions made the travesty even more gruesome. her name was Elena Tolburt. She'd been arrested for prostitution during a sting operation directed at one of Nashville's finest escort services. Highly skilled artisans, the women were beautiful, intelligent, and they could fake an orgasm better than the best porn stars. The particular escort service Ms. Tolburt had worked for charged a measly $500–1,000 an hour, depending upon the job description. When she'd been arrested, she had a portable electric charge card stamper in her purse. She could put her services on Visa or American Express, and the john could include it in his expense account.

Chapell saved the form he'd been working on. He then gave the computer a three-week time frame and ordered it to search the murder files of women below

the age of forty after the fourth Toy Duck murder
five years before.

There were two. One of them had been a married
woman, a schoolteacher. He was pleasantly surprised
to see that the other had been found floating in a
transparent plastic garment bag in the Cumberland
only two days after the dead horse and its inhabitant
had been discovered in the pasture. Roberta LaBarge.
She had been another $1,000-a-squirt bed bunny—if
the job description included metal and leather. The
river's current had conveniently placed the bag between the paddle wheel and stern of the *General Jackson* at its berth next to Opryland. The *General* was
one of the largest paddle wheelers in the United States
and took hundreds of passengers on trips up and down
the Cumberland on a daily basis. An alert crew member had seen the bag and had tried to remove it to
keep the wheel from fouling. When he saw what was
inside, he'd almost fallen overboard. Her arms and
legs had been cut off and stuffed into the bag with
the rest of her. Evidently, she wouldn't fit in one piece.

The cop checked the case records for the woman
five years before that—ten years ago. Nothing.

He went into the TBI files, which covered the entire
state, not just Davidson County, and did the same
search. Bingo! Six days after Randi Barnes had been
found sewn inside a Tennessee Walker, Judy Moeller,
another high-priced prostitute, had been pulled from
the Cumberland in Trousdale County not far from
Hartsville.

*We know about Elena Tolburt—after Bella Rose.
How abut after Snowy Lockhart? Come to papa, you
gorgeous . . .*

There it was—a twenty-year-old naked woman had
been found four days after Bella Rose was murdered.
The automated debris-removal mechanism at Cheatham Dam had plucked her from the water above the
turbine intakes along with a couple of tons of logs,
tires, pieces of styrofoam, and a hundred kinds of junk

that were routinely thrown into the river to avoid paying landfill fees. the dam was thirty miles down river and in Cheatham County. No mutilation, no cocoon. The woman had been identified by her mother in Ashland City. Croschay Hull had been a student at Tennessee State. She had not had a record for prostitution. There were several snapshots included in the file. Chapell pulled them onto the screen one by one. She was a looker, that's for sure. If she had been hooking, she was young enough, and, so far, smart enough, that she didn't have a record.

She may have been in the water a couple of days before she floated.

The normal human body had a specific gravity that was only a little denser than that of water. With the temperature of the Cumberland well into the eighties, a corpse would stay under one or two days before the resident bacteria generated enough gasses to float it to the surface. The longer a body was in the water, the more bloated and less recognizable it became. If it had been there long enough, identification could be made only from fingerprints, scars, tattoos, dental and bone X rays.

The detective checked after Maudry Evans's murder—nothing. *If there is a victim, and he hasn't put her in something that made her float, she won't have surfaced yet. Obviously, he only wraps up the ones he mutilates—probably to keep the car from getting all messed up on the way to the river. Why the hell haven't we seen this before? Probably because there wasn't a definite pattern—they weren't all in Metro, they weren't all mutilated, nor were they all wrapped in something. God knows, we have enough prostitutes murdered every year in this state. I know nothing has come in today. If the pattern holds, there could be a dead, naked woman somewhere in the Cumberland River.*

This would get the brass off his ass for a while. No longer could they accuse him of stonewalling. If the good doctor had indeed sacrificed some of the meticulous technique he had used for the Toy Duck murders . . . if an investigation could prove . . . Chapell would never let them actually get to his brother. At the last minute Dr. Chapell would simply do that amazing disappearing act in the South American jungle—or perhaps six feet below the bottom of the creek a quarter mile up the hill from the house.

"Gene, you got a minute?" Chapell had called the sergeant on the phone.

"Sure."

McCurty entered the open door a few seconds later, and Chapell looked at him with perhaps the first ray of optimism he'd had in three weeks.

"I want to show you something."

He brought up the four murder-rape victims' cases on the screen one by one.

"Notice the dates."

"I see exactly what you're doing, Rides. Toy Duck, five, ten years ago, Bella Rose, Snowy Lockhart. Anything on the ones fifteen, twenty years ago?"

"No, but I'll bet we'll find something in the paper records. We weren't totally computerized back that far."

"Fooling with those naked women—putting them into the horse, handling them—makes the son of a bitch horny, doesn't it?"

"You bet your ass it does. For some reason he doesn't have a girlfriend whom he wants to go to for relief." *Ponder, damn him, has never had a steady girlfriend. Says they're more bother than they're worth— won't keep them around.* "The Toy Duck women are inviolate. He can't rape them—that's taboo, for whatever deranged reason. But he has to get his rocks off. So he picks an expensive prostitute and plugs her using a rubber—no DNA. Water eliminates pubic hair, fibers, or any other evidence. If he can't keep from mutilating her, he wraps her in something to keep the blood off his car, then dumps the body into the Cumberland." *That way she'll never be able to say*

*that Rae Willie Chapell's boy was one of her clients
when she writes her tell-all book and goes on Oprah.*

"Extremely interesting, considering a lot of these
psychos get off on just the killing—no penetration."

"Not this guy. This opens a whole new field of in-
quiry. We can reinvestigate these victims. Maybe he
wasn't quite so careful with them. *We'll sure as hell
see, anyway.*"

"Here, I scratched down the case numbers." Chapell handed the sergeant the paper. "Get the TBI to
fax us the files on Judy Moeller. Get Ferraro and Cain
to go over Tolburt, LaBarge, and Hull, looking at
them in this new light. We'll see if Alicia can help us
out with the ones fifteen and twenty years ago. That
woman's got a memory like . . ." He let the sentence
dangle. "See if she knows of any old-timers who
worked the cases."

"Ted Wagner might have been on the team back
then."

"He's in the nursing home on Belmont, isn't he?"

"Yeah. I'll give him a call."

"Also, check the escort companies for charge cards
taken by any of the dead women on the nights they
were murdered. It'll probably be a lark—I'll guarantee
he paid cash. If you have to, go reinterview the people
who knew these women. I'll get the choppers on the
river. We need a thorough look all the way from Car-
thage to Clarksville. I'll also call the Coast Guard and
get them to broadcast it on Channel Sixteen. Any
boats out there with a radio can keep an eye out.
First, I'm going to go tell the captain personally about
this. Maybe he and the old man will cut us a little
slack." *I am walking a very fine line between them
catching Ponder—if it is Ponder—before I do, but
maybe this will give me a little breathing room so I can
see what kind of fun and games the bastard is up to.*

The pickup truck Slater Howe was driving sloshed
through the holes and ruts in a dirt alley that a few

hundred feet ago had been sort of a street. It had rained through the night. As he drove farther and farther toward the back of the old industrial complex, the large warehouses became progressively more and more rundown. It didn't matter—the size and surrounding buildings were right, and the rental price had been cheap. It had taken him more than a month to locate the old warehouse park in South Nashville. The buildings had to be in a semblance of proportion and size to the originals.

"What you gonna do with that old building, mister? The roof's shot, the windows are all busted out. It'd take a hundred grand to put it in good enough condition to use it." Howe didn't need to use the inside.

As he turned the last corner, the building gloriously revealed itself. "MGM Soundstage 14." He had told the rental agent that he was creating a set for a movie that would be filmed in the fall. It had taken two months of work, including Saturdays and Sundays, to construct the huge facade with its rounded roof. Before that, the trailer had taken much longer. After a year of putting ads in trades, he'd located one that was in reasonable shape in a junkyard in North Carolina. It had been even tougher finding parts and furnishings. More than once he'd thought of forgetting the idea of making the thing so real and just going ahead and reconstructing it out of what was available in K Mart. But the perfectionist in him wanted to leave nothing to chance. It had to be clearly authentic; the effect had to be overwhelming. Then there was the little matter of the FX inside the trailer. The toughest task had been rigging the eight special lines from under the trailer through the floor and into the right locations—one for each "burn." Getting them to work off the remote had been tricky. He had extensively tested the apparatuses before installing them. They had to fire simultaneously, and it was for sure that they couldn't be tested once fixed in place. The one window large enough to jump through had been swapped for

a custom-made bulletproof-glass window that was
framed in solid steel. The only question he'd encoun-
tered so far had been the door—maybe the weakest
link. Without tearing the side of the trailer down to
the frame and reinforcing it with steel beams, he'd
had to settle on two four-inch bolts and believe that
they'd be more than strong enough in the "heat" of
the moment.

Jeni had been a quick learner. She had picked up
the accent almost absentmindedly. He would have to
correct her only once, and she would not make the
same mistake again. He had told her what to have the
hairdressers do at the expensive salon, and they had
done it perfectly—the color, the cut, the styling. She
had tried the makeup herself after looking at scores
of pictures and a lot of old television footage, but it
had taken both of them experimenting to get it right.
Unfortunately, they didn't have the expertise of a Hollywood makeup artist. The day the look had locked
into place was one of the highlights of Slater Howe's
life. While he was working on "the face," he had been
in total concentration, not looking at the overall effect.
He'd thickened and darkened the eyebrows just a little, working from memory only. She was already wearing the tiny cheek pads, but he'd lifted the cheeks a
few millimeters more with a new blush. He had taken
a break to go to the bathroom and had not looked at
her as a whole before he'd left the room. While he
was gone, she had inserted the teal contacts which she
had still not adjusted to and didn't wear all the time.
He came into the room, head down, in deep thought—
it was now time to begin working on the other voice—
the child. She had given him several versions, and he
knew, with a little work, he could get the right one.
He was still working on what to do about the fact that
she was an inch taller than Rae Willie, but perhaps it
wouldn't be noticed.

When he returned from the john, she had slipped
into one of the outfits he'd put together—charcoal

short shorts and sandals, and a sleeveless pink blouse with a scooped collar.

"Hi, baby."

He had lifted his head at the sound of the all too familiar husky voice. A tremendous, terrorizing jolt hit him in the heart and throat, and for a few seconds he could not even breathe. Rae Willie Chapell stood smiling at him, hip shot, twirling a flowered scarf in her left hand.

"What's your pleasure, cowboy, the couch or the floor?"

He had not taught her the smile. He had not taught her how to stand like that. He had not taught her how to twirl the scarf. That stuff would have come after the look was right. The *ferae naturae* animal stood before him once again, and it seethed in contempt for the entire world. Granted, the Canadian woman had watched a lot of films of Rae Willie, but this was too real. The look and posture were *there*, and the effect was chilling. Not even Rae Willie's mother could tell that this woman was not her daughter.

"Sweetie, you just earned yourself an additional five grand."

Slater Howe was trembling from shock, and the old mind-lacerating feeling of desire for the dead singer broke over him like a busted wave on a surfer. He was doing a good job of hiding it until Jeni deliberately unbuttoned the blouse, then the shorts, and let them fall. As Rae Willie had before, she wasn't wearing anything underneath. The eagerness of a first-grader swept over the fifty-six-year-old man exactly the way it had every time he'd made love to the star over twenty years before. Fortunately, one of the few things that had not been burned twenty years before was the rod of 440 stainless that had just sprouted between his legs.

Chapell had split the task force that was still working on the Toy Duck murders. One-third was now reinterviewing friends and acquaintances of the murdered hookers; two-thirds remained on the Toy Duck murderers, interviewing everyone who had known Maudry Evans, trying to find one coincidental name that was common to the other murdered women.

Chapell had personally called and warned the known escort companies in the city. "The next client you schedule for a prostitution gig could be a sick bastard." They all thanked him and assured him that their girls didn't do that sort of thing.

He had also invited Jon Rheinhart to the initial briefing that took place on the last Thursday in August.

"Who won last night?"

The detective's team, minus him, had played Rheinhart's team the night before on the ice.

"You did. Five to three."

"Jeez, they're not supposed to do that without me."

The agent grinned. His life hadn't been easy lately. Follow-up stories on the bureau's debacle in Homer's Trace were still bouncing around the airwaves and the newspapers.

"We may have a serial killer with two M.O.'s, Jon. I'd appreciate it if you can get the B.S. boys to work up another profile on this new one fast. It may give us a leg up on the bastard."

"I'll put it in the 'emergency' hopper." The meeting had broken up. The two men were talking in the hall. "We did miss you last night. Or let's say, I missed going around your sorry ass last night."

"Sure. Dream on. I haven't done anything since I've been back except work and sleep. Maybe next game. If we could find this maniac, we'd all get some time off. The guys are getting tired. It's been over a month of twelve-hour days for some of them."

"That's why we chose law enforcement, Rides. To stay out of the house and away from the wife."

"Maybe, if I'm ever able to find a wife."

"Hey, I told you twenty-years ago—in college—

you're too picky about your women. There just aren't enough goddesses who can play tennis, cook diet food, give incredible back rubs, sing like Nancy Westbrook, hit the upper left corner with a slap shot from the blue line . . ."

Chapell grinned. "You've got a great memory, Jon. There's going to be women's hockey in the ninety-eight Olympics. Maybe there's hope."

"Why don't you come over for dinner tomorrow night? It's Friday night. You don't have a date, and Teri would love to see you." Chapell had introduced Rheinhart to his future wife when they were seniors in college. "You haven't come to eat with us in years."

"Thanks, a rain check, please. Maybe when this is over. I've got a pile of paperwork on my desk that's going to keep me busy all weekend. Somebody's got to proof, sort, and sift all the shit we're generating. You got your basic vouchers to verify, overtime records to compile, reports to write . . . And they keep calling goddamn meetings. The other day the chief called a meeting to schedule the meetings. I'd give a lot to be back on the street doing interviews—chasing perps."

"Well, the front door's always open for you. We're getting old too fast, Rides. You look behind and before you know it, you'll see that forty has come and gone. Have some fun somewhere besides on the ice for once."

"I'll have my fun watching our Toy Duck friend on his arraignment for murder one." *And if you believe that* . . . "He's broken his pattern, for whatever reason after all these years, and if we don't get him quickly, I'm afraid some more girls are going to die."

"Well, don't put so much pressure on yourself—it's not your fault."

Bullshit, it's not my fault. Maybe I should just shoot the bastard now and bury his body in a cement piling for the new bridge. "See you, Jon."

*   *   *

Since he'd been back to work, the fatigue had got worse. Chapell would go home exhausted, then lie in bed unable to go to sleep. He'd finally relent, take a Seconal. With booze it worked fast and thoroughly— too thoroughly. In the morning he'd have to drink three cups of very strong coffee in order to get out the front door. *I'd gladly murder and pillage for some Eskatrol spansules.* He often wished that Uncle Sam hadn't made the pharmaceutical companies stop manufacturing speed. You could get the stuff on the black market, but that's all a cop needed—to be caught with illegal drugs—tough way to end a career. *Shades of* Valley of the Dolls, *Jacqueline.*

It was going to get worse.

With increasing horror Chapell had watched an overwhelming advertising blitz the last few days—in the papers, on television and the radio—even a billboard had been erected near Music Row. Beginning Friday night, HBO was going to begin showing the television premiere of *I Only Dance to the Blues,* the film Rae Willie had been working on when the fire in her dressing trailer had killed her. Fortunately, everything had been shot except a few long shots, and a double had done those. The movie had never been shown on TV. Fox had recouped its investment in the theaters, then out of respect for the artist had put the film back in the can. With the insatiable demand for Rae Willie Chapell that had infected the world market, there was too much money to be made to bother with respect any longer. If there was ever a prompt for another Toy Duck killing, this was it. Chapell intended to stick closer to his brother than August ticks on a stray dog. If he was with Ponder and there was another killing, Ponder would be in the clear.

The detective left work at five p.m. on Friday afternoon. He wanted to make sure he saw Ponder leave his office. He had spent part of the morning on the phone, renting three cars and having two of them delivered to special spots. He would start the weekend tail with a dark blue Taurus that he picked up personally from the rental agency at the downtown Stauffer Hotel—the half-block-long, skinny skyscraper buried in the skyline. The hotel was connected to the downtown convention center, which was across the street from the Ryman—the old home of the Grand Old Opry. Across Broadway, to the south, the new $120 million-dollar arena was under construction. Progress had gradually eradicated Lower Broad's adult book stores and sleaze joints, which had dominated a few years before. Some of the bars had been institutions for the writers and artists when country music had its first beginnings. Tootsies was still there. Just across the alley from the Opry, it had been made famous by the likes of Hank Williams, who used to duck in for a quick one, or two, or three, between Opry shows on Saturday nights. Its disheveled lavender front seemed to defy the ages. Earnest Tubb's record shop was still across the street. If the city planners had their way, the whole of Lower Broad would be leveled to put up more convention centers, hotels, Hard Rock Cafés, and assorted tourist traps. Then the money grubbers could boast that their colossi were built on top of some of country music's most significant historical sites.

In addition to the Taurus, Chapell had rented a Dodge Caravan, which was parked in the lot at the Sheridan Inn on Harding Place. The hotel was close to the I-65 entrance-exit nearest Ponder's home. At an abandoned lot behind the McDonald's on Eighth Avenue South—an alternate route Ponder might use to come into town—was an off-white Geo Prism.

The garage had told him that morning that the Jaguar would take another three weeks. He would be glad to have it back, but would probably trade it in for one that hadn't been wrecked. For now, he was driving the Cherokee, and he parked it in a dark corner of the Church Street Center Garage, which was beneath the downtown mall across the street from the hotel. After carefully donning an expensive wig, fake mustache, and Serengeti sunglasses, he plopped on a baseball cap and admired himself in the mirror. The elevator took him to the enclosed bridge that spanned Commerce Street and led to the hotel lobby. There was a bar located on the bridge, and he was tempted to snatch a quick one.

You can't stay awake now, stupid. forget the booze.

The express desk gave him the keys to all three cars with only a quick signature. He used a fake ID that had its own untraceable company credit card account. The bill would end up in a rented box in Chicago, never to be paid. The fake ID, along with the disguise, should be more than adequate. He'd brought a satchel full of different beards and mustaches, hats, jackets, glasses, and a few other necessities just in case.

He drove one block south to Broadway, then turned west. The street eventually passed Ponder's clinic in Belle Meade, but not before it had changed to West End Avenue, then Harding Road. Some of Nashville's streets had been fooling both tourists and locals for years. Harding *Road* was on the west side of town and, if followed far enough, would lead all the way to Memphis as Route 70. Harding *Place* ran from the airport, which was in the southeastern quadrant of the city, across the full width of the city's south side for almost fifteen miles before it dead-ended into Harding Road in Bellemeade, but not before it had changed its name to Battery Lane for a couple of miles, then back to Harding Place. Whether the modifier was Place or Road could separate a driver from where he, or she, wanted to be as much as fifteen miles, and Nashvillians casually referred to both as just plain "Harding."

Old Hickory Boulevard was even worse. Broken into dozens of jagged and erratic pieces, the street, and sometimes country road, circled most of the city, but nowhere was it designated by adjectives like northwest or southeast. Without specific directions, Old Hickory could be in Scottsboro, White's Creek, Madison, Hermitage, the Knollensville Road area, Brentwood, the Hillsboro Road area, in Percy Warner Park, Bellview, and a number of other places. From the village of Old Hickory to Percy Warner Park was twenty-four miles, and heaven help the lost tourist who was trying to get from one to the other by way of Old Hickory.

Ponder's Jaguar was still in its parking place. Chapell pulled the Taurus into a Texaco station, took a leak, filled the thermos with coffee, and picked a parking spot in a small shopping center where he could see both the front and back doors to the clinic. He poured a cup of coffee and settled down to wait. The police radio was on the seat next to him, but he had turned it off. If they needed him, they'd beep him on his beeper. Probably his beeper would be malfunctioning again, and he'd never get the message—at least until he'd seen what his brother was up to. If they tried the cellular, it wouldn't be on either.

Ah, he's actually going to call it a day.

The cop had been sitting, watching for over two hours. At seven-thirty, Ponder emerged, got into the Jag, and headed back into Nashville on Harding Road/ West End/Broadway. Chapell followed him, remaining well back in traffic.

Ponder drove four miles back into the city and turned south, on Seventeenth, toward Music Row. Chapell followed at a distance, timing the light as they zigged around the building on the corner that had once been part of Hank Williams' home, most of which was still located on Franklin Road. The innocuous brick building, and attached garage, had been neatly sliced off Hank's house, moved by truck, and plopped onto the site of a former gas station which had been next door to what is presently Gilley's. The place had never caught on as a tourist attraction and over the years had fallen into some disrepair. It had

at one time seen service as a bar, the front decorated
with neon beer signs. Now it was a music store/
recording studio/tapes and equipment store. Hardly
anyone cared that it had once belonged to Hank
and Audry.

They zagged back onto Seventeenth, and the new
ASCAP building slipped by on the left, as did RCA.
Elvis had cut in RCA's old Studio B. Reba McIntyre's
monstrosity was still emerging from a large hole in the
ground. While the hole was being dug, the noise from
the jackhammers and dynamite had generated so
many lawsuits from local studios trying to record that
her lawyer began just handing out his card to the companies who were complaining. In Larry Gatlin's studio
across the street, the jackhammer sounded like someone was beating on a guitar case with a couple of
drumsticks.

The two brothers continued down the street, which
was lined with old homes that had been turned into
offices long before scores of modern office complexes
had sprouted like weeds all over the area. Both types
of buildings housed managing, promotion, booking,
and publishing companies along with law firms and
a hodgepodge of satellite businesses. At the corner
occupied by the Opryland Music Group's building,
Ponder turned right onto Grand. As Chapell eased
through the intersection, he saw the Jag pull into a
parking spot in front of the building that had once
been Ray Stevens's studio and publishing company.
An accomplished pianist, in addition to playing every
other instrument in the world, Ray would lay down
all the rhythm instruments on the track, including
drums. He would sing the solo—on the song he had
written and was publishing with his own company—
then put on all the backup parts. With classic Ray
Stevens humor, he had been heard to say, "Man, I
make *all* the money!"

Chapell continued slowly down Seventeenth until he
found a narrow driveway which would cut through to

the back alley. Most of the blocks in this area of town had an access road that split the block in half. He drove the Taurus slowly down the alley's broken pavement until he could see Ponder's car. The detective backed the Taurus into a parking spot behind a small garage and waited. Ponder was about seventy yards away and was sitting in the car reading a paper. He looked like he was waiting for someone. Chapell left the engine on, in order to run the air conditioner, and its vibrations and sound soon put him to sleep. He awoke confused when his head smacked against the side window. Panicky, his eyes flew first to where Ponder was parked, then to the clock on the dash. The doctor was still there, and the clock had only moved eight minutes.

"Jesus, I've got to get some quality sleep."

He had fortuitously awakened just in time to see a blond woman wearing short, tight dress and heels come out the front door of Ray's old building. She strutted down the sidewalk and got into a Mercedes 500-SL. When she pulled out, Ponder followed discreetly. The caravan turned south on Twenty-first Avenue and proceeded by Vanderbilt on the right, then Peabody College on the left. The woman stopped at the First American Bank's twenty four-hour teller on the corner of Twenty-first and Wedgewood, then continued south on the street, which had now turned into Hillsboro Pike. The three cars threaded their way through the Friday night traffic in Green Hills, and she finally turned left—east—to wind her way through a series of short streets. When she pulled into the driveway on a street off Lealand Lane, Ponder slowed noticeably, and Chapell had to dart into a driveway to avoid getting too close. They were now less than a mile from where someone had tried to kill his Jaguar with an elephant gun.

Bastard's stalking her.

Chapell couldn't find a number on any of the houses. In fact, he hadn't even been able to get the name of the street they were on. It was almost dark, and where there *were* signs, they were hard to read. Had he been able to get both, he might have called dispatch and asked who lived there. Of course, then he'd be on record, and the question might come up, "How did you get the woman's address before she was sewn inside that horse, Lieutenant?"—if she were murdered. Maybe Ponder wanted to have an affair with some music executive's wife, and he was checking out where she lived. A Mercedes, no less. And maybe the executive's wife did a fair imitation of Rae Willie Chapell. . . .

And a nice house—what I could glimpse of it. Hey, I'm not going to let him sew her inside any horse, and you can bet the farm on that, boys.

He picked up his brother's taillights again, but Ponder was obviously headed home. When Chapell saw him pull into the street that led to the mansion, he said to himself, "This would be a good time to switch vehicles and disguises."

Within five minutes, he had parked the Taurus in the back lot of the Sheridan and was on his way back in the Dodge Caravan wearing a dark, full beard and mustache along with a black cowboy hat.

It was eight-thirty and almost dark when he parked the van on the side of the street and made his way onto the grounds of Rae Willie's mansion. August's canopy of sopping night air had descended with a thud upon the area's bowl—a giant gouge in the earth that had been gouged by the serpentine squirming of the Cumberland River during a distant ice age. Chapell thought of how nice it would have been to have gone to the Sounds' game. This kind of night would dim the outfield with a hazy mist and amplify the crack of the bat as it bounced off the giant guitar-shaped scoreboard. Beer would flow in rivers, and T-shirts and shorts would be soaked from the night's moisture when the spectators got home. Most of the city's residents who had remained at home for the evening had already made their way from backyard pools and patios to the air-conditioned relief of indoors.

Sticking to the hedgerow, the cop made his way to an old hiding place. When it was totally dark, he crept to the shrubbery outside the window in the den. Except for the television, the room was pitch black. He couldn't make out the features of Ponder's face in the dark, but Chapell knew beyond a shadow of a doubt what was on the screen. The soundtrack's orchestra was playing "I Only Dance to the Blues." Rae Willie had written the tune. It had been number one on the charts for over two months. There was just enough light from the television set for Chapell to see the reflection of the big man's streaming tears.

Not as tough as you think you are, brother dearest. We certainly loved our mother, didn't we? In spite of everything she did to us. God, if this doesn't set him off . . .

The detective decided to get comfortable. Ponder was obviously going to watch the movie before doing any sewing. Chapell needed something to sit on so he wouldn't have to stand stooped over in order to look in the window for two hours. He was incredibly tired. He carefully made his way around the house and stole a chair from the pool deck. Placing it inside the shrubbery, he could see through the window and still remain unseen. He settled down with the patience of a cop, and awaited Ponder's move after the movie.

Maybe he'll just go to bed, folks. Regardless, I'm here until dawn. Just got to keep out of sight, that's all. Big place. Won't be hard. No-body knows . . . the hiding . . . placcces . . . beeetterrr thhhaaaan . . .

The will to direct the muscles weakened, and the mind space slowly emptied of any, and all, resolution to move; no reason to change positions; statuesque; *flexibilitas cerea;* wax. All is wax. Time slowed geometrically until the movement of the world sloshed through his mind in a soundless frame-by-frame plastic-melt parade. The insect symphony and distant street sounds glissandoed lower and lower in a great slo-mo Doppler effect, as each of the night sounds became more and more liquid. After sitting only an eternity, he had lost the will even to accomplish the most basic bodily functions. The mind still ran, although cursed with rust and corrosion. The body had all but ground to a halt. For all it mattered, it could stay that way for ever more. To move the muscles would grind metal-armored body viscera, and they would shriek and groan in protest; they might even shatter. Once shattered, heart, lungs, liver, could never be repaired.

The roar of a car, very near, made him jump.

"Shit!"

He fought desperately to get back to reality, pawing, clawing, screaming his way out of the abyss.

When he arrived, he saw Ponder barreling down the driveway in the Jag. The Pirellis complained loudly as the Jag turned onto the street, and the car roared out of sight.

Chapter Ten

Heart beating like a bad drummer, Chapell was already in full flight.

He raced across the lawn, vaulted a low granite wall, and quickly made it to the van, which was parked a few yards down the street. As he started the engine, he could just see Ponder's taillights turning north onto Franklin Road. The cop left the headlights off as he rutted lawn and peeled rubber in pursuit. He screamed up the short hill and turned after his brother just in time to catch the familiar Jaguar taillights turning onto Battery Lane.

"The bastard is going after that woman. I'll bet you my house."

Chapell was sure Ponder had not seen the Dodge; was sure the veterinarian had not seen the Taurus that afternoon. He would have to believe no one was following him, and no one would know where he was going. By the time he got the woman anesthetized and made the trip to a farm near Homer's Trace, it would be after eleven o'clock. The detective barreled around curves and turns on his way back to Lealand Lane and the short street the woman lived on—if he could find it! The street layout in that area of town was irregular and complicated with short dead ends, right-angle elbows, and loops that went nowhere.

"Fuck!"

Another wrong turn—dead end.

"Sssshhhhhit!"

Nothing familiar on this one. He was tired—too

tired—not up to the level of concentration it would take to retrace his route.

"Must be the next one."

There was a car coming toward him. He just caught a glimpse of Ponder's Jaguar as it flashed by in the dark. Ponder must have just walked into the house and stuffed a rag soaked with ether in the woman's face.

"Fuck *and* shit!"

He wheeled into the first driveway and had to wait as not one but two cars came down the street too close for him to back out.

"Come on, you bastards!"

He was soon on the bumper of the car in the rear. There was no place to pass that wasn't hills or curves.

Finally, one of the cars turned off. He managed to squeeze by the one still in front of him by passing it on a curve. He was going fifty when he topped the last hill before Hillsboro Pike—the main drag through Green Hills. The Caravan almost left the road on the sharp hilltop. As he came down to the light on Hillsboro, he thought he caught a glimpse of Ponder's car going up the hill on Hobbs, which was the street straight across. The Jaguar was headed in the general direction of Homer's Trace. The detective gunned it through a red light, much to the chagrin of a Papa John's Pizza delivery boy, and he quickly ran the van up to sixty-five going up the street's long hill. When he broke over the top, the Jaguar was nowhere in sight.

"Re-fuck and re-shit!"

There were no cars anywhere.

Might as well head toward River Road. Maybe I'll pick him up.

Ten minutes later, he was winding around the sharp curves up, over, and down Sullivan's Ridge. For miles the road snapped back and forth in wild bends. There were only three places, until well into Cheatham County, where it would be straight enough to pass. Chapell sailed around three cars on one of them. He threw a microglance at the speedometer and thought that it said he was doing over ninety. None of the cars were Ponder's Jag. As he neared the area where the murders had taken place, his thoughts became more and more frantic.

He must have been going almost as fast as I am. I'm not going to find him on the road. Maybe if I stake out one of the previous sites, he'll show up. Let's see, there have been two recent killings at the Stratten farm; one recently and one fourteen years ago at McNulty's; and the last one was at Tenebrae's. Plus, Nolan Tyres was found on the Summers farm. My bet is on none of them. I'm going to bet he's going back to one of the old farms—one from ten years ago. No, belay that! Out of the five sources of horses in the area, I'm going to bet the son of a bitch is going to go all the way back to twenty years ago and that first little girl that was killed. These other places are too predictable. Thurman's. That's where the first murder took place. We've both ridden with Gale on that farm. Unless he goes to a totally new area ... I'm going put my money on George Thurman's place. There are some thick woods back of the pasture and, if I remember, an exposed farm road that runs through the fields all the way back to the woods. He might get the car into the woods from the back side by using one of the dirt roads off Pond Creek Road in order to keep from being seen, but I'm going to risk it and go in from this side, lights out. I'll look around for the Jag, then settle down and watch the horses. It's as good a bet as running to these other farms and searching twenty square miles for the hidden car. Damn, how did I ever lose him in the first place?

It was four minutes to eleven when he swung the ten-foot steel gate open and drove the van onto the access road. There were posted signs plainly visible. Tough. That hadn't stopped Ponder before. Thousands of acres of woods bordered the back of the farm, but hunters were allowed into them only by written permission. Too many horses, cows, dogs, and people had been shot over the years. One year a turkey hunter had shot his hunting partner out of a tree. Another year a deer hunter had shot a Volkswagen—had torn most of a front fender off with double-ought buck. Chapell had turned off the van's headlights, even though the area was well out of sight and earshot from the house, which was three-fourths of a mile down the road. He got out of the van and closed the gate behind him. The road ran beside the pasture for four hundred yards, then entered thick woods that would gradually mount the valley's west ridge all the way to the top, where all semblance of civilization ceased. The terrain back there was rough—steep hills with broad ridges that were separated by deep, creek-inhabited hollows. There was no open ground. Logging roads crisscrossed the area, some of them still in use for scattered lumber operations. Most of the unused roads were kept open by someone running a mower down them two or three times a year so that there would be access in case of fire.

Chapell drove slowly. There was just enough light from a frazzled moon to see the double dirt lane. Once in the woods, he removed the itching wig and beard, got out, and scouted until he found a place to back the van off the road where it would be out of sight if Ponder happened to use the road. He sprayed himself liberally with insect repellent, another staple carried in the tote bag. That done, he took his Steiner binoculars and looked for a place that gave an overview of the field below. Twenty minutes later, after his eyes had adjusted to the dark, he could see the horses grazing about a quarter mile away. There were about a dozen of them.

Now, friends and neighbors, we'll see if we're gonna have a show tonight.

At eleven thirty-five, he returned the fifty yards to the van to get the lunch he'd picked up on the way to Ponder's clinic. From his office he'd faxed an order to a sandwich shop on West End. He also got his windbreaker. The temperature was about seventy, and with the dampness the air was on the chilly side.

Cicadas were concertizing, as were several bullfrogs from the two small ponds below in the pasture. He could see an occasional car whizzing down River Road. A tug with its tow of barges struggled upriver against the current in the distance, the drone of its engines echoing back and forth between the ridges on either side of the river. The pilot was playing with the searchlight, panning the fields on either side of the river. *Probably looking for deer.* The light—millions of candlepower strong—would burrow through the night for two or three miles with little effort. A few miles to the north a woman had missed the curve at the bottom of Dump Hill and had driven into the river because the light had blinded her. She had drowned; her infant son had been rescued by a passerby as the car sank in twenty-five feet of water. The state finally put up a guardrail. Chapell speculated whether the pilots of the tow boats played games to stay awake— see who could spot the most deer during one shift. Were there cars in remote parking spots with sweat-covered lovers steaming windows—windows that had to remain mostly up to keep out the mosquitoes?

It was peaceful. So peaceful, in fact . . .

. . . that he awakened with the sun in his face, his hair, jeans, and jacket soaked with dew, nose and sinuses clogged from lying on the damp ground for hours—sound asleep!

"God damn it, Chapell! Have you got to screw up everything you touch?"

Maybe it wasn't so bad. He remembered looking at the tritium dial on his watch at twelve-fifteen. Nothing had happened. He'd had a clear view of the pasture, and the horses had remained undisturbed.

Using the binoculars, he scanned the field. The horses were still about a quarter mile away. Three of them were lying down.

That's okay. Don't panic, Rides. Horses lie down.

He'd walk down there and make sure nothing had happened. Just his walking toward them would be enough to get them on their feet.

It did—two of them. The third remained on its side.

I don't like this. Better go see.

Fifty yards.

"Yo! Haw! Haw, girl!"

The others ran off in a huff, then stopped at a safe distance and glared at him.

Oh, God, no. Don't let this be . . .

The mare didn't move. Her belly was facing him, and the closer he got, the sicker the feeling became in his stomach and bowels. He wanted to squat and defecate.

From fifty feet he could see the terrible, wonderful stitching. There were no cries for help; nothing appeared to be moving inside the animal's swollen belly. Rider Chapell knelt on the pasture floor and vomited—not from what he knew was inside the horse's belly—he'd seen death and gore in all its glory for seventeen years; the sickness came from the fact that he was now ninety-nine percent positive that his brother was the sickest son of a bitch that God had ever shat from his perverted ass! If the woman curled inside the travesty lying before him lived on that short street off Lealand . . .

When the retching had petered out, the panic began to set in.

"Jesus, if someone sees me out here . . ."

He wouldn't have a prayer as far as explaining to billions of people around the world how Lieutenant Rider Chapell knew who the killer was—had suspected for some time. However, instead of turning the sick bastard in and getting him arrested, the murderer had been allowed to sew another miraculously created, intelligent—above all other creatures on earth—wonderfully warm and loving, childishly playful fellow human being into the bowels of a horse, where she

died one of the most horrific deaths man in all his
creativity had been able to dream up.

The cop bolted for the van, and as he reached for
the keys in his pocket—no keys! However, there was
something that hadn't been there when he'd gone to
sleep. Instead of the keys, there was a single gold
spangle that perfectly matched the ones stitched into
the dead horse lying down there in the pasture. The
keys that had been in his pocket were now in the
Caravan's ignition, and Chapell never left the keys in
the car, not even in his own garage.

*Sweet Jesus, he's playing games again. Now he
knows that I know, and the only reason he didn't
whack me was he wants to scare the shit out of me
first. Well, my dearest brother, bring on your best. We'll
see if I can't win my first one in the last thirty-odd
years.*

Chapell had had a deep-seated, irrational fear of
his brother since childhood, even though Ponder was
younger, Ponder wasn't like other kids. He had the
cunning and patience of his father, the hunter, and the
"I'll rip your heart out to get what I want" ruth-
lessness of his mother. Chapell had seen his brother
in action too many times. Had seen him during his
board-breaking, brick-busting phase; had seen Ponder
do things that other boys couldn't do—make impossible climbs up cliffs; make ridiculous shots with a gun
or bow. Through a high-powered spotting scope,
Chapell had watched his brother break a beer bottle
from a thousand yards with a rifle when they were in
high school. Ponder had customized a 300 Weatherby
Magnum. One summer he had spent weeks practicing
by himself in a remote part of northeastern Tennessee,
living in a motel, loading his own cartridges, experimenting with bullets and powder measures. In spite of
all the training Chapell had undergone over the years,
he still had a deep and abiding fear when it came to
taking on his brother. The mild-mannered veterinarian

image Ponder projected to his wealthy Belle Meade
clients was a far cry from the calculating and savage
machine that had got in a fight in a bar in northern
Idaho one summer when the boys were on the road
with their mother for a week.

And now Chapell's simple failure to remain awake
and catch the son of a bitch in action had caused a
big problem. The detective couldn't take a chance on
driving the van through the pasture and out the gate.
The road was filled with Saturday morning unfortu-
nates who had to work six days a week or who worked
shift work and got stuck with every other weekend.
There was a curve in one direction, a hill in the other.
With the stiff early morning breeze that was blowing
up from the river, he couldn't hear the cars coming
either way. He would be totally exposed when he got
out to open the gate—someone would remember him,
or the van, when the murder hit the airwaves. He
could wait for an opening in the sporadic traffic, hope
for the best, and just crash through the fence, but
there would be paint that could easily be traced to the
van. He could wear the beard, sunglasses, and a stupid
hat, but not even a general description could be allowed—not him, not the van. If they checked the
rental agencies ... A clerk gives them a composite
picture on the computer—it's manipulated to remove
the beard and hat. ... He could only hope that he
hadn't been spotted in the pasture so far. There was
a small hill between where the horse lay and the road,
so unless someone was out wandering the hills and
dales when the rest of the county was sleeping, he was
probably safe.

*Take the road up the hill. Find out where it goes. I
know there's much less traffic on Pond Creek Road—
if that's where it comes out, and if I can get through.*
The logging roads were passable, but sometimes it
took a four-wheel-drive vehicle.

Damn, I wish I had the Cherokee!

He climbed for a quarter of a mile; then for another

half mile the road wound its way along the spine of
the ridge, following every curve and dip. It finally
began to descend, and halfway down the steep hill he
was confronted with a long section that had been
deeply gutted by the rain. In several places steps of
flat, naked limestone had been exposed. The van
would negotiate the steps, but the gulleys were over
three feet deep in places.

"Take it slow and easy, Rides. You can do this. Just
straddle the damn ruts."

There was no going back; there had been no alternative routes. He inched the van down the hill, keeping the left-side wheels on the center ridge, straddling
the first gulley. The road made a sharp curve and the
single rut split into three deep furrows. Now he had
to keep the wheels on a narrow six-inch ridge or they
would slip into one of the trenches, grounding out the
van. He made it through the section, breathed a sign
of relief, and carefully banged the van down a series
of one-foot limestone steps. He could see that the last
of the steps was more like two feet, and if he didn't
get a little run at it, the back bumper would hang on
the ledge's lip. He gunned the unfamiliar engine a
little too much, and the van leaped off the ledge, the
front wheels bouncing hard when it landed. When the
back wheels hit, and vehicle bucked violently and
began to skid on loose pieces of limestone. All braking
control went out the window, and Chapell watched
helplessly as the van was propelled into the chaos of
ruts, holes, and ledges that lay ahead. There was nothing he could do except ride the brakes and try to
minimize the slewing. The trail steepened even more,
and the car continued to plunge down the hill. Steering the road became a good joke, and whenever he
did hit the brakes, no matter how lightly, the van
would slide and skid. The grade was now much too
steep, and with all the loose gravel in the trail, there
was no footing.

The headlong dive ended abruptly when the right-side wheels slid into a three-foot trench after bouncing over a series of basketball-size rocks. There was a loud, metallic ping, followed by a prolonged scraping noise. The van lurched violently to the side, almost tipping over, and forward progress halted. The cop's body had gone airborne, and he was dribbled between the seat and the ceiling several times before coming to rest mostly against the driver's door. The world outside the windshield appeared to be tilted dangerously. The gas pedal was still in the right place, and he began to gun the idling engine out of sincere frustration. It was a lost cause.

"God damn my ass!"

When he got out to look, he could see the left front wheel canted at an odd angle as it hung in space. The axle had snapped.

"Well, Rides, old fella, let's see you get out of this one."

He spent a half hour sterilizing the van of all evidence of Rider Chapell's presence. He carefully wiped fingerprints with his handkerchief, then took the floor mats out and shook them. He meticulously scoured every square inch on the seats and floor where he could possibly have deposited a hair, a fiber of cloth, or any other telltale piece of evidence that would be caught in Forensics' vacuum filter and placed under a microscope. It was a long way from being foolproof, but he did the best he could without a high-pressure hose and a few gallons of hydrochloric acid. He thought of burning the van, using its own gasoline, but that would attract certain attention to the area.

"It may be enough. I wasn't in the damn thing that long to have made much of a contribution to the evidence pool."

He took a look at the sun and headed southeast through the woods. He'd have to walk the entire six miles back to town, and none of it could be on the road where someone would remember the description of a man walking away from the area of a murder, regardless of the disguise. What if someone stopped to give him a ride who was an expert on disguises—a theater manager or a private detective? What about giving away his height and build? It would be easy to call a cab. He had the cellular in his bag. However, there would then be a record. The hike was not going to be easy. The terrain was nasty, and a lot of the hills could be negotiated no other way than straight up and straight down—to go around would expose him to somebody's view. Fortunately, except for the chronic fatigue due to the ungodly stress he'd been under for a month, he was in excellent shape—especially his legs. Good legs was one of the benefits from playing hockey. He could only pray that no one spotted that dead horse and called the cops. One of the first calls the cops made on Toy Duck murders was to Lieutenant Rider Chapell. If that didn't work, then they called his cellular.

"Oh, I'll be there in a while, guys. I'm stuck out in the middle of the boondocks without a car. How'd I get here? Well, I was trying to get away from . . . Aw, fuck you!"

At nine a.m. he called the rental agency and reported that the van had been stolen sometime during the night. By five o'clock in the afternoon he had finally made it to Charlotte Pike. With an exposed half-mile walk, wearing a wig, full beard and mustache, sunglasses and the cowboy hat, he was able to catch a bus downtown after a forty-five-minute wait. There was no other choice. From there it was a four-block walk to the garage where the Cherokee was parked. Neither the phone nor the beeper had rung. Hopefully, it'd be a long time before the horse was discovered.

Goddamn lab will go over that van with an electron microscope. You'd better hope that the cleaning job was good enough, Chapell. At least they won't be able to trace the rental to me.

*   *   *

He was totally exhausted when he pulled into the long drive to his home, and he'd still not one hundred percent verified the fact that Ponder was the killer—he had not seen it happen with his own eyes. However, it had shaken him badly to be ninety-nine and nine-tenths certain. For the last month he'd held out hope that he was badly mistaken. Hope was dissipating fast.

He had driven a few dozen yards up the long drive when there was a tremendous explosion behind him. The Cherokee's back window and windshield had exploded a fraction of a second before.

"Jesus!"

Another elephant gun.

"You son of a bitch, now you've made me mad!"

Covered in glass, he slammed on the brakes and jumped out the door, rolling for the ditch. There was another explosion and a tree shattered over his head. He was up and running into the woods, angling back toward the main road, where the shots were originating. The Beretta had magically appeared in his hand.

"You bastard, this time I'm going to ring your bell and bury you in the goddamn swamp!"

He sprinted through the brush and woods, tearing his clothes and skin on briars, leaping over rocks and roots on an all-out sprint for the main road. He arrived panting hard and realized that he'd been making so much noise crashing through the brush, he hadn't been able to hear if there'd been an engine starting, followed by a squeal of tires burning rubber.

No! He's still here some place. There was no time to get to a car hidden on one of the little roads in the woods along here—no time for him to get away. I was here too quick. Now, you bastard, I fully intend to see you before you see me. If I were you and I was only trying to scare my quarry rather than kill him—and that's what you were doing, dearest brother, shithead that you are, or you would have easily blown my head off with that cannon—if I were you, I'd get into the woods on the other side of the road.

Chapell had been moving while he was thinking, but he was moving on adrenaline only. His nerves were badly shot. Arms and legs were noticeably shaking. He turned off his beeper. A distraction at the wrong moment could cost him his life. Cautiously, he pushed into the woods on the road's far side, crouching, searching thoroughly, identifying every form in his path. Twice he jumped out of his skin and swung the Beretta as squirrels bolted for cover. Years of training on the department's live-target-simulation set had kept him from pulling the trigger. Ponder could be wearing his camo outfit, and when Ponder went into invisible mode . . .

The detective searched for almost an hour, slowly, noiselessly making his way from tree to tree, watching for any movement, listening for giveaway sounds. There was nothing. He finally gave up and cautiously made his way back to the road, then up the driveway, leaving the Jeep where it was. When the lab crew came to investigate, they'd want the scene left intact. In his agitated state of mind it had never occurred to him that someone could have pulled up in a car at the entrance of the driveway, shot at him without leaving the driver's seat, then sped off as he was brushing off glass.

The phone started to ring just as he let himself into the kitchen.

"Rider Chapell."

"Lieutenant, it's Gene. We've been trying to reach you."

"Sorry, what's wrong?"

"We got another one."

"Oh, great goddamn, not on Saturday."

"Sorry. This time he left some evidence, though. We found where he parked his car and where he may have been watching the horses. We even found a candy bar wrapper. The lab's going over it for prints."

Oh, sweet Jesus, I didn't leave any candy bar wrappers out there. Did I? I'll bet my loving brother planted it just out of my sight. God damn you, Ponder, you're going to get yours!

"Rides?"

"Yeah, Gene. Sorry. I just walked into the house. Somebody just pulled the elephant gun routine on me again. Blew out the windows on the Cherokee. I'm still a little shaky. Where is the farm?"

"Hey, we can handle it. You want to get a team started at your place? Maybe we got another mystery going here—I mean, we were fairly certain that Nolan Tyres was the shooter last time, right?"

"Shit, you're right. We'd better follow procedure. They won't find anything except a couple of monster hunks of buried lead. I looked for the son of a bitch for over an hour, starting the second I got out of the car—my radio was on the dash and he shot the shit out of it. I wasn't smart enough to grab the cellular when I jumped from the car, and I turned off the beeper so if it went off it wouldn't give me away. That cannon scares the bejesus out of you. I've never heard anything like it." *Except for the two or three big-game rifles Dad had.* "There was no time to call for backup. I looked for empty shells where the shots came from. Nothing. Didn't hear any cars leaving. If this is the same guy that did it last time, he's good. I never caught a hint of him beforehand—nor did I catch a glimpse of him afterward. The frame on Tyres was brilliant."

"Do you think it's our Toy Duck friend—you know, warning you off? Flaunting his success? Whatever?"

"My gut feeling says yes. He could have killed me either time. He's playing with me—after murdering lookalikes of my mother. Now he's got himself another howitzer, and it works for me."

"You'd better stay put until we get a lab crew out there."

"Shit. I need to see this last Toy Duck scene. He finally left something behind?"

"Yeah. Ground was too hard to get a tire cast, but from the size of the impression in the grass, the width of the vehicle, we're thinking it might have been a truck or a van. I'll give you directions, anyway."

McCurty gave directions that were totally needless. Chapell said he'd be there if he could get away soon enough—he'd have dispatch call on the radio first. Actually, he didn't have any intention of going out there. He knew what the scene looked like. It was indelibly inscribed in his memory. He just hoped that any prints on that candy wrapper were useless. Thank goodness he always crumbled his wrappers severely before he stuck them in his pocket. Ponder had taken it out of his pocket when he took the keys. Bastard. If the wrapper was cold-ironed and the prints reconstructed by computer . . . Could the lab do that kind of shit? Could the FBI? If they found *his* prints at the scene of the crime . . .

I was a senior, Ponder a sophomore, at Dartmouth. At the end of the summer we flew to Boise to spend a few days with Mom—at her request. "I'm lonely out here, sweetie. Like to see my boys once in a while." That was a laugh. Rae Willie Chapell didn't get lonely. She had too many friends surrounding her twenty-four hours a day—Jack Daniels, George Dickell, Evan Williams; there were Mr. Coke and Mr. High, Mr. Low and Mr. "We're not sure what this one will do at any given time." We never did figure out why she asked us to come see her. She spent no time with us other than to say hello and "What the hell are you doing here?" Typical whim, I guess. Ponds and I ducked out during the middle of the last night's show and went bar hopping.

We were minding our own business, drinking beer in a dark corner. The bar was almost empty, probably because most of the patrons were at the concert. Ponder

*was telling me how the Koreans did certain things—
eat, have fun, drive, sex, fight. He had spent part of the
summer that year in South Korea, totally immersed in
some obscure martial art taught by a master in Seoul.
I'd been working for the sheriff's office in Williamson
County—gophering mostly. It was a plum that had
been afforded only because I was the son of a star, but
I didn't care. It was a chance to see law enforcement
in action.*

*Anyway, a couple of drunk construction workers
come into the bar and take issue with the fact that two
college boys have been born on Mother Earth. They
squeeze into the booth with us and start making fun of
our clothes and Ponder's long haircut. The bartender
doesn't interfere, figuring two kids were helpless and
would never come back anyway. When I say politely
that my brother and I would like to leave, one of the
men makes these kissing noises and remarks that Ponder has a nice ass. He puts his hand on Ponder's arm,
and Ponder reaches with his other hand, removes it,
and asks him to leave. The guy puts his hand back,
this time on Ponder's hand. Ponds removes it once
more. The guy slides closer, puts his arm around
Ponds, and once more foolishly takes my brother's
hand. That was enough. Before the moron can even
wipe the smile off his face, his nose is displaced a full
inch by Ponder's elbow. Blood's spouting all over the
table like a broken water pipe.*

*The guy jumps to his feet, holding the mess on his
face with both hands, and the other guy reaches across
the table for Ponds. Ponds is already out of the booth
and on his feet.*

*"You little son of a bitch. You didn't have to do that.
He was only playing with you. Now I'm going to have
to teach you a lesson."*

*Ponder wasn't little. He was six-two and weighed
two-ten. He turns to the bartender and says, "Mister, if
you know how to call this asshole off, you'd better do
it now."*

"Jimbo, leave the kids alone. You guys started it. It's over."

There's the typical "Like hell. This little shit needs a lesson in manners." The tone of voice and the dialogue sound like a bad movie. The man pushes Ponds toward the door. At least he's got the presence of mind not to pursue the entire cliché inside. Ponder goes willingly. The guy with the broken nose goes to the bar and gets a towel for all the blood. Ponder goes through the door, followed by Asshole, then Broken Nose holding the towel to his face, followed by me, followed by three more patrons who had just walked in when Ponder moved the nose.

"You don't want to do this, mister."

Ponds is holding up his hands, protesting.

"You long-haired little college pricks think your shit's white and don't attract no flies. We was just havin' a little fun, and you went and broke Carl's nose. Now I'm gonna remove a piece of you so you'll have something to remember us by."

Guy's got a knife. None of the people watching tried to do anything to stop it. I guess they all figured Ponds is going to get cut a little, get a little scar to remember the night, and that's it. They were wrong.

Asshole makes his first, and last, lunge with the knife. Ponder, lightning fast, steps to the side, grabs the arm, and brings it down hard on his knee as if breaking a stick in half for firewood. There's this horrendous crack, and the guy starts screaming bloody murder. The ends of both bones in the forearm are sticking right out of the skin. He drops to his knees holding the arm, blubbering like a baby. The other guy throws the towel aside and takes this huge jackknife out of the snap scabbard on his belt.

"Call it off, mister." Ponder's holding up his hands again.

I see the knife and am about to tackle the guy from behind so Ponds can get it away from him, but Ponds *sees what I'm going to do. He says, "No, Rides. You'll get hurt. I've got it covered."*

Broken Nose circles, feints a couple of times, then makes a serious swipe. The rules have changed now. You can see that he's got more on his mind than just leaving a scar on the college boy. I see the bartender in the doorway. I say, "Mister, you'd better call the cops. This guy's trying to kill my brother, and you're not going to like the way it turns out." The idiot doesn't move.

Ponder easily steps back from the first swipe. I swannee, you could see the change come over him— concentration, whatever. The first man was an exercise. This guy's the real thing. He allows the sucker one more swipe, but this time when he jumps out of the way, he pops into the stance. Before the dumb bastard with the knife can recover his balance—before he could even short-fart—Ponds spins three-sixty, and his foot catches the man behind the left ear full force. I never knew anybody could move that fast, much less my brother. Jesus, it was just a blur. There's this sickening splat, and the man drops like a bag of wet feed. Other than some twitching in his fingers and feet, he doesn't move. I bend down to check his pulse and he ain't breathing. Blood coming out his ear and left eye.

"I think he's dead, Ponds," I say.

Indeed he was. It was the sheriff's department that showed up at the scene first. A deputy took us to jail while the local cops questioned the witnesses. They never mentioned an arrest, so we never called a lawyer. I knew it would be useless to call Mom. At that time of the morning neither she nor the road manager would be in any kind of shape to understand what was going on. The bus didn't leave until noon, anyway. In the morning the sheriff came to the cell personally to release us. He told us to get on that bus and never come back to Boise.

Jesus, he was fast. So unbelievably fast. Unlike the Chuck Norris and Stephen Segal movies, when the vil-

*lain gets up from blow after blow, real life is entirely
different. So many people don't realize how serious it
is. And what's really crazy is the fact that in real life
there actually are a few martial arts fanatics who are
dumb enough to meet in isolated places in order to
fight without a referee and without pulling punches the
way they are forced to in competition. They meet in
old barns, warehouses—one on one—full contact. Usually, they dope themselves up on painkillers before the
fight in order to endure the pain of a possible broken
jaw and other bones. Occasionally, they actually man-
age to kill one another. It only takes one full-force
blow, well placed. Ponder had purposely used that
blow—one super shot to the mastoid process, causing
the brain stem such violent trauma it shuts down for
good. He had not hesitated for an instant to kill that
man.*

Chapell stayed put while the two detectives found
the slugs. One of them was buried in the dirt next to
the drive; the other was in a large walnut tree, and the
cop patiently cut out the section of the wood around it
with a saw Chapell loaned him. They did the measure-
ments from the car to where the slugs had ended up,
and then from the position in the brush next to the
drive where the shots must have originated. Prelimi-
nary diagrams were sketched, and extensive notes
were taken on time, date, weather conditions, setting,
kinds of trees, and all the other minor details that
might have to be produced in court if the perp were
caught and put on trial. They took a lot of pictures
and asked the same questions at least twice. It was
standard procedure to have another detective investigate any crime in which a police officer was personally
involved. The premise was that the officer would be
shaken enough to prejudice the evidence.

By the time they were finished, it was almost dark.
Chapell had dispatch put him through to McCurty.
The detective said they were just putting the woman's

body into the ambulance—to stay put; there was nothing he could do.

If her address is on that short street off Lealand, Ponder's in big trouble.

It was.

And she could do a good imitation of Rae Willie Chapell—had even recorded a novelty tape of it. The woman's frantic husband has disclosed this information when he'd called missing persons later that evening. He was definitely scared after watching all the media hype about killing Rae Willie look/sound-alikes. The poor man had been given an invitation he couldn't turn down, and he'd identified his wife through the small window in the dented stainless steel door. Ferraro had called Chapell, had awakened him at three a.m. to tell him this.

At six a.m., the phone rang again.

"Rides?"

"Yes?"

"Well, don't you recognize your own sister's voice? It's Gale."

In spite of a horrendous six-mile walk and using the bare ground for a bed the night before, Chapell had been sleeping in fits and starts. He was exhausted, mentally and physically, but he was not so far out of it that he couldn't recognize the voice on the phone. It instantly brought him to a full state of wakefulness—and terror. It wasn't Gale's voice. It was the thinly disguised, feathery voice of a half-drunk Rae Willie Chapell.

Chapter Eleven

Depleted and frazzled, partly from the booze he'd downed before going to bed, the voice on the phone shook Chapell badly.

"Who the hell is this?"

There was a familiar giggle, and she said, "Who do you think it is, silly?"

"This is a real sick joke, lady."

He hung up.

Immediately he was sorry he had. There was a soothing aftereffect from hearing his mother's voice. Of course, it wasn't his mother's voice. Someone was trying to shake him. It was obviously more strategy on the part of the maniac who was killing women by stuffing them alive into dead horses and shooting at him with large guns. Why? What had he done to piss Ponder off so badly? Where had Ponder found the woman who sounded like their mother?

He was about to go back to sleep when the short introduction to "We're Just Convenient" came blasting up the stairs and down the hall from the stereo downstairs. His mother's voice quickly followed.

There comes a time to write the story's end.
When soul's are wearing thin and love is too ... long
    ... gone;

"Jesus Christ! What the hell ..."

Chapell leaped out of bed, naked, grabbed the Glock that was on the nightstand next to the bed, then

sprinted down the hall, jumping the stairs six at a time.
The CD player was on, and it was playing so loudly,
the music was shaking the walls.

"When warmth from summer sun has been replaced
   by winter's wind
When the harmony no longer fits the song—"

"I didn't know the damn system could play that loud."

"We're just convenient,
Convenient,
Not lovers, we're not even best of frien—"

He quickly shut it off, and glancing at the patio
through the open door, he caught a soul-shaking
glimpse of an all too familiar figure.

"My God, he's going for broke, isn't he?"

The familiar smell of Electrique hung faintly in the
air. It was a perfume that had been discontinued in
the sixties. Rae Willie had bought a special supply
from the manufacturer because she loved the scent.
She wouldn't wear anything else.

Chapell sprinted toward the patio door with full in-
tentions of chasing down Ponder's little "trick" and
slapping the hell out of her.

"Goddamn bitch!"

He bolted out onto the deck with the expectation
that she would be running down the drive. Nothing.
He wheeled and ran around the far side of the house
to catch her running into the woods. Nothing.

"Where the hell could she have gone?"

Unless she'd gone straight into the air, there was
no place where she could have been lost from sight.

He made a complete circle of the house again just
to make sure. The phone rang as he returned to the
deck. He made his way inside and answered it.

"I want to see you."

"Goddamn it, where the hell did you go? How did you do that?"

"I would like to meet with my brother."

"You bitch, you are not my sister!"

"I want to see you."

"I think you just saw about all of me there is to see."

She giggled. As cruel as this prank was, it was hard to stay mad at the actress. She was too good. The voice was too real. It wasn't Gale, and he didn't understand why Ponder, in his bizarre way of thinking, would want her pretend she was Gale—why not go straight for the jugular? The woman sounded like their mom—imitating someone else. Why the charade? Why not say she was Rae Willie? Gale should have been back today. God knows, he'd gone through enough to make it possible, but this wasn't Gale. Gale didn't sound anything like her mother.

"Why not come see me? What have you got to lose?"

"No, thanks. Good-bye."

He hung up and went around the house unjacking the wires from the phones.

His cellular rang. It had been sitting on the kitchen counter. He picked it up.

"Come on, just one more teensy drinky poo."

That was Rae Willie's favorite saying when she was mostly snockered.

"Who is putting you up to this? How much are you being paid?"

"Oh, come on, Rides, does a boy's mother need to be put up to wanting to see her own son?" The voice had changed—dramatically!

"So you've just switched from daughter to mother now? Neat trick, lady."

"You knew I wasn't Gale. I could never fool you."

The voice had deepened, matured; it was scary. Now she was Rae Willie.

"Remember your fourteenth birthday, when I told

you I had forgotten to get you something—I'd been too busy?"

"My mother did forget. She'd been drunk for three days straight."

"I had you believing it, didn't I?"

"This is a kitschy little story, lady. Does it have a point?"

"Well, I was hiding the dirt bike in the garage all the time, honey. Point is, I didn't fool you. You knew I had that silly old motorcycle all the while."

I knew that the road manager, or somebody, had gone and bought the bike—you didn't have anything to do with it. Out loud, he said, "You didn't buy the bike. Fain or Slater or somebody bought the bike and sneaked it into the garage. I just happened to stumble on it because I was looking for an air pump for the basketball."

"I'd like to see you."

"Lady, I'm extremely tired. I've been working long days and not sleeping too hot. Why don't you take your high-priced act somewhere else?"

"I know about Toy Duck."

Oh, oh. Out loud, he said, "Go on, what could you possibly know that's not in the media?"

"Darling, I know about the box in the attic. You know the one that's full of the stuff horses are sewn up with?"

"*Jesus*! And exactly how is it that you know this?"

She giggled and said, "I live there, silly."

There was a pregnant pause while he tried to catch his breath. The woman continued when he didn't answer:

"I can tell you a lot more."

Maybe he'd better see her—Ponder was playing a serious card. Maybe the woman could be turned—could be used to pin this whole travesty on the veterinarian. Then all doubt would be removed once and for all.

"All right, come in the house."

"Oh, I left the house a long time ago. I waded along the side of your wonderful pool and down the creek. I've been riding in the car talking to you. Why don't you meet me at a special place this evening—give me a chance to fix up a little?"

Fix up was another of Rae Willie's terms.

"All right, you win."

She gave him a time and complicated set of directions which he had to write down. The woman had done her homework, and a lot of the stuff hadn't been in the books and movies. Someone had coached her well. His stomach was starting to swirl with acid again. He went to the kitchen cupboard and got the jug of Tums. If Ponder was indeed indicting himself, there would be no alternative but to do that unthinkable thing—kill him. If Chapell turned his brother in, the man could hold up the system for years. The Chapell brothers were both multimillionaires, and Ponder could afford a battery of the best lawyers in the country. Not only that, the man would remain free on bail regardless of how high they set it. He'd be free to continue the killings. He might also eventually skate on some kind of insanity defense—God knows, the Toy Duck killer was crazy. In addition, Lieutenant Detective Rider Chapell would never work in this town again—or any other town! God Almighty, how did he ever get into such a mess?

His beeper was sitting on the kitchen counter along with his Beretta and badge. It went off, and Chapell walked over to the kitchen phone, plugged it back into the jack, and dialed the number that was showing on the tiny LCD screen.

"McCurty."

"Gene, this is Rider. What's up?"

"Hey, Lieutenant. Happy Sunday morning. We just got a break on the rape-murder cases."

"It's about time we got a break on something. I'll be there in a half hour."

"No, no, stay put. We'll run it down, get some

rest. Peters found a witness who saw Croschay Hull get into a dark-colored Jaguar the evening she disappeared."

"Did the witness get a plate?" *Jaguar! Ponder, you son of a bitch! How could you be that stupid?*

"No, but he got a look at the guy driving. Witness was taking out the trash at one in the morning. The Jag drives up; woman comes down the walk from her apartment house, gets in; the car goes right by the witness, who steps behind a tree."

"What'd he look like? Anyone we know?" Chapell's heart had begun to pound furiously.

"Curly, dark hair. Beard. Good-looking. Said the guy got out of the car under a streetlight, opened he door for the girl, and then got back in. Tall. Said he looked like class. That's why he took the pains to notice. What's a guy in a Jaguar doing picking up a college girl at one in the morning?"

"That may be why we've had no witnesses—he's picking the girls up in the middle of the night. Probably promising to pay them big bucks."

"Works for me. We've got the witness looking at mug shots."

"It'll be a waste of time." The heartbeat thing was going into orbit. Chapell was scared, but he refused to allow it to show. He continued, "This guy, if he is Toy Duck, is not going to have an arrest record."

"Just in case, we'll let him work with Sergeant Tenely on the computer to see if they can come up with the guy's face."

"Outstanding. Let me know if something happens. Does the captain know yet?"

"No. Why don't you call him?"

"I will. I'll be in a little after lunch."

"See you then."

Chapell's face was prickling with sweat. He was afraid he was going to have a heart attack. He had set the squad on this track of investigating, but he wasn't prepared for such quick success. If the witness came up with a good composite picture ... But Ponder had been wearing a beard and wig ... That damn computer could switch things around in a heartbeat.... If the squad put it all together and found out the lieutenant's brother was the cause of the worldwide publicity, Chapell would be lucky to escape a prison term. If Ponder told them that his brother had suspected him and said nothing—if he proved it by telling them about the box in Howard Peretti's shed, about the suturing material in the attic ... Now was the time to step in and made Ponder disappear. It was time to cross the Rubicon—throw the die. If he could only be absolutely sure. *How much proof do you need, stupid?* The black minidevil was back. Well, perhaps tonight would push it one way or the other.

She had told him to be there at nine o'clock. However, Chapell wasn't about to walk in on this little operation cold—not when he knew how well his brother planned things ahead of time. An hour and a half early, he parked the Cherokee in the parking lot of an electrical-contracting company. The industrial park was unfamiliar to him, and he would sneak in carefully, making sure no one saw him. And wasn't this a weird one? This area was hardly the part of town you'd expect to set up a meeting between a mother and son.

The Beretta was in the shoulder holster, as usual, but he removed the gun and racked a round into the chamber. He ejected the magazine, took a loose round from his pocket, and pressed it into the clip to replace the cartridge that had gone into the chamber. Then he did the same for the .22 High Standard that fit the silencer in his jacket pocket. The bullets had been dum-dummed. Once they hit, they would explode into fragments. Severe damage—no ballistics match. The .22 went into a holster on the back of his belt.

He made his way down a series of alleys, always

hugging the darkest side of the dilapidated warehouses. He had negotiated four blocks of them before,
even in the dark, he could see that the far end of the
old industrial complex ended in a large, undeveloped
open area. As he'd moved farther and farther from
the main road, the streetlights had become more
scarce. One of the buildings on the street where he'd
been told to meet the woman proved fortuitous. At
its back there was a fire ladder that went all the way
to the roof. The roof would be the perfect place to
hide for an hour and watch anything that took place.
It was still an hour and ten minutes before he was
supposed to be there.

He climbed the iron ladder carefully, making sure
that his sneakers made no noise on the rungs. There
was a light breeze that would both hide and carry
noise, and the cop wasn't about to take any chances.
Ponder could well be in the area already, and struck
just right, the ladder would reverberate like an enormous tuning fork. At the ladder's top he could see
that the roof had a tar surface—good, less noise.
Spaced down the fifty-by-forty yards of flatness there
were several shedlike structures that housed some
type of equipment. Chapell silently made his way toward the front of the roof, always keeping a structure
between him and the facade that ran the width of the
building's face about four feet above the roof. The
facade would make a perfect place for Ponder to hide
and watch whatever was supposed to take place
down below.

Shit!

Something moved.

It was dark, but not dark enough that Chapell
couldn't see the man sitting on a stool while looking
over the facade. The figure's attention was totally focused on the dark street below. Chapell stayed hidden
about fifty feet away, and he saw the man reach into
his pocket and take something out. A tiny light illumined a wrist and watch. He replaced the penlight,

then reached over the top of the facade and aimed
something. Suddenly, there was a burst of light below
on the street. He must have turned the lights on with
a remote switch—interesting. Chapell could now see
that the silhouetted figure was dressed in black, was
wearing a black cap and probably had his face blackened. The cop saw the man pick up a handgun, then
heard the safety click on and off several times. Ponder
was nervous. Maybe he wanted to make sure the
safety was off. There were a few snipers who wanted
their weapons ready to fire when working this close
to the target. They would flip the small lever and then
leave their pulling finger on the trigger guard until the
target was accessed, not leaving the chance of the
safety lever snapping too fast at the most inopportune
time—under stress—regardless of how many times the
small operation had been practiced. The tiny click had
spooked quarries and got snipers killed too many
times to count.

*Cheap, brother of mine. You're going to bushwack
me with a handgun? You could hit me with a knife
from up here. Big letdown—not your usual panache.
Maybe, like me, you're just tired of it all. What I still
can't believe is that after all these years it comes down
to something as stupid as this.* There was a tremendous
mental sigh inside the cop's head. He wanted badly
to cry. The soliloquy continued. *Well, we might as well
get this over. It's going to be a bitch getting his corpse
off this roof.*

Chapell had unholstered the .22 and silently screwed
the silencer onto the barrel. Muffling the safety with
his left hand, he carefully thumbed the lever downward. The gun's trigger was now live. Inch by inch the
cop moved from his cover. The lights below proved a
godsend. He could now see the small piles of debris
that had been deposited by forty years of wind. Stepping on a small twig or dead leaf would have given
him away. He wanted total surprise, giving his brother
no advantage.

At twenty feet, he dared go no closer. He leveled the gun and said, "Ponder?"

"Wh—!"

The man whirled and the weapon whirled with him on a dangerous arc toward the cop's stomach. Chapell could not give Ponder the chance to fire that gun. With a heavy heart and the greatest reluctance, he pulled the trigger three times. The seated figure was knocked off the stool, and the "gun" dropped to the roof. It didn't go off. Chapell approached, gun leveled. He had put only three shots into his brother, but he was ready to empty the clip if Ponder was still able to reach for a weapon. Depression dropped like a water-soaked blanket. He had wanted to talk to Ponder, discuss what had been going on—give his brother every opportunity to explain. Maybe there was some miraculous explanation that would take them back to the time when they were kids. Chapell had needed that desperately. The last thing he'd wanted was for it to happen like this. He kneeled down beside the dark figure, and with a hand that was shaking so badly he had to brace it with the other hand, he raised the blackened face in order to examine the eyes for any trace of life.

It wasn't Ponder!

Chapell tore off the cap, then using his handkerchief, he squatted before the dead man and desperately scraped at the black grease paint.

"Jesus Christ! Slater!"

Confusion fell like the worst Alaskan blizzard, and the cop fell into a sitting position next a television monitor, his back against the facade. Something fell over that had been standing against the facade. He only barely noticed that it was a safari rifle, complete with sling and scope. The detective was shaking violently and on the verge of throwing up. Something was radically wrong here, and his mind was light-years away from being capable of analyzing the evidence before him. He glanced down at his feet to see the gun that Howe had leveled at him in order to reassure himself that this death hadn't been in vain—that it had been pure and simple self-defense. The gun wasn't a gun at all. It was the remote mechanism in the rough shape of a gun. Another wave of revulsion and fear washed down his body. He trembled, less and less, until his mind threw the circuit breaker and he blacked out.

When he awakened, it took a minute for it all to sink back in. The nausea returned in small, uniform ripples. He had killed a man who had been one of his dearest friends when he'd been a kid. Slater had tagged him "Polliwog" after pulling the floundering six-year-old out of a shallow pond. He'd been trying to catch tadpoles, had slipped and fallen, and was covered with mud. The bus driver had taken him home, cleaned him up, and Rae Willie had never found out. Slater had teased him about the nickname until he was twelve years old.

The woman . . .

The woman! Was she really going to meet him? What had Slater planned to do? Why? Why would Slater Howe . . .? She said she had a small trailer. Trailer? What a ridiculous place to park a trailer. Naw. The meeting was a ruse. But Slater . . .

Chapell, the cop, jumped to his feet and was once more shocked at what he saw before him. He was thrown violently back in time. In the street below, his mother's dressing trailer was parked in exactly the same spot it had been twenty years before—in front of MGM's Soundstage Number Fourteen! He could see the sign with her name on it in gold letters over the door.

"My God!"

The trailer's inside lights were on.

He ran to the ladder. If the woman was actually there, maybe she'd have some answers.

He knocked.

No answer.

The door was unlocked, and when he opened it, the smell of whiskey overwhelmed him. There was an empty bottle lying on the carpet just out of reach of his mother's outstretched hand. She was lying on the sofa, naked and unconscious.

"Oh, God!"

A flurry of mixed emotions swirled around his head as the scene focused and then slowly merged exactly into the original of so many years before. The effect made him dizzy, syncopal, more nausea.

Love-loathing.

Adoration-abhorrence.

Desire-disgust.

Passion-panic-*parricide*!

There was a lighter on the floor next to the couch.

"No! Maybe that's what Slater wanted—had set up, but I won't do it. I'm not crazy. Where the hell was his mind? This is all so unbelievably senseless!"

Unnoticed, the door quietly swung shut, as if normal. He was much too involved in the flashback to notice the faint click after it had latched. The woman moaned, stirred, then fell silent again. She was beautiful. So was his mother, all the times he'd seen her exactly the same way. The perfect breasts, the blond swatch ... Rae Willie, ever meticulous, had dyed her snatch to match her thatch.

The first time it had happened he'd been nine. She had gently called him into her bedroom one rainy afternoon. The doors to the balcony were open, and the smell of wet earth wafted through on a long skinny breeze. He had seen her naked many times, but never this close.

"Get up here—beside me, sweetie." She patted the bed.

He had been wearing a pair of camo jeans and an olive green T-shirt. She'd pulled the shirt over his head as he sat on the edge of the bed. The small rose-colored circles at the tip of her breasts seemed welcoming, familiar. He saw the perfectly formed nipples shrivel and harden. It was as if they were reaching for him.

"Here, lie down beside me."

She said no more, but began kissing him on the face. Her mouth opened wider, and he could feel her tongue swishing, each touch leaving a wet spot for the air to fan. She moved the kisses down his neck to his chest, lingering on his nipples, sucking gently, then tongueing rapidly. A breast dragged back and forth across his bare skin as she switched back and forth several times. Her tongue made a long, wet mark and slowly drifted down to his lower stomach. Something was happening inside his pants. He'd never felt like this before, and although it was strange, it felt very good—like the sub-dued delight of a new kind of candy or the first ride on a new bike. She undid his pants, pulled them off with his underpants, then resumed the kissing around his groin. He had become hard. That was nothing new. He awakened most mornings with an erection from needing to pee. However, this was different—he didn't need to pee. Instead there was something like having to pee going on down there along with a growing awakening. She took him into her mouth and began sucking, pulling him in and out. The new feelings intensified greatly, the peculiar urge building pleas-antly. Finally, she lay back on the bed and pulled him on top of her. He remembered the tremendous feeling of relief when she reached down and inserted him inside the cotton candy place. It was so soft in there—softer than her tongue, which came into his mouth when she began kissing him again. There was such an incredible feeling of completion, being inside her. There had been a part of him missing, and now it was fitted snugly into place. She began moving, taking him into her in gentle gulps, releasing him slowly, reluctantly. Bumping, he'd called it when ea-gerly reliving the scene alone in his own room. In the times to come, the growing boy-man had quickly learned how to "bump" back, and over the years the two lovers had become expert at exacting every ounce of pleasure from, and for, the other.

When he exploded, he found, to his surprise, that she was screaming with him, the teeth of both mother and son gritted in hereditary coincidence against such tumultuous intensity, as bodies bucked and convulsed without control while slaved to the violence of the gratification.

"Well, sweetie, I think you're probably going to stay put a while—he must have drugged you. I need to take care of a small detail on the roof across the street."

Jesus. After all those years of paying his medical bills, I was the one who recommended hiring Slater as curator at the museum. But I certainly can't leave this little charade in place, because they'll connect him to me. I could come clean, say I was lured here by a woman sounding like my mother, then killed a sniper when he tried to kill me. But that won't wash—too many background questions I couldn't answer—they'll want to know why I didn't report it all, maybe bring backup.

Out loud, he continued, "God damn! Was Slater killing those women all along? Is he Toy Duck? He was crazy over Mom. Maybe he resented imitators—all these poor girls. Maybe Ponder is innocent."

"Ponder is innocent!"

"Maybe . . ."

One of the minidevils in the back of his head muttered, "Son, Slater Howe was in ga-ga land for fifteen years. He couldn't even pee by himself for five years. Good try, Sherlock, but . . ."

His line of reasoning was cut off abruptly by a loud *phut* that came from beneath the sofa.

"What . . ."

Flames sprang up around the sofa, then leaped across the carpet, hungrily devouring the spilled liquid.

Within three seconds the sofa had turned into a rapa-
cious hell. Chapell screamed and danced backward out
of the way. He saw his mother's hair blaze in a fireball.
Wispy little yellow curls eagerly licked away her eyebrows. She moaned loudly and moved in unconscious
pain. He yanked off his jacket and began beating the
flames around his feet. Within seconds the coat was
aflame. He looked frantically for something else to
beat back the fire with, but there was nothing. The
curtains were already ablaze. To dash unarmed into
the inferno around the couch would have been suicide.
He ran to the back of the trailer and into the bedroom, frantically looking for something to beat out the
fire, but the room was already a hellish furnace. There
must have been a separate igniting device. In the bed
he could see two blazing figures—one appeared to be
smaller—a child, perhaps.

"Goddamn Slater! You're fucking crazy!"

The scene was too much for an emotional caldron
that was already brimming over the sides. Chapell
panicked and bolted for the only door out. The door-
knob burned his hand when he turned it, and the door
refused to open. He kicked it, but it held steadfastly,
locked in place by the four-inch dead bolts that had
been closed by an electromagnet on an automated
cycle set in motion by remote control. Slater Howe's
fully automated barbecue machine continued to function flawlessly. Unfortunately, Slater was unable to
turn on the closed-circuit monitor and watch from the
roof across the street. However, the VCR at his just-
seconds-dead feet meticulously recorded it all for pos-
terity. A fiber-optic lens in the cupboard door relayed
the scene faithfully for another forty seconds before
the intense heat fused the camera's circuits and it all
shut down.

Chapell ran to the window and battered it with his
elbow until he was sure his arm was going to shatter.
Everything that could be thrown through the glass was
engulfed in flames. The window wouldn't break. He

was sweating profusely from the tremendous heat, and wisps of smoke were rolling off his T-shirt and jeans. A thick cloud of battleship gray slowly unfurled through the trailer, and he squinted more and more as it stung his eyes mercilessly. He ran at the door, battering it with his shoulder.

Solid.

Another run.

Unforgiving.

He was choking and coughing violently.

Too much smoke. Gonna have to drop to the floor to breathe. Can't batter the door on your stomach, stupid. One of the minidevils . . .

One last, desperate body check on the son of a bitch who had just hooked him in the face with a stick.

He was flabbergasted to find himself flying through space, then hitting the ground and rolling away from the godawful heat. The striker that had housed the dead bolts had softened just enough in the heat to become susceptible to the blows.

"Can't stay here and whine, fella." He struggled to his feet and began loping away from the fire and back toward the main street where the car was parked. "Fire trucks will be coming. God, I'd like to stay and watch them. Oh, shit, what am I going to do about Slater? Hey, nobody's going to look up there. This is just a tourist who found a secluded place to park for the night, set the damn thing on fire, end of story. Leave Slater until the scene is clear. Now, get the hell out of here."

The .22 slugs had gone about shutting down Slater Howe's life-support system very effectively. The heart and breathing had stopped, but while his killer sat in a cage, back against the wall, on sheer will alone the former bus driver had reached for the remote and pushed the button that had set in motion the events across the street. Had it been another two inches from his reach, it wouldn't have happened. As is usual in many cases, the brain continued to function for a cou-

ple of minutes, its electrical impulses refusing to die
the same way an old television set that's just been
turned off refuses to immediately give up the ghost.
There was no tunnel with a blinding light at the other
end; there were no phantom demons arriving in a
hoard to spirit his soul off to Charon's ferry dock on
the banks of River Styx. The bio-electrical computer
was running on a few seconds of stored battery power,
and it continued to process thoughts, mind images,
worries and fears, just as it had for over half a century.
Slater's last thoughts were totally rational. "Did I return the Nitro Express and the crossbow to Jay Jr.'s
collection in the museum? If he were alive, he'd kick
the piss out of me for borrowing them. Maybe I should
have left the windshield busting alone after I framed
dickhead Nolan Tyres. Too bad I wasn't as good at
sewing the son of a bitch up as our poor, pathetic
psychopath who's been doing it seriously all these
years. Well, Rae, maybe I'll find you where I'm going
next. . . . Sure like to be able to turn on the monitor—
watch the fun. . . . Sorry, Jeni . . . but business is business. You . . . would tell . . . on me. Burn . . . in . . .
hell . . . Po—"

The thoughts had been verbalized in a slow *morendo*—
a piece of music that decrescendos and ritards at the
same time—a dying away. A black, moisture-laden
breeze kicked up briefly as if celebrating a premature
memorial, but Slater's mind was exiting the one-way
gate and too far gone to appreciate it. He was on his
way to the place where Puss Killian, her brain ridden
with a malignant tumor, wrote Travis McGee, "It's
real black out there, and it lasts a long time." Death
pressed on his chest like an obese woman sitting on a
small stool. The stool broke and Slater Howe was
gone.

Five minutes later, when Chapell had reached the
Jeep, there was an orange glow marking the darkness.
The trailer had ignited the old wooden warehouse that

Slater Howe had fixed to look like MGM's soundstage.

"Damn, that's beautiful! I should have been a firefighter." Chapell had climbed a set of outside stairs on the side of the four-story building where the car was parked. He could not be seen in the darkness. From a half mile away he could see the flames skittering into the black where the rounded jaws of low clouds nipped and snapped at them in self-defense. It was going to storm. He watched, mesmerized, as the fire trucks, one after another, screamed down the main street and turned into the old industrial complex. Probably a night watchman somewhere in the area had seen the glow and turned in the alarm.

As far as Chapell was concerned, Slater Howe's ingenious plan had been a waste of time.

The thunderstorm had almost worked up the support from its constituents to go public when the cop walked into his own home an hour later. Lightning jumped continuously from cloud to cloud, the echoes of Thor's gleeful approval rolling across the Tennessee landscape in great sonorous waves. The door slammed shut behind Chapell just as the "foot of the anvil" swept up the hollow, raking leaves and branches too old, too weak, onto the drive and decks.

He had thrown the .22 and its silencer off the Briley Parkway Bridge. Another load of guilt had been shoveled onto the heap of discarded duties—duties that went with a badge cherished and lovingly polished for seventeen years out of choice, not out of the necessity of having to work for a living.

Wearily, he made his way up the stairs and was about to turn on the light when he spotted it. Sitting innocuously in the middle of the bedspread's smoothness, the outside security light shone just bright enough to see it. It took a flash of lightning to reveal the caked blood. The yellow plastic duck sat as if bobbing on a small pond, looking for its mother. Seeing it desecrating the sanctum of his own bedroom blew the frayed fuse inside Chapell's head. Weeks of going without sleep; the trauma of shooting an unarmed man without the benefit package that came with police support; watching his mother's death—again; withholding evidence that was pertinent to solving Nashville's worst serial killings; being shot at repeatedly—the tremendous overload blew the circuits for the second time of the evening, and Rider Chapell collapsed on the bedroom floor in unconsciousness.

He awakened in the darkness, and the grogginess and confusion were immediately swept away by the awareness that someone was in the room with him. The storm had hit—force six. Rain and hailstones pelted the bedroom's French doors mercilessly.

The shadow stood motionlessly in a darkened corner of the room. A slight movement had given it away. Chapell grabbed in slow motion for the Beretta, but it wasn't in its holster. Panicky, he lunged through the molasses for the nightstand, where there was a 9mm Glock in the drawer; it wasn't there either.

The shadow moved again. Chills flowed up and down the cop's back, fanning down the arms, down the backs of his legs.

"Who's there?"

He had to shout over the sound of the rain against the glass.

Nothing.

It moved again.

"Goddammit! Is that you, Ponder?"

A familiar voice broke the darkened corner's silence.

"Well, little brother, how was your evening?"

In spite of the fact that Chapell was older, Ponder had always referred to him as "little brother" because Ponder was, physically, considerably larger. Ponder had always automatically assumed the responsibility in the fights. Ponder had achieved a mature greatness through his intelligence, cunning, and years of dogged practice in the fighting arts.

"Ponder, what the fuck are you doing, scaring the shit out of me?"

"Well, after your barbecue trick, I think it's time we had a talk. You may not be around long enough if we don't."

"You were at the trailer?"

"Of course. I had been following you all evening."

The doors to the deck were backlit with a blinding flash, followed immediately by a room-shaking crack of thunder. The light illuminated a serene look on the too familiar face, which was framed with long, thick hair neatly settled on either shoulder. Chapell jumped noticeably.

"Then why the hell didn't you get me out of there? I almost burned to death."

"I did get you out of there, stupid. How do you think the door got opened?"

"I didn't see you."

"You took off like a bat out of hell, excuse the simile."

Chapell's wits were beginning to return. It was time he assumed his role as a cop—took charge. He knew he could not kill his own brother. When he'd thought he'd killed Ponder a few hours before, the remorse was too much. Seeing Slater's face had, in a way, been a godsend. Killing his own flesh and blood was not acceptable. That left only one way out, as difficult as it was. Chapell was a cop, a good one. Perhaps one final act of performing his duty by the book would avenge for all the wrong decisions he'd made in the past few weeks.

"Ponder, why have you been killing these women?"

"Because they were pretenders, little brother. There was only one Rae Willie Chapell, and she doesn't deserve to be imitated by a bunch of hacking amateurs."

So it's finally out. He's finally admitting it. There was an overwhelming relief that swept over the cop. Out loud, he said, "Ponder, we've got to turn ourselves in. I'll spend some time in prison for withholding evidence and for shooting Slater, although I might be able to convince a jury Slater was a perceived threat. But you—*you* can get help. We'll get the best lawyers, we'll plead 'guilty while insane.' Hell, you'll spend some time in an institute; I'll make sure you get the best help in the country. A couple of years, you can be out, free and healed. You can't kill any more innocent women."

"I have a better idea."

Another flash, another crash. This time the illumined face was anything but serene. A thousand darkened lines seemed to have crawled onto it.

"There is no better idea, Ponds. We've got to turn ourselves in." An exaggerated heaviness dripped from his voice; it sounded like he was going to cry.

"You're the only one who knows, Rides. I'm enjoying life the way it is and have no plans to allow it to change. Logic dictates that the only witness to my little hobby should disappear." Even in the dark, Chapell could tell his brother was smiling.

"No! If you don't come with me, I'll have to come after you. If I don't, someone else will."

"You don't have to come after me, Rides. I'm right here."

The big man stepped into the light, grinning, and Chapell could see the strips of rawhide and spangles draped over the doctor's hand. So it had finally come down to another fight between the brothers—this one to the death!

Ponder placed the suturing materials on the dresser and walked out of the corner's darkness. More chills went skittering over Chapell's skin. There wasn't a doubt in his mind that Ponder was going to try to knock him out, then sew him inside a dead horse. As his brother got closer, Chapell saw the folded cloth in his hand and he could smell the ether.

"Jesus, no!"

Panic bubbled from his throat as he bolted for the door. If he could make it downstairs, maybe he could get the shotgun; maybe he could get outdoors and get into the woods. There was a loaded .38 Special in a drawer in the desk.

He was too slow. Ponder was at the door before him, and Rider felt a blow to his solar plexus. The pop was just enough off so that it didn't knock the wind out of him as planned. Rider hesitated for a half second, reeling from the sudden, sharp pain. Cat quick, he grabbed the lamp from the end table and swung it at his brother. Having expected the cop to fall to the carpet, Ponder was a fraction late in reacting. The lamp shattered into a thousand pieces on the man's face, and he staggered backward. Rider recovered from the tremendous swing he'd taken with the lamp and then lunged for the door one more time. Ponder beat him to it again, in spite of the dark rivulets of blood now flowing from numerous deep cuts on his face. Before the detective could catch himself, he felt another blow to his stomach, followed by one to the side of his head. The warm blood from his brother splattered across his face. The panic quickened and he charged Ponder, head down, grunting and straining like a three-hundred-pound lineman. Again, the move was unexpected, and Ponder was thrown backward into another table. Another lamp shattered against the wall. Legs driving, Rider continued to push until Ponder, table and all, blasted through the French doors, across the deck, and into a heavy wrought iron breakfast table with an umbrella over it. The storm's fury was now at its peak, and rain and hail screamed across the deck in slashing horizontal drapes. Rider tried to check his drive, but he slipped on the inch of hail that had accumulated and fell hard on his back. Ponder did a backward somersault over both tables, and Rider lost track of him. After three desperate, windmilling tries the cop regained his feet and bolted back into the house through the broken door. He was sure Ponder was going to grab him any second.

"Gotta get that gun! The only way to stop him is to shoot his ass!"

He sprinted down the hall, jumped the stairs ten at a time, and fell hard at the bottom. He felt an ankle turn and the immediate sweat-popping pain. He was up quickly, hobbling for the loaded twelve-gauge that stood in the corner next to a bookcase. He kept it handy for cottonmouths in the creek. He had almost reached it when the French doors exploded. Blood and rain streaming down his face, Ponder leaped for him. The look of rage on the man's face was something Rider had never seen before. The cop grabbed the gun and swung around, but it was knocked from his grasp with a tremendous kick. It flew across the room and smashed through the window in a teak china cabinet. Arms numb, Rider dived across the carpet, rolling and squirming—seeking the gun before Ponder could recover his balance. He heard another lamp break as Ponder dived over an end table to stop him. The detective felt his legs grabbed. The pain from the ankle went ballistic. Both men were prone on the living room floor, with Rider kicking and screaming in abject terror. Panic welled up once more, blowing through the top of his head, and with one last tremendous kick he broke free. He grabbed the gun, punched the safety off, and began firing at the man who was in the midst of an airborne leap. He kept firing until the gun was empty, and he could hear the walls, lamps, light fixtures and furniture, exploding violently from the #6 shot. When the echoes had finally died, except for the rain splattering on the lower deck's slate, the only sound to be heard was his own keening. Ponder was lying on top of him, and blood from the wounds was pouring onto the cop's face, drenching his clothes. Rider screamed and wrenched himself free, tossing the shotgun away as if it were a live grenade. Soaked in hysteria, he went out the door screaming, dragging the useless foot behind as he hobbled down the long drive to the road. Ponder would be on him any second.

Ponder would not die. Ponder would tackle him on the very next step. Ponder would not quit until he had sewn his brother inside a goddamn horse! The cop hit the main road and fell in front of a car that was just coming over the hill. He was up on one knee, waving his arms frantically, standing his ground until the car slewed to a stop in the pouring rain. He couldn't believe his eyes when the blue strobes came on behind the car's grille and McCurty and Johnson jumped out.

"He's coming! He's right behind me! For god's sake, help me! Give me a weapon!"

Ponder ran screaming out of the darkness, eyes bugged in fury, his long hair a wet mat. He was holding the elephant gun at his hip, firing, working the bolt, firing again. Chapell had already jumped inside the unmarked car and grabbed the shotgun bracketed on the floor next to the door. He came out of the car, wheeled and fired, cringed, dodged and fired again and again until the magazine was empty. Ponder fired back, zigged, zagged, fired, rolled, and expertly avoided the shotgun's blasts until his own gun was empty. By the time Chapell had emptied the magazine, his brother, already out of ammo, had disappeared into the woods, and he was still a-fucking-live!

The two cops had dived to the road. They slowly got to their feet just as Chapell threw the empty shotgun onto the front seat of the cruiser and wrenched the glove box open, looking for more shells.

He screamed at them, "Did you get him? Did you get a shot off? I didn't hear your shots! Dear God, did you hit him? I missed him every goddamn shot! Jesus, he's slippery! That goddamn elephant gun—blow your ears off. Sorry about the car, Gene. Big mother holes, aren't they?"

"*Lieutenant* what's going on? Who the hell were you firing at?"

"My own goddamn brother, Gene! The son of a bitch has been sewing those women inside the horses! He finally admitted it. I found the suture stuff inside his attic. Goddamn, my own brother! He was trying to kill me. Said he was gonna sew me inside. He could do it too. If anybody could do it, he could. Jesus, you ought to see my house! It's a wreck. Lamps, doors— all busted to hell! Bastard's too good—all these years ... I couldn't kill him. Think I got a piece, though. He's hit. You can be sure of that. Motherfucker's hit. Gale's gonna shit a brick. Now she's gonna know our precious brother is for real, goddamn it! I got the proof. She won't piss on my face this time! You hit him, Gene? Did you get him too?"

The two cops had been looking at each other in total amazement.

McCurty finally holstered his Beretta and said, "*Rides ... Rides*?"

"Yeah, Gene. You okay? He didn't hit you, did he? Goddamn elephant gun—four-sixty Weatherby mag." Chapell was still examining the spot in the woods where Ponder had disappeared, as if the man was going to return any second.

"Sir ... you were the only one shooting. What did you say about your brother?"

"You know, my brother. Jesus, you've met him enough times. There's me, and ... me, and ... and Gale. Gale's gonna ..."

Chapell stopped and turned to look at McCurty with a face that portrayed pure horror. He sniffed, wiped his mouth with the back of his arm, and looked away quickly.

McCurty said calmly, "Sir, you don't have a brother. It's a matter of fact that Rae Willie Chapell had only two kids—you and Gale. Your sister burned to death twenty years ago in the fire with your mother!"

McCurty and Johnson took Chapell to Central State's psychiatric ward after calling the captain. Later, they drove back to the house of the wild-eyed man and went room to room looking for anything un- usual. Other than the holes in the ceiling and walls from several shotgun blasts, the house was in perfect order. There were no broken lamps or smashed doors or windows.

The captain came to the hospital at midnight to question Chapell personally, but the man steadfastly refused to say a word. However, at the mention of his brother and Gale, he went berserk, throwing chairs at the window to smash it into smithereens, tipping the bed and dresser over before they could subdue him. It ended with four cops holding him down while a doctor gave him a powerful sedative; then they tied his arms and legs to the frame of the bed. Several noses were bleeding, and there would be a number of dark bruises the next day. Once he was asleep, he was transferred to the psychiatric ward.

The next morning, armed with an open search warrant, two cars carrying all seven members of the Murder Squad turned into the long drive. A sign at the gate said:

> Rae Willie Chapell Museum
> Country Music Foundation
> 9 a.m. to 5 p.m. Tuesday through Sunday
> Adults $4   Children $1

McCurty and Johnson had been on the way to Chapell's home the night before because of the terror-stricken man's appearance on the tape they had found in the VCR next to Slater Howe's body. It wasn't as if *his* face wasn't well known in Nashville. After the fire had been extinguished, the fire inspectors had discovered, along with an unidentified woman's remains, all the remote-control gadgetry that had been custom-built into the trailer. It hadn't taken long to locate Slater's hiding place.

The deceased, with the bullet holes, was the curator emeritus of the Rae Willie Chapell museum; Chapell had told McCurty and Johnson that he had found his brother's suturing material in the attic; Fallingstream didn't have an attic, but the house he'd grown up in did. The mansion had been turned over to the Country Music Foundation only a year after Rae Willie had died. Chapell had a full set of keys on his key ring. It had taken the men a half day to find the secret hiding place.

"Look at that stuff. There must be enough to suture another twenty, thirty horses. Where the hell did it all come from?"

"No wonder we couldn't find the sources. Must have been stockpiled years ago. I've seen enough catalogs from craft manufacturers to last me a lifetime, and a lot of this stuff isn't even made anymore."

"These chemicals . . ."

"Over a dozen toy ducks left. It'd be awhile before he'd have to do any shopping, that's for sure."

The squad found several men's wigs, beards, and mustaches—in assorted colors, along with shoe lifts, cheek pads, and a set of surgical instruments. There were also a half-dozen stolen license plates. Three of Rae Willie's favorite Jaguars were on display in the museum's garage.

"You know, this stuff is the exact paraphernalia needed for the 'night-after' rapes and murders that followed the Toy Duck killings." Tweedy was holding a black wig in his hands—one that fit the description the witness who had seen the jaguar pick up Croschay Hull at one o'clock in the morning.

Efforts were underway to collect hard evidence proving whether or not Howe was the Toy Duck killer. Pictures were being shown. Witnesses were being sought who could establish his whereabouts at pertinent times. Even though no evidence was found that would establish him innocent or guilty, the cops became more and more certain that Howe was the Toy Duck murderer. He had motive—he'd been in love with Rae Willie, and he was eliminating pretenders to her posthumous fame; he had opportunity—he had an ear to the music community, could select his

victims as they presented themselves; he had the
"weapons" which were found in the attic at his place
of work. Chapell had got caught in some kind of bizarre trap and had, unfortunately, killed Howe. He
must have thought of Howe as "a brother." It was a
well-known fact that they had been close when Chapell was growing up. The effect of finding that Howe
was the Toy Duck killer, then being forced to kill him,
had caused the man to crash and burn.

The night the cops had come to his house, he had
been out of his mind—crazed with fear—probably
from what he'd just gone through at the trailer. He'd
simply cracked. Because he had refused to utter a
word, there had still been no explanation about his
brother and sister.

Three days later, he was transferred to an expensive
sanitarium at the request of his lawyer. Whenever his
sedatives wore off, he went into a frenzy that made
the average speed freak look like a snail on a wet
sidewalk. He thrashed violently at his straps until his
arms and legs bled, gnashing his teeth and screaming
until he lost his voice. Had he been left unattended,
he would have died from exhaustion.

Chapell's breakdown was kept a closely guarded secret among only a handful of people who had a need
to know. If the press got hold of the fact that one of
Nashville's finest hometown boys . . . It couldn't even
be revealed that he might have killed the Toy Duck
murderer—the evidence in the attic was enough to
make the Murder Squad believe that Howe was the
killer; however, without collaborated proof it was still
too circumstantial for a court of law. Theoretically,
anyone could have planted the stuff in the attic. Two
questions remained unanswered. How could Howe
have killed the first two or three women—especially
the first one? The man had been recovering from terrible burns in hospitals and nursing homes for years.
Was he faking it? Did he use some serious painkillers?

The second question had so far gone unasked by anyone in the department. Was Rae Willie's own son the diabolical son of a bitch who had killed all those women who looked like his mother?

Chapter Twelve

"The line that separates very sane from very insane is infinitely thin."

Two mornings after the patient had been admitted to the small, expensive hospital, two psychiatrists sat in the conference room discussing the case history. The room was paneled in varnished mahogany and lined with original paintings, each with its own brass lamp. There were two large, elaborate chandeliers overhead, and brass sconces lined the walls in concert with hidden indirect lighting that was recessed in the perimeter of the ceiling. The men sat at one end of an ornate teak table that appeared almost long enough to land a small airplane. A thick file folder lay before one of the doctors. He was Dr. George Thessalonica, an energetic man of average height who was in his sixties. A fifteen-hundred-dollar tailored suit, thick, wavy white hair, and gold-plated pilot-type glasses gave him a cosmopolitan look—the kind of man who was a staple at the best cocktail parties. The other man, Dr. Thomas Arquette, was considerably younger. His hair was chicory brown but cut badly—a couple of locks hung in his face. His gray slacks and white smock were neatly pressed, but his appearance emanated the impression that his neatness was a product of the environment and necessity—that left alone he would have been unacceptably disheveled, that he was much more interested in his work than in how he appeared. Dr. Arquette was the head of staff at the small, expensive hospital.

Dr. Thessalonica said, "When the patient was in high school, he had several schizophreniform episodes. We knew, of course, even back then that schizophrenic behavior usually begins in late adolescence, early adulthood years, and Rae Willie made no bones about mandating that her son maintain therapy—throughout his life! She knew that there's no cure for the disease. Not long before her death, she even had her will changed to say that if anything ever happened to her, he would maintain therapy or his inheritance would be cut off and his share go to charity. Of course, she didn't know that he would eventually receive the entire estate. She also knew that the disease had not been proven to be genetic, but with three preclusive strikes against her family already, she wasn't about to take any chances. Her mother, born and raised in Nashville—like her daughter—had been diagnosed with full-blown schizophrenia and spent most of her adult life in institutions. Rae Willie was the product of a rape by another schizophrenic patient, and when she was nineteen, she began to exhibit schizophrenic symptoms herself. Thinking processes began to fragment—there were delusions and hallucinations. She was hospitalized after she walked into a police station and told them that the CIA had a thought transmitter planted in her head. She later told me that she could see the antenna barely sticking out an ear whenever she looked in a mirror just right. At times she would talk to me in the typical 'mind salad' gibberish. I'll never forget her looking at me one day in a session and saying, 'The green jelly is safe in the cat's mouth—the one who lives inside the refrigerator.' I was young. It spooked me. I later figured out what she was trying to say."

"What was she trying to say?"

"She was on a diet at the time and about ten pounds overweight. Green jelly was pistachio ice cream, about which she was fanatical. She also kept cat food in the refrigerator. If she visualized that the ice cream was in a dirty can of cat food, it would be easier to refrain from eating it. After we got the disease under control . . ."

"Chlorpromazine?"

"Yes. It worked like a miracle on her. That and the therapy. She was able to pursue her career, and it never became an issue with the public. She told me one time that the most pernicious aspect of the disease was the utter frustration at not being able to say—or sing—what her mind was thinking. She said it was as if her mouth was several paces behind her brain, which was thinking several things at one time. She was one of my first schizophrenic cases, and she provided me with a great deal of insight as to what goes on inside the head of someone who's suffering from the disease. She told me that they removed her from her mother's funeral because she was laughing uncontrollably. Said a good joke had flown through her mind, and it had triggered several other jokes. She never experienced catatonia, nor did she ever go frenetic, but she did see a patient die of exhaustion from a frenzy because they didn't sedate him in time."

"What were the patient's symptoms when he was a kid, Doctor?"

"When he was fourteen, he became rather schizoid—he'd get into fights when someone made fun of him—couldn't take a joke. He became withdrawn, didn't want to go to school, didn't want to obey his parents. He told them the only authority he would bow to was the law. During one of the episodes Rae Willie found a cop to befriend him, and everything was fine. The boy would accept the authority of the police, but was quite unwilling to submit to his parents."

"Interesting. It's usually something like religion that takes the substitute place of the parents—parents who don't show love. His mother and father don't give him the love he needs, so he gets it from God—becomes fanatic."

"Yes, exactly. A couple years later, not long after his mother's death, he began having delusions. Felt that someone was after him—trying to kill him. Someone wanted the family fortune. He became obsessed with the law enforcement field—began studying textbooks, befriending policemen, always asking questions about the work and procedures. I still believe he thrust himself into a role of authority because there was no one left to assume it for him. Imagine the trauma of losing your entire family in the space of a year. You may be sixteen years old, but suddenly you're all alone in the world and all of your so-called adult friends and guardians are interested only in separating you, piece by piece, from your considerable fortune. He outgrew the delusions and obsessions with time, and the normal healing process. He finished his schooling without too many problems. An occasional fight, if I remember—might have been a residual manifestation. He was always fighting on the hockey team."

"What kind of tests are you running on him?"

"I'm looking for schizophrenic evidence, of course. We just ran a PET scan. There was no difference in the evoked potentials when we exposed him to both light and sound flashes—nothing jumped at us; brain tracings were perfectly normal; and there was no reaction to the gluten compounds."

"How about a CAT scan—abnormal brain ventricles?"

"I've done one every other year during routine physicals. Anatomy is perfectly normal."

"Nothing out of the ordinary. Maybe there is no mind splitting. Maybe he just cracked up from stress and only needs rest."

"I could believe that if it wasn't for his family's history and the frenetic episodes he's been exhibiting. And then there's this matter of a brother and sister. There was a reference in the police report that he made to his brother. Could be a hallucination. It's not fractured enough, nor has his behavior been abnormal enough to be hebephrenic."

"You said brother?"

"Yes, he called him his brother. I know that the patient and Rae Willie's bus driver—the man's name was Slater Howe—were very close when he was growing up. There might have been some kind of blood-brother ritual. He might have been talking about Howe."

"There must have been quite an age difference, wasn't there?"

"Yes, but who knows . . .? We have to remember that this is an extraordinary and enigmatic man, Doctor. He's extremely bright. He's been Nashville's darling since the death of his mother. The media have always loved him; they're always doing feature articles on him for one reason or another—raising money for charities, his hockey team, his work. He's one of the best in the world at what he does. If he's been hallucinating, he may have kept his sanity and his profession viable by old-fashioned superhuman effort just to keep from losing it all. His mother was seriously affected by the disease. Drugs and therapy helped, but that woman regained and maintained her sanity by sheer determination and will. She fought it daily by mentally scratching, biting, and clawing her way clear of what her brain wanted to do—in spite of the substance abuses. In all the years I've practiced, I've never seen anyone who could do that. We are all at the mercy of the mind's frivolity."

There was a knock on the double doors at the end of the room. Dr. Arquette said, "Come in."

Dr. Thessalonica closed the file, and both men stood as detectives McCurty and Johnson entered the room. Introductions were made and the cops were seated opposite the two doctors at one end of the table.

In his soft, lilting voice Dr. Thessalonica said, "I was the Chapell family doctor when they were all alive, and I've been treating our new admission since he was a kid."

McCurty asked, "We've known your patient fairly well for a number of years. A couple of the guys go all the way back to high school with him. Can you tell me what's wrong?"

"I can tell you very little right now, sir."

McCurty continued, "What was he talking about— this brother stuff? It's a well-known fact that Rae Willie had two kids; she had no illegitimate children and neither did her husband. The family's life was too well documented for an extra son to have fallen through the cracks."

"Detective, I really don't know. All I can tell you is that he's suffered a severe mental breakdown. He's under heavy medication. We're not sure what the prognosis will be. When he's able, you can talk to him all you like. However, since he's been here, he hasn't uttered a word."

McCurty asked, "Has he been under psychiatric treatment for all these years?"

Thessalonica continued, "Sergeant, I'm sorry. You know I can't give you that kind of information. Regardless of how benign, it's the stuff lawsuits are made of.'"

"Well, we have a lot of questions. There are nineteen murders that he may know something about."

Dr. Thessalonica continued. "Let me ask you a question. The admissions report says that when you picked him up, he told you his brother was trying to kill him? Tell me more about this brother. Did he elaborate any? Call him by name? I'm going to need all the help I can get to open him up."

McCurty took a small loose-leaf notebook from the inside pocket of his coat, thumbed through several pages, and said, "I quote, 'My own goddamn brother, Sergeant. The son of a bitch has been sewing those women inside the horses. He finally admitted it. I found the suture stuff inside his attic. Goddamn, my own brother! He was trying to kill me. Said he was gonna sew me inside. He could do it too. If anybody could do it, he could. Jesus, you ought to see my house. It's a wreck. Bastard's too good—all these years.' "

There was silence in the room as the men digested what had been read. The cop put the notebook back in his pocket, then looked down at his hands on the table. He finally said, "This was in the heat of the moment, you understand—just after we'd pulled up. He had evidently run all the way down the drive in the rain and, in fact, almost ran right into the cruiser. When I got out, he lunged into the car and grabbed the shotgun. We hit the deck, but when we saw he was just shooting at the woods, we didn't shoot him. He was in an extremely agitated state, disheveled, was limping. When he realized we were there, he seemed to catch himself. You could see that he immediately regretted what he'd just done, as if he'd let the cat out of the bag. When we questioned him about what was going on and about his brother, he clammed up."

Dr. Thessalonica asked, "And he said his brother had been stalking him?"

"Yes."

"Perhaps he was hallucinating."

"The shots someone took at his car with at least two different high-powered rifles weren't hallucinations. The first gun, we believe, was the big game rifle we found in Nolan Tyres's trunk. The second rifle belonged to the museum but was in the possession of Slater Howe. We think that Howe probably set up Nolan Tyres. Tell me, Doc, do you think Chapell considered Slater Howe to be his brother?"

"It's possible, I suppose. There was also mention of his sister. Can you tell us what he said about his sister?"

McCurty took the notebook out of his pocket again, flipped the pages, and read, " 'Gale's gonna shit a brick. Now she's gonna know our precious brother is for real, goddamn it. I got the proof. She won't piss on my face this time.' "

"That doesn't sound like Slater Howe to me. If Howe wasn't the so-called brother, our patient was hallucinating both a brother and his sister. Interesting."

Johnson interjected, "Can he do that?"

Dr. Arquette, who had been quiet, interjected, "Over twenty centuries ago, the Roman poet Horace observed schizophrenia in a man whom he said sat each day in an empty theater and enjoyed a performance no one else could see or hear. He even applauded his imaginary actors with gusto."

The two cops became briefly mired in the mind image.

Dr. Thessalonica broke the spell. "Unless he was talking about some sort of cemetery headstone conversation, it sounds like he believes she's alive. You know, the patient had tremendous guilt feelings when his mother and sister were burned in that fire. He never forgave himself for not being there to rescue them—as Slater Howe was. After the fire, when the Hollywood police went to his hotel room a few blocks from the movie studios, he was sleeping so soundly they had to get the desk clerk to let them in the room. Cops said they banged on his door for five minutes. He was there—in bed—but once they got in the room, they still couldn't wake him."

Johnson said, "I read the report on that fire again, just recently, Doctor. The fire investigators said that a spilled whiskey bottle was the accelerator that ignited the room from the cigarette. Do you think Chapell was capable of setting that fire deliberately? How did he feel about his mother?"

The doctor continued, "That much I can tell you. It's no secret that he had a love-hate relationship with her. I can't figure him killing her, though—when his sister, whom he adored, was in the trailer too."

McCurty spoke next. He said, "I just finished the new biography on Rae Willie by Nolan Tyres. He maintains that twelve-year-old Gale was voluntarily sleeping with Rae Willie's lover—that there was a sex triangle going on. I got to thinking about Slater Howe and his poignant rescue that night—I've read the fire report too. We all have. If Howe was hanging around the trailer at that time of night, maybe he knew what was going on inside. He could have been Tyres's source." What McCurty did not say went unspoken between the two cops: *Did Chapell kill Slater Howe because the trailer was a setup to lure him in so Howe could burn him to death? Did Howe know something—see something that nobody else had? Had the kid deliberately set the fire that killed his mother and sister?*

"This guy was certainly involved to be just a bus driver." Dr. Arquette was working his chin with his fingers as if pondering the situation.

Johnson said, "Right now the evidence points, circumstantially, to the fact that Howe was the Toy Duck murderer and that he had also been taking potshots at Chapell. Evidently, Chapell suspected something, for whatever reason, and he conducted his own search of the museum's attic. He may have confronted Howe with the suture material. We'd like to know what took place on the rooftop where Howe was killed. It looks like self-defense. Gene mentioned that we found the rifle that had been used to shoot at the car—it was within Howe's reach when he was killed. We dug a slug out of the dirt beside Chapell's driveway this last time somebody shot at him, and it was a perfect match ballistically. Evidently, he beat Howe to the draw, but we haven't found the gun he used if he did. We'd also like to know what the trailer fire was all about. I guess it'll have to wait."

"When he is ready to talk to you, I'll let you know."

Five months after the celebrity patient's admission to the sanitarium, there was a serious fire in the offices. It started a little after midnight, and the automatic sprinkling system extinguished it when it spread beyond the suite of offices that belonged to Dr. Thessalonica. For some reason the sprinklers did not work in the doctor's office. The rooms were destroyed along with most of the files. The first fire crew into the office found the dead doctor lying in the middle of an inferno. The charred remains were tentatively identified from a bracelet. Later from dental X rays.

The fire inspector quickly determined that the fire had been set deliberately—gasoline fumes were still pervasive. There were also numerous stab wounds on the blackened corpse. The inspector immediately called the Murder Squad. The doctor's body had been found just outside his private bathroom, which, with its thick wooden door mostly closed, had been only slightly damaged. When the lab crew had finished, the detectives began sifting through the debris that was scattered through the office suite. In the bathroom Sergeant McCurty was surprised to find an audio cassette on the floor. The tape's label was in code, and the detective initialed the cassette and placed it in a plastic bag. Preoccupied, he stuck it in his pocket and forgot to deposit it in the box that held the suite's other gleaned evidence. Later, in his office, he discovered the cassette, and carefully handling it so that any fingerprints would not be destroyed, he popped it into a Walkman to see what was on it. For the better part of an hour, he sat mesmerized by the chilling voices of the doctor and patient. He spent two more hours typing the transcripts himself rather than trusting a stenographer from the pool with the information on the tape.

CONFIDENTIAL
EYES ONLY
TRANSCRIPTS OF CASSETTE C-36 FOUND IN
LAKEVIEW SANITARIUM FIRE

PATIENT: She loved it, you know? Twelve years old, and she was fucking like she was thirty. Mom's boyfriends would do them both at the same time, sometimes.

DOCTOR: You saw it?

PATIENT: Goddamn right I saw it. Many times. She probably deserved what she got, but God knows, I didn't mean for her to burn. I was gonna get her out, but before I knew it the whole place was a furnace. I can see it just as clearly as if it were a few months ago. (*giggle*) Mom lying on the couch; fire out of control.

DOCTOR: You never told me that you started the fire.

PATIENT: (*mumble—unintelligible*)

DOCTOR: Is that what Slater Howe was doing? Making you relive it?

PATIENT: I brought her back, though.

DOCTOR: Whom did you bring back?

PATIENT: I rebirthed the little whore. A couple of weeks after the fire. Worked like a charm too.

DOCTOR: Sewing the women who looked like your mother into the horses?

PATIENT: Who looked like Gale would look. Womb.

DOCTOR: You felt the horse was a womb to rebirth them?

PATIENT: Only thing big enough. She loved horses.

DOCTOR: Didn't it make you feel guilty? Killing innocent women?

PATIENT: The first one did a little. She was only a kid—twelve, thirteen. Back then they had to be Gale's age, you know. Wouldn't work ... Later, when finding someone the right age became a royal pain, I found out it didn't matter. Twenty became thirty.

DOCTOR: And the other women?

PATIENT: Tore the hell out of me. (*giggle*) Tough work, but somebody's gotta do it. I needed my sister. She'd start to fade, and I'd slit open another whore—excuse me, horse. (*giggle*)

DOCTOR: I was talking about the prostitutes. You mentioned the other day that you needed release. . . .

PATIENT: Oh, that. That's nothing. Forget that.

DOCTOR: I'm curious about the duck.

PATIENT: Gale wouldn't take a bath without her little ducky. If we were on the road and it got lost, we'd have to find a toy store and get another one. She wouldn't get in the tub without it. Nice touch, the duck ... eh?

DOCTOR: Why did you have to keep rebirthing her so many times?

PATIENT: Is the zebra in the slap shot cage yet? He was coming on the last train, wasn't he?

DOCTOR: I know you're not now, nor have you ever been, hebephrenic. You're fooling around. In fact, I'm not sure but what this whole story isn't a fabrication. And it may be awhile before you get to play hockey again, whether you hate the referees or not, if you don't work at the therapy.

PATIENT: Good for a laugh.

DOCTOR: What happened on the roof with Slater Howe?

PATIENT: Do you remember when Gale and I were kids, we used to do the make-believe things? The stage in the attic, all that?

DOCTOR: Yes. They worried your mother—you both took them too seriously, she said.

PATIENT: I loved those games. All the imaginary characters. I should have become an actor. We used to keep them going for days—offstage—around the house, on the road. They were a great way to relieve the boredom on the road. The rich get much more bored than the poor, you know?

DOCTOR: And . . .

PATIENT: Sometimes I'd get carried away.

DOCTOR: How?

PATIENT: The game became reality—art imitating life, or something. I loved that—kept it going as long as possible. The imaginary people became real. We would live the fact that we were, say, a poor family in Poland during the war. We'd even talk in accents of the country. We'd go without food, pretend that the bodyguards were the Gestapo, and that they were after us; pretend that our father and mother were spies, and they were going to turn us in.

DOCTOR: Tell me about your brother.

PATIENT: What brother?

DOCTOR: Why did you kill Slater Howe?

PATIENT: That was a mistake. He turned a gun on me. I surprised him and he turned around so fast, I really thought he was going to shoot. Turned out it wasn't a gun at all. It was the remote to activate the sensor on the door. Once the sensor was triggered, the door locked on a timer and the fire was ignited. Can you imagine? That son of a bitch wanted to fry me alive.

DOCTOR: He saw you coming out of the trailer the night your mother and sister burned, didn't he?

PATIENT: The little slut! Twelve years old and she fucks like she's thirty! I really was going to get her out, but a whiskey bottle spilled, and before I knew it, the whole place was a furnace. I saw Slater when I ran out the door. He didn't think I did, but he was standing in the shadows. He's been stalking me for months. He killed my Jaguar using the gun he planted in Tyres's trunk. Or was it Trunk's tires. (*giggle*) Then he shot the Jeep with one of Dad's safari guns.

DOCTOR: Why didn't you turn him in? Have him arrested?

PATIENT: He shot it the first time with one of Dad's crossbows. That was fun.

DOCTOR: Weren't you afraid?

PATIENT: Hell, yes, I was afraid. But I knew he wasn't trying to kill me. Slater was an excellent shot. If he'd wanted to hit me, he'd have done it the first time. He was just trying to soften me up.

DOCTOR: Why didn't you have him arrested?

PATIENT: What, and let the fact get out that I burned my mother and sister to death?

DOCTOR: So you did light the fire . . .

PATIENT: What do you think, Doc?

DOCTOR: Would you like to tell me why?

PATIENT: Not particularly, but I will. You can't testify against me.

DOCTOR: No, I can't.

PATIENT: Obviously, I started that fire because she was turning Gale into a whore. I'd think you could see that! My mother did a lot of horrible things, but sex outside the family is going too fucking far. Nobody would, or could, stop her. Daddy didn't give a shit. I'm not even sure if Gale was Daddy's child.

DOCTOR: What do you mean, sex outside the family? (*room noises*) Did your father ever molest Gale?

PATIENT: Don't be ridiculous.

DOCTOR: Did you ever have sex with your mother?

PATIENT: (*unintelligible*) Goddamn ... gander ... not fucking ... goose ... (*loud noises as if chair is thrown— much agitation, room noise. Tape machine turned off and on*)

DOCTOR: So you did rape and kill those women—the prostitutes?

PATIENT: Hey, a man does what he's gotta do. You get horny, handling those sweet young naked things and not being able to fuck the shit out of them—hell, a man needs to purge the pump once in a while, doesn't he?

DOCTOR: Why didn't you rape the women who looked like your sister before you killed them?

PATIENT: Hey, Doc, who said I killed them? They were alive when I sewed them inside. All I did was a little recycling—saving them from themselves—born again, you could call it. That's as worthy a cause as you can get—a second chance? Start with a fresh slate? Shit, they loved it.

DOCTOR: How did Gale return to you?

PATIENT: Oh, usually a phone call. We'd go have lunch. Sometimes with ... (*long silence*)

DOCTOR: Why won't you tell me about your brother?

PATIENT: What brother?

DOCTOR: Did you ever have sex with your sister?

PATIENT: (*Increased room noise, mumbling, but no answer.*)

NOTES ON SESSIONS BETWEEN DECEMBER
21 AND JANUARY 21

After treating this patient for over twenty years for schizophrenia, I have come to the conclusion that I have badly missed some other diagnoses. I was always aware of his brilliant mind, but I reluctantly have to admit that he may have been misleading me for the entire twenty-two-year period he was under my care. The symptoms of schizophrenia were manifest enough. Paranoia, catatonia, and frenzy have all been clearly exhibited and have been successfully treated by drug intervention and therapy. He has led a relatively normal life. In this aspect my diagnosis was correct. However, the patient has been successful in hiding some extremely important revelations from me—revelations that have only come out in the past few weeks since he's been confined to the institution—revelations I would have thought not possible, considering all the hours we spent in therapy over the years. At no time did he ever reveal, even slightly, any psychotic tendencies. I knew about a few neuroses: for instance, he'd never been able to stop wetting the bed. But this sociopathic behavior is extremely disconcerting to me, because had I diagnosed this capability, perhaps lives would have been spared. I must admit, he kept the propensity brilliantly hidden and probably would have fooled any psychiatrist. In the sessions over the past few months when he has admitted to the reality of his brother, he has related many episodes where both individuals exist concurrently, and they interact with one another! Apparently, he was so successful in creating—rebirthing, as he labels it—his sister, he also created an imaginary brother, complete with all the details of quotidian life. They have lunch together, they play racquetball; there is an elaborate history of the brothers growing up—fights, daily chores, recreations, interplay with their mother. I'm convinced that most of the relationships carried on with his siblings take place when he is alone—at home, for instance, while he's lying on the sofa or in bed. Occasionally, however, there are times when he manifests these hallucinations in public places. I do believe he is aware enough that the characters are not real that he carries on his conversations with them only in his head. To be seen talking to an empty seat in a restaurant wouldn't do in his position of prominence in the community, and he knows it. The imaginary brother acts as an authority figure and seems to do things independently that the patient finds out only by secondhand discovery—spying, stalking, gathering evidence of guilt. This fantasy world is consistent with the hallucinations of paranoid schizophrenia, although the visual aspects are more well developed than usual.

Unfortunately, this psychosis appears to be much more complicated than just schizophrenia. The patient is additionally suffering from a definite multiple personality disorder. At times he totally *assumes* the identity of his imaginary brother. I have been successful in bringing the brother out on several occasions. Compounded with more hallucinations, he even assumes the life his brother would live—eating, drinking, working—even to the extent of extensively and intricately carrying out the duties of his brother's job description. It's an ingenious way of transferring guilt, justifying his actions because of the inability of the authority figure to stop him. He appears to routinely weather stressful situations and crises in his life by assuming his brother's identity—a classic defense mechanism.

The ritual of rebirthing his sister was always precipitated by some monumental event involving his dead mother—a newly released CD, a movie, the biography by the murdered author. Gale's corporeality would dissolve from the direct competition from Rae Willie herself, and he would again have to perform the ritual that would bring her back.

On numerous occasions he has even hallucinated himself as seen through his imaginary brother's eyes. I'm not sure he hasn't also assumed the personality of his sister too, but so far I've been unsuccessful in bringing her out.

It will take many months, perhaps years, to unravel the intricacies of his personality. I also believe that because of the sociopathic proclivity, I can conceive of no circumstances where I would feel safe returning him to society. The police department has closed the Toy Duck cases because they believe Slater Howe was the murderer. What is most tragic is the fact that I am bound by doctor-patient privilege from revealing the fact that this patient has admitted to me that he killed nineteen people—nine of whom were asphyxiated by being sewn, alive, inside a dead horse!

He stood naked, one with the cold February night. It would be warm soon enough. He lifted his hands to the hills, the miraculous cords of life draped across them in supplication. A large animal had been selected this time. In the dark he had opened and cleaned out the entire visceral cavity; he would need the room—feet where the lungs used to be—head, torso, arms in the belly of the Great Womb.

He fell to his knees in anticipatory joy, said the chants, and quickly lost himself in the rhetoric, tears and ritual. When he had tired of it, he returned, mentally, to the field, and could not help giggling at the absurdity of it all.

Poor Thess. All these years he sincerely thought he was successfully keeping my "mental illness" in remission. The fool never figured out that I didn't even take the medicine. I should have stopped seeing him twenty years ago, but the sessions were always such a hoot—matching wits, staying one step ahead of him, telling him nothing. In all those years the good doctor never once considered that I was as sane as he was. Sustained performances that merit the finest Oscars, to say the least. They never suspected that I just loved having fun! The game is the thing. The game is everything. Almost pushed the game too far, though, with the box full of shit in Peretti's shed. Rheinhart and his big mouth after the game I got the hat trick in. I gave them their chance—they were too stupid to put it together. And that goddamn Slater almost killed me. First he blows my car practically in half with that cannon, then he tries to burn me to death. After all I did for him, he was still harboring a grudge all these years. Poor bastard. I'll have to admit, it was a good job, even the mannequins in the bed. Unfortunately for the chick that got crisped, and for him, it wasn't good enough. I was

*too good for him. Too good for them all—twenty years'
worth. Why can't they just accept the fact that some
people are special? We're smarter, stronger, we've got
the world by the scrot, and we're going to take what
belongs to us, like it or not. My perks are simple
enough. All I ask is to kill a couple sluts once in a
while!*

The soliloquy continued out loud, "Well, here goes,
folks. Step right up, get yourself born again. Spin the
wheel. What *will* come out on the other end this
time?"

He slipped inside the "womb," feet first, like a kid
in a sleeping bag. He would take this ride for all it
was worth, sucking out every last ounce of experience
the way a fanatical reader sucks out each metaphor
and simile to hold and digest with intense pleasure.

The cord of life began to weave its magic across
time and space. This time the wondrous stitches would
be found on the inside.

Epilogue

Only when the air ran out and the darkness inside his head began to swirl did he hear the gentle popping of the rawhide strings as they were cut one by one.

Pop.

Pop.

Pop, pop ... pop ...

Before he could stop himself, he slid onto the grass, where the cold night air licked his blood-bathed body with expectation. He savored the feeling for a few seconds, lying on his back, feeling the texture of the grass—admiring the grain of the stars, which were stunningly clear.

"Rider, you dickhead! You've ruined my game!"

He didn't have to look to confirm the presence standing in the pasture's darkness a few feet away. He began to laugh. Soon the guffaws were echoing dangerously off the trees bordering the pasture.

You crazy bastard. I ought to turn you in. The familiar voice had a grin to it.

"Well, after tonight they're gonna know it wasn't Slater, aren't they?"

Who cares? The voice was insouciant.

The blood-covered man stood and perfunctorily smeared any prints on the duck he'd inadvertently grabbed as he was tumbling from the horse. He had read enough police procedure books over the years that it was an automatic gesture—no clues. He'd even been inside the Metro Police Department more than

a few times as a guest. He picked up the towel lying
on the grass and, after wiping his hands, carefully
cleaned the surgical knife in his hand. An artist
needed to take care of his tools. Finishing, he grinned,
looked at a man-size space of empty darkness, and in
an ostentatious gesture, took a long, exaggerated lick
down a blood-covered arm with his tongue. Head
bent, but eyes still focused on the imaginary brother,
he flicked his eyebrows up and down twice in a
Thomas Magnum gesture. The figure finally muttered,
"*Gross,*" in approval. Had anyone seen the bizarre
behavior, they would have wondered if the man had
taken leave of his senses. They certainly would have
wondered what the one-sided conversation was all
about.

The cops had got him on not one but two goddamn flukes! Meanwhile, he'd obligingly gone ahead
and given them a shit load of fuel for the fire.
They'd been coming to question him at the exact
time when he happened to be in the middle of one
of his favorite games—a game that had taken on a
frightening reality. Unfortunately, before he could
extricate himself, he had blurted out something that
was at the head of the "Stupid and Incriminating"
column in the circles that cops run. Unforgivable,
after all these years.

The first fluke: his face turns up in Slater's remote
VCR act. How the hell was he supposed to know
that the crazy bastard was taping the barbecue
scene?

Then, the very next day, while he's lying in the hospital room, strapped to the bed and helpless as a newborn, the second fluke: they find the dropped knife!

The shit had hit the fan in solid, earth-shuddering
chunks. It had all ended three days later when the
powers-that-be had quietly stuffed his ass in a nut-
house without so much as a "Thank you, kind sir,
for twenty years of painstaking labor and exceptional
reliability." Mental evaluation, they called it. Maybe

being the only living relative of Rae Willie Chapell had something to do with the case not going immediately to court—do not pass go, do not collect ... And the fact that all their hard evidence was only circumstantial—it could have been planted. There had been no clear prints. They couldn't trace the Caravan's rental to him. Bless Slater's heart, the old boy had provided just enough doubt. They also knew Rae Willie's boy had a few hundred million dollars to pay the best attorneys in the country to keep the thing going forever.

That goddamn dropped scalpel! He'd never missed it. They'd found it late the next afternoon, Sunday, near the broken van on the logging road. Unfortunately, it was one of a set of surgical instruments given to him as a present for graduation, and the entire set had been engraved with his initials—PAC. Not too many veterinarians with custom-engraved surgical instruments in Nashville whose mothers resembled all those dead women.

This little soiree would fuck their heads up. The maniac escapes and he leaves an empty horse with no woman? What will he think of next? America, beware! He's loose! Lock up your women! More like South America beware, now that every cop in the country would be looking for him. Fuck Fallingstream. Place was always full of mildew—noise of the falls never quit, although sometimes it was nice to open a door and listen.

He began to wipe the blood from his face and hair with the towel. When he'd finished, he said, "Little brother, you'd fuck up a wet dream."

Hey, you were jumping around in there worse than a one-legger trying to tup a ewe.

"Bullshit. I was just having some good, clean fun. I was taking the tour, that's all."

Tour, hell. You'd have been dead in another few minutes.

"Well, come on, let's get out of here. It's almost dawn."

With his imaginary brother in tow, Dr. Ponder Allegro Chapell broke into a slow trot and headed toward the spot where he'd left his clothes.